LONESOME ROAD

Mollie Lee
Pryor

D0555558

Titles by Patricia Wentworth

LONESOME ROAD

PATRICIA WENTWORTH

HarperPerennial
A Division of HarperCollinsPublishers

This book was originally published in 1939 by J. B. Lippincott Company.

HarperCollins books may be purchased for educational, business, or sales promotional use. For information please write: Special Markets Department, Harper-Collins Publishers, Inc., 10 East 53rd Street, New York, NY 10022.

First HarperPerennial edition published 1993.

Library of Congress Cataloging-in-Publication Data
Wentworth, Patricia.
Lonesome road / by Patricia Wentworth. — 1st HarperPerennial ed.
   p.   cm.
ISBN 0-06-092406-3 (pbk.)
1. Silver, Maud (Fictitious character)—Fiction. 2. Women detectives—England—Fiction. I. Title.
PR6045.E66L65   1993
823´.912—dc20   92-54860

93 94 95 96 97 ❖/CW 10 9 8 7 6 5 4 3 2 1

Look down, look down that lonesome road
Before you travel on.

NEGRO SPIRITUAL

LONESOME ROAD

CHAPTER 1

Rachel Treherne got out of the first-class carriage in which she had travelled to London, gave up her ticket at the barrier, and after walking a little way in the direction of the exit stopped and looked up at the station clock. It was only eleven. There was plenty of time for a cup of tea. Tea, or coffee. It was always a moot point whether refreshment-room tea was nastier than refreshment-room coffee, or less nasty.

As she entered the refreshment-room Miss Treherne decided that she would have coffee. She liked it less than tea, and would therefore not mind so much whether it was good or bad. It would at any rate be scalding hot. In spite of a warm suit and a fur coat she was cold. It had been snowing when she left home, but here in London there was no fall, only the feel of snow in the air, and an overhead gloom which looked as if it might turn to fog. Rachel Treherne shivered and began to sip the hot, sweet coffee. She did feel a little warmer by the time she had finished it. She looked at her wrist-watch and found that it was now ten minutes past eleven. Her appointment was at half past.

She crossed the station, hailed a taxi, and gave the address: "Montague Mansions, West Leaham Street, S. W."

As the engine started up and the taxi began to move, she leaned into the corner and shut her eyes. She couldn't go back now. When she wrote to make the appointment she had said to herself, "I needn't keep it. It will be quite easy to write and say that it is no longer necessary." But she had not written. Miss Maud Silver had replied that she would be very pleased to see Miss Treherne at 11.30 on Wednesday, November 3rd, and

Rachel Treherne was on her way to keep this appointment.

All the way up in the train she had thought, "I needn't see her. I can ring her up and say that I've changed my mind. Then I can shop, and do a matinée, and go back home—" No, she couldn't just go back. She had borne it too long. She couldn't bear it any longer without some relief. Having come so far, she must see Miss Silver. She need not tell her anything, but having made the appointment, she must keep it. If Miss Silver did not impress her favourably, she could always withdraw, say she needed time to think the matter over, and then let it fade. . . . Something in her shuddered. "No—no—there's no relief that way. I must—I must tell someone. I can't bear it alone any longer."

She opened her eyes and sat up straight. Her heart felt cold in her, but her mind was made up. She had played with the idea of seeing someone, talking to someone, shifting this dreadful burden of fear. But now the make-believe was over. Her mind was firmly set. Whatever came of it, she would not go back without unburdening herself.

The taxi drew up. She paid the man and mounted half a dozen steps to the modest entrance of Montague Mansions. It seemed to be a block of flats. No porter, stone stairs going up, and one of those small lifts you work yourself. Rachel Treherne was always rather afraid of them, because twenty years ago when she was a girl her dress had caught in the iron grill of the lift shaft and she had had a narrow escape from being killed. She remembered Venice, and being nineteen, and the American who had wrenched her free, tearing the muslin of her dress with his square, powerful hands. How odd things were. She had forgotten his face, and she had never known his name, but she could still see those very strong hands which had saved her life. She had never felt really comfortable in an automatic lift since then, but of course one did not give way to such a foolish feeling.

She managed the lift very well, and found herself presently standing in front of a door with the number 15 upon it. And, just over the bell, a small brass plate with "Miss Silver. Private Enquiries." She rang quickly, and had a momentary sensation of relief. If you have been brought up as a gentlewoman you don't play the errand-boy's trick of ringing a bell and running away.

A stout, old-fashioned woman opened the door. She had a big white apron over a dark print dress, and she looked like the comfortable sort of cook whom you do not expect to see in a London flat. She smiled pleasantly and said,

"Come right in out of the cold. Terrible draughty, all these stone passages, and the street door standing open. Miss Treherne? Oh yes, Miss Silver will see you at once, ma'am."

She opened the second door, and Rachel Treherne came into a room which was much less like an office than a Victorian parlour. There was a brightly flowered Brussels carpet, and plush curtains in a cheerful shade of peacock-blue. There was a black woolly hearthrug in front of an open coal fire. There were odd little Victorian chairs with bow legs, upholstered laps, and curving waists. There was a row of photographs in silver frames upon the mantelpiece, and over it a steel engraving of Millais' *Black Brunswicker*. On the opposite wall *The Soul's Awakening,* and *Bubbles*. The wallpaper, covered with bunches of violets, put the clock back forty years.

In the middle of the Brussels carpet stood a writing table of carved yellow walnut, and at this table sat a little woman in a snuff-coloured dress. She had what appeared to be a great deal of mousy grey hair done up in a tight bun at the back and arranged in front in one of those extensive curled fringes associated with the late Queen Alexandra, the whole severely controlled by a net. Beneath the fringe were a set of neat, indeterminate features and a pair of greyish eyes. In complexion Miss Silver inclined to being sallow, but her skin was smooth and unlined. At the moment of Miss Treherne's entrance she was engaged in addressing an envelope. She completed the address, blotted it, and setting the letter upon one side, looked up with an air of grave attention and slightly inclined her head.

"Miss Treherne? I hope you did not have a very cold journey. Pray be seated."

A chair had been placed in readiness on the far side of the table. Miss Treherne sat down, and was aware of scrutiny, not prolonged but keen. Miss Silver's small greyish eyes raked her and dropped to the knitting which she had taken from her lap and which now appeared to engage her whole attention. The garment on her needles was one of those small coatees which are showered upon expectant mothers. In colour it was of a delicate shade of pink. A large white silk handkerchief protected the wool from contact with Miss Silver's snuff-coloured lap.

What the grey eyes had seen was a tall and slender woman who might be anything between thirty-five and forty years of age—good carriage, good skin, good eyes, good hair. The colouring should have been dark and rich, but there was a blight upon it—a chill. The lips held an anxious line. The eyes went here and there like those of a startled horse. The hands held one another. So much for the woman.

Miss Silver looked up from her knitting, took another glance, and could have written a complete inventory of Miss Treherne's habiliments—a hand-knitted suit in a beige and brown mixture, heavy silk stockings, and excellently cut low-heeled shoes of dark brown leather; a very good fur coat; a single modest row of real pearls; a small brown felt hat. Everything betokened the woman of taste and means who lives a country life.

Everything also betokened a woman driven by fear. Whilst Miss Treherne made answer that the weather was very cold for November, Miss Silver was noting the nervous movement of those clasping hands. She knitted half a row before she said,

"You are very punctual. I appreciate punctuality. Will you tell me why you have come to see me?"

Rachel Treherne leaned forward.

"I don't think I should have come, Miss Silver. I wrote to you, but I think I have only come to apologize and to say—"

"Second thoughts are not always best," said Miss Silver primly. "You are very nervous. You wrote to me because you were alarmed and you felt that you must speak to someone about what was alarming you. This gave you some momentary relief, and you began to think you had been foolish—"

"How do you know?" cried Rachel Treherne.

Miss Maud Silver nodded.

"It is my business to know things. And it is true, is it not? May I ask who recommended me to you?"

"No one." Miss Treherne leaned back again. "Hilary Cunningham—she—the Cunninghams are connections of an old friend of mine. I met them there, and Hilary was talking about you—oh, months ago. And then when I felt I couldn't bear it any longer I remembered your name and looked you up in the London directory. But, Miss Silver, I don't want anyone to know—"

Miss Silver nodded again.

"Naturally, Miss Treherne. All my work is extremely confidential. As Lord Tennyson so beautifully puts it, 'Oh, trust me all in all or not at all.' I very frequently quote those lines to my clients. A great poet, now sadly neglected. And really very practical, because it is no use expecting me to help you if you will not tell me how I can do so."

"No one can help me," said Rachel Treherne.

Miss Silver's needles clicked briskly.

"That sounds very foolish to me," she said. "And—" she coughed slightly—"just a little impious too. No one will help you if you will not allow yourself to be helped. Now suppose you tell me just what is worrying you, and we will see what can be done about it."

Rachel Treherne was irresistibly reminded of her schoolroom days. Miss Barker of estimable memory had displayed just such cheerful efficiency as this when confronted by the intricacies of *Nathan der Weise* or the inaccuracies of a muddled problem in arithmetic. Something in her responded to the click of the needles. She looked across the table with her dark eyes wide and said,

"I think someone is trying to kill me."

CHAPTER 2

Miss Silver said, "Dear me!" Her needles clicked reassuringly. She looked up for a moment and said,

"What makes you think so?"

Rachel Treherne drew in her breath.

"I came here to say that, but I don't think I ever really meant to say it. Because when you say a thing like that nobody believes you, and now that I've said it, it sounds even worse than it did when I thought about saying it. Even then I knew that you wouldn't believe me."

"People so often say that," said Miss Silver placidly. "The thing that is troubling them appears to be unbelievable. But then of course they have not, fortunately, any experience of crime. I, on the other hand, have a great deal of experience. I assure you, Miss Treherne, there is very little that I cannot believe. Now I think it would be a good thing if you told me the whole story. First of all, why should anyone want to kill you? Secondly, has any attempt been made, and if so, in what circumstances? And in the third place, whom do you suspect?" She laid down her knitting as she spoke, took a bright red exercise-book out of the top right-hand drawer, laid it open before her, dipped a pen, and wrote a careful heading.

These actions had a curiously composing effect upon Miss Treherne. The calming influence of routine made itself felt. Whatever she said would go down in that little book and be on record there. The book touched the schoolroom note again. Upon just such a page had she inscribed such classic phrases as

"Have you the pen of the gardener's aunt?" By the time Miss Silver looked up she was ready with what she had to say.

"I don't know if you will believe me or not. You see, I don't quite know what to believe myself. You don't know me, but if you were to ask people who do know me, I think they would tell you that I am not naturally suspicious or hysterical. I have always had a great deal to do. I haven't had much time to think about myself at all. I have had other interests."

"Yes?" said Miss Silver. "What interests, Miss Treherne?"

"You know the name of Rollo Treherne?"

"Ah," said Miss Silver—"the Rollo Treherne Homes. Yes, indeed. You are associated with those Homes?"

"I am Rollo Treherne's daughter. He made an immense fortune in America—you probably know that—and he left it to me as a trust to administer. He died seventeen years ago. It has kept me very busy."

"The Homes were your own idea?"

Rachel Treherne hesitated.

"I think so. I had an old governess—we were all very fond of her. She made me feel how unfair it was that people like her should work for others all their lives and then have a bitterly poor old age. When I had to consider what I was to do with all this money I thought about Miss Barker, and that gave me the idea of the Treherne Homes."

"You devoted the whole of your father's fortune to the Homes?"

"Oh, no—I don't want you to think that. There were certain sums I could touch, but a great deal of the capital was tied up—rather curiously tied up." She paused, and her voice changed. "I could leave it by will, but I couldn't give it away. It is a little difficult to explain. Legally I have entire discretion, but actually I am bound by my father's wishes. That is why he left all the money to me—he knew that he could trust me to consider myself bound."

Miss Silver's eyes lifted again. She looked for a moment at Rollo Treherne's daughter. Width of brow under the dark hair; eyes widely set; nostrils very sensitive; lips pressed together for control, but not thin—no, a good mouth, generously cut and meant to smile; chin firm. She thought she knew why this woman had been burdened with wealth. Just because it would be a burden to her, and not a toy. She said,

"Just so. You are a trustee—morally. I quite understand."

Miss Treherne leaned an elbow on the table and rested her cheek upon her hand.

"It's very difficult," she said. "I had to give you the background, because without it you wouldn't understand. About three months ago I got an anonymous letter. Of course, I've had them before, but it was different—"

"I hope you kept it, Miss Treherne."

Rachel shook her head.

"Oh, no, I destroyed it at once. And it wouldn't have helped you. It was just words cut out of a newspaper and stuck on to the commonest white writing-paper. There was no beginning and no signature. It said, 'You have had that money long enough. It is other people's turn now.'"

"Did it come by post?"

"Yes—with a London postmark. That was on August the twenty-sixth. A week later there was another, very short. It said, 'You have lived long enough.' And a week later again a third letter, 'Get ready to die.'"

Miss Silver said, "Dear me! And you did not keep any of them. What a pity. How were the envelopes addressed?"

Rachel Treherne moved, sat back in her chair, and said,

"That is the strange part of it. The address in each case had been cut from a letter which I had already received."

"You mean the envelope was an old one?"

"No, not the envelope. But a couple of inches with my name and address had been cut from a letter which had come to me through the post, and gummed on to a new envelope."

"From what letters were they taken?"

"The first from a letter addressed by my sister Mabel, Mrs. Wadlow, the second from a letter from a cousin, Miss Ella

8

Comperton, and the third from another cousin, a young girl, Caroline Ponsonby. But of course it had nothing to do with them. Their letters had reached me and been read, and the envelopes thrown aside."

Miss Silver said, "I see—" She went on knitting. When she thought the pause had lasted long enough she spoke. "I would rather hear the whole story before we examine the details. I suppose you did not come here just to tell me about these letters. There has been something further—" The pause extended itself. Miss Silver continued to knit.

In the end Rachel Treherne managed two words.

"Something—yes—"

"Then will you please tell me about it."

Miss Treherne dropped her brow upon her hand in such a fashion as to screen her eyes. When she spoke, it was in a low, even voice.

"A day or two after the last letter I had a narrow escape from falling downstairs. I had been washing my dog, and I was carrying him. I didn't want him to shake himself until I could get him downstairs, so I was hurrying. And just as I came to the top step my own maid, Louisa Barnet, caught me by the arm. 'Oh, Miss Rachel!' she said, and she pulled me back. We have been together since we were children and she is very devoted to me. I could see that she was white and shaking. She held on to me and said, 'You'd have got your death if I hadn't stopped you. I nearly got mine coming up, but you going down and your hands taken up with Neusel—oh, you wouldn't have had a chance!' I said, 'What do you mean, Louie?' and she said, 'Look for yourself, Miss Rachel!'"

"And what did you see?" enquired Miss Silver in an interested voice.

"The stairs go down in a long, straight flight from a half-way landing. They are of oak and uncarpeted. I was on the landing when Louisa stopped me. I don't allow the stairs to be too highly polished, but when I looked I could see that the first three treads were like glass. Louisa had just come up. She said her feet went from under her as if she had been on ice. She came down on her hands and knees, and just saved herself by catching at one of the banisters. With the dog in my arms I should have been quite helpless. I mightn't have been killed, but I should certainly have been very badly hurt. The house-maid is a local girl, steady and not too bright. She said she had done the stairs just as usual." Rachel Treherne gave the ghost of a laugh. "I've never had to complain of her polishing anything too much!"

"And when did you come up those stairs yourself—or when had anyone else been up or down?"

"Not all the afternoon so far as I know, but I didn't want to make a fuss or ask questions. The house was full. I was in my room writing letters. My sister was resting. The girls were somewhere in the garden. Everyone else was out. I finished washing Neusel at half past four, and I shouldn't think anyone had come up or down since three o'clock."

"Plenty of time to polish three steps," observed Miss Silver.

Rachel Treherne made no answer, but after a moment she went on speaking.

"I shouldn't have thought of it again if it hadn't been for the letters. I tried very hard not to attach any importance to it, but I couldn't get it off my mind. You see, the stairs would be done before breakfast, and if they had been like that all day, someone would have slipped on them long before half past four. But if they were polished in the afternoon when everybody was out of the way, then it was done on purpose to make someone fall. And after those letters I couldn't help thinking that I was the someone. I couldn't get it off my mind."

"What polish had been used? Could you tell?"

"Oh, yes. It was some the housekeeper got to try—a new stuff called Glasso, but I wouldn't have it used on the floors because it made them too slippery."

There was another pause. Miss Silver laid down her knitting and wrote in the shiny exercise-book. Then she said,

"Is that all?" and Rachel Treherne took her hand from her eyes and cried,

"Oh, no—it isn't!"

Miss Silver gave a little cough.

"It will be much easier if you will go straight on. What happened after that?"

"Nothing for about a week. Then Louisa Barnet found the curtains on fire in my room. She beat the fire out, and there was not much damage done, but—it couldn't have been an accident. There was no open flame in the room, or any way the curtains could have caught. I wasn't in any real danger, I suppose, but it wasn't a pleasant thing to happen on the top of everything else."

Miss Silver's needles clicked.

"A fire is always unpleasant," she pronounced.

Miss Treherne sat back in her chair.

"The worst thing happened four days ago. It is what brought me here, but I've been wondering whether I could tell you about it. It's so vile—" She said the last words in a slow, almost bewildered manner.

Miss Silver picked up her pink ball and unwound a handful of wool.

"It would really be much better if you did not keep breaking off," she said in her most practical manner. "Pray continue."

At another time Rachel Treherne would have been tempted to laugh. Even now a flicker of humour crossed her mood. She said,

"I know. I will tell you about it as quickly as possible. On Saturday I did some shopping in Ledlington. One of the things I brought home was a box of chocolates. I am the only one in the family who likes soft centres, so I chose a good hard mixture, but I made them take out just a few and put in some of the ones I like myself. The chocolates were the sort that have the name stamped on them so that you can tell what you are taking. I handed them round after dinner, and they were very good. I had two with soft centres, and enjoyed

11

them. I took the box up to my room because Louisa Barnet is fond of chocolates too. She is like me, she doesn't care for the hard centres. She was with me when I bought them, and I knew she would expect her share, so I told her to help herself. She took one, and almost immediately ran into the bathroom and spat it out. When she had rinsed her mouth she came back. She was terribly upset. She said, 'That chocolate was as bitter as gall—there's someone trying to harm you, Miss Rachel! You can't get from it.' She brought the box of chocolates over to me, and we examined them thoroughly. The ones with the hard centres were all right, and we put them aside. There were about a dozen left with soft centres. Three of these had had a little hole made in the bottom and filled up again. It was quite cleverly done, but you could see it. I touched the filling of one of these chocolates with my tongue, and it had a strong bitter taste. I burnt all the chocolates that were left."

"A very foolish proceeding," said Miss Silver briskly. "You should have had them analysed."

Rachel answered with a hopeless gesture and a single word. Her hand lifted from her knee and fell again. She said,

"Impossible."

CHAPTER 3

Miss Silver waited. No other words followed. She knitted to the end of her row, and then remarked,

"This is for Hilary Cunningham's baby. A sweet colour—so very delicate."

Rachel Treherne's dark eyes rested for a moment upon the pale pink wool. She said in an absent voice,

"I didn't know that Hilary had a baby."

"Not till January." Miss Silver began another row. "And

now, Miss Treherne, I think we had better proceed. I asked you to tell me three things. Firstly, why should anyone want to kill you? You have not really replied to this, unless your statement that you are Rollo Treherne's daughter, and that he has left you discretionary powers over his very large fortune, is an answer."

Miss Treherne said without looking at her,

"It might be."

"I asked you, secondly, whether any attempt had been made on your life, and if so, in what circumstances. To this you have replied very fully. Thirdly, I enquired who it was that you suspected. It is very necessary for me to have an answer to that third question."

Rachel said, "I suppose so," and then remained silent for quite a long time. Her hands were once more clasped in her lap. She looked down at them, and when she began to speak she did not raise her eyes.

"Miss Silver, I believe that I can trust you. My difficulty is this—I do not see how you can help me unless I am frank with you, unless I tell you everything. But that is the trouble. With the best will in the world, one can't tell everything. I look at the problem, at the people, and I look at them through my own temperament, my own mood—perhaps through my own fear, my own doubt, my own suspicion. These things do not make for clear vision. And, not seeing clearly myself, I have to choose, I have to select what I am going to tell you, and then I have to find words to convey these troubled impressions to you, a stranger. You have no check on what I tell you. You don't know the people or the circumstances. Don't you see how impossible it is to give you anything except an unfair picture?"

"I see that you are very anxious to be fair. Now will you tell me who it is that you suspect?"

Rachel Treherne looked up.

"No one," she said.

"And who is it that Louisa Barnet suspects?"

Rachel turned abruptly. She faced Miss Silver across the table now.

"No one," she said—"no one person. She's afraid for me, and it makes her suspicious. It is because of these suspicions that I have felt bound to come to you. I can't go on like this, living with people, seeing them constantly, being fond of them, and these dreadful suspicions always there between us."

"I see," said Miss Silver. "If I may quote from Lord Tennyson's poem of *Maud*—'Villainy somewhere! Whose? One says, we are villains all.' And again:

> 'Why do they prate of the blessings of peace? We have
>   made them a curse.
> Pickpockets, each hand lusting for all that is not its own.
> And lust of gain, in the spirit of Cain, is it better or
>   worse
> Than the heart of the citizen hissing in war on his own
>   hearthstone?'

Really very apt, I think. I fear that the lust of gain in the heart of Cain is responsible for a great deal of crime."

Rachel Treherne said "Cain—" in a sort of whisper, and Miss Silver nodded.

"Impossible not to realize that it is some member of your family circle who is suspected by Louisa Barnet, if not by yourself."

"Miss Silver!"

"You had better face it. When it comes to attempted murder, it is no use just letting things slide. I am sure that you must realize this. For your own sake, and for the sake of your relatives, the matter must be cleared up. Your fears may be groundless. The attempt may have come from some other quarter than the one which is causing you so much distress. We will attack the matter courageously and see what can be done. Now, Miss Treherne, I would like full details of your household, the members of your family, and any guests who were staying with you at the time of these attempts."

14

Rachel Treherne looked at her for a moment. Then she began to speak in a quiet, steady voice.

"I have a house at Whincliff. My father built it. It is called Whincliff Edge, and it stands, as the name suggests, on the edge of a cliff overlooking the sea. There are very fine gardens on the landward side. It is in fact a kind of show place, and the house is big enough to accommodate a good many guests. I have therefore to employ a considerable staff outside, and a housekeeper and five maids indoors. I don't employ any men indoors. My housekeeper, Mrs. Evans, has been in the family for twenty years—she is one of the nicest women in the world. The maids are local girls and from no farther afield than Ledlington—I know all about them and their families. Maids generally stay with me until they marry. They are all nice, respectable girls. None of them could have the slightest motive for wishing to harm me. My guests—" She paused, and then went on. "The house is often full. My father built it not just for himself and me, but to be a rallying point for the family. They regard it in this light, and I am very seldom alone there."

"You mentioned a sister, I believe."

"Yes—my sister Mabel."

"A younger sister?"

"No, five years older. She married young, and my father made a settlement on her then."

"He did not leave her anything more in his will?"

"No."

"And was she satisfied?"

Miss Treherne bit her lip. She said,

"There was no quarrel. My father did not expect his will to please everyone, but he had his own reasons for what he did."

Miss Silver coughed slightly.

"People's reasons so seldom appeal to relatives," she remarked. "Pray continue, Miss Treherne. You said your sister was married. Has she any family, and were they staying with you at the time of these occurrences?"

15

"Yes. Mabel is not very strong. She had been with me all through August. Her husband, Ernest Wadlow, was coming down for the week-ends. He is a writer—travel, biography, that sort of thing. Their two children were also coming down for the week-ends. Maurice, who is twenty-three, is reading for the Bar, and Cherry, who is nineteen, is engaged in having a good time. The other guests were my young cousin, Richard Treherne, who is a grandson of my father's brother; a first cousin on my father's side, Miss Ella Comperton—she has a little flat in town, but she is always very pleased to get away from it; a first cousin on my mother's side, Cosmo Frith; and his young cousin and mine, Caroline Ponsonby—"

"One moment," said Miss Silver. "Which, if any, of these relatives were staying with you on the dates upon which you received the three anonymous letters?"

"None of them," said Rachel Treherne, "except my sister Mabel. She was with me all through August and September, but the others only came down for the week-ends."

Miss Silver put down her knitting and took up a pencil.

"I should like those dates, if you please."

Rachel Treherne gave them as one who has a lesson by heart.

"The first letter, Thursday, August 26th—the second, Thursday, September 2nd—and the third, September 9th, also a Thursday."

"And the incident of the polished steps?"

"September 11th."

"A Saturday?"

"Yes, a Saturday."

Miss Silver entered these particulars.

"And the fire in your room?"

"The following Saturday, September 18th."

"And the incident of the chocolates?"

"Last Saturday, October 30th."

Miss Silver wrote that down, then looked up, pencil poised.

"Nothing happened between 18th September and 30th October?"

"No. I was away a good deal. I had no guests—" With a sudden realization of what she had said, a brilliant colour flushed her cheeks. She looked beautiful, startled, distressed. "You mustn't think—" she began.

Miss Silver interrupted her.

"My dear Miss Treherne, we must both think—calmly, quietly, and above all dispassionately. No innocent person will be harmed by our doing so. Only guilt need shrink from investigation. Innocence will be vindicated. Pray let us continue. I have here a list of your relatives, written down as you gave them to me—Mr. and Mrs. Wadlow, your brother-in-law and sister. Mr. Maurice and Miss Cherry Wadlow, their son and daughter. Mr. Richard Treherne. Miss Ella Comperton, Mr. Cosmo Frith, and Miss Caroline Ponsonby, all cousins. You have told me that none of these relatives except Mrs. Wadlow was in the house upon the dates on which the anonymous letters were written, posted, or received by you. I should now like you to tell me which of them was staying in the house on September 11th, the day of the polished steps incident."

The colour had left Rachel Treherne's face again. She said,

"They were all there."

"And on the following Saturday, September 18th, when the curtains in your room were found to be on fire?"

"They were all there."

"And during the six weeks when you had no guests there were no more occurrences of a suspicious nature?"

"Miss Silver!"

"Let us be dispassionate. There were, in fact, no more occurrences during that period. But on Saturday, October 30th, there was the incident of the chocolates. Which of these relatives was in the house on that occasion?"

Miss Treherne repeated the phrase which she had already used twice, but in a tone that was almost inaudible.

"They were all there."

Miss Silver remarked, "Dear me!" turned a page, wrote a heading, and said in a bright, matter-of-fact tone, "Now if you

will give me a little information about each of these relatives—just the merest outline, comprising age, occupation,
financial position—"

"Miss Silver—I *can't!*"

Miss Silver looked at her kindly but firmly.

"Indeed you can, my dear Miss Treherne. It is best for us to
speak quite plainly. As matters stand, you are in continual
fear of being obliged to suspect one or other of your relations.
The situation is quite impossible, and it must be cleared up. If
you withhold information, I cannot help you. Let us continue.
We will begin with your sister Mabel, Mrs. Wadlow."

CHAPTER 4

Miss Silver's notes:

"*Mabel Wadlow:*—Age 44. Nervous semi-invalid. Reads a
great many novels—thrillers. Very fond of husband and children. Some sense of injury over father's will.

Ernest Wadlow:—Age 52. Dilettante. Traveler. Writer. Never
made much money by his books. Wife's money not much in
evidence. Miss Treherne obviously assists them.

Maurice Wadlow:—Age 23. Reading for the Bar. Socialisti-
cally inclined. Perhaps dearer to his parents than to Miss T.
Anxiety on her part to be fair to him very marked. Probably
clever, bumptious young man, too pleased with himself to
please others. This merely conjecture.

Cherry Wadlow:—Age 19. Pretty girl. Out for a good time.
Rather giddy. Nineteen usually either too giddy or too serious.

Ella Comperton:—Age 49. Daughter of Rollo Treherne's
elder sister Eliza. Spinster on small income. Small flat, small
interests, small life. Some jealousy that younger cousin
should be rich woman? Miss T's tone that in which we speak

of someone whom we commiserate but cannot really love.

Cosmo Frith:—Age 45. Another dilettante, but of a different type. All the talents but no executive ability. Jack of all trades and master of none. Unmarried. Fond of society, fond of pretty faces—*Wein Weib und Gesang.* Is a first cousin on the mother's side, and Miss T. has a good deal of affection for him. Finances precarious.

Caroline Ponsonby:—Age 22. First cousin once removed of Miss T, Mrs. Wadlow, and Cosmo Frith. Miss T. has a great affection for this young girl. Described her in v. warm voice as 'the dearest child.' Small independent income.

Richard Treherne:—Age 26. First cousin once removed on the father's side, being grandson of Rollo Treherne's younger brother Maurice. Architect. Foot on bottom rung of ladder. Ambitious. Miss T. has put a certain amount of work in his way. From manner in which she spoke of there being no blood relationship between him and Caroline it is clear that she would welcome a match between them. Lord T. says, 'In the spring a young man's fancy lightly turns to thoughts of love.' Have not noticed that November has any chilling effect. Miss T. very warmly interested in both these young people."

CHAPTER 5

Having taken down these notes, Miss Silver sat back in her chair and picked up the pale pink coatee.

"There—that is over," she said, and began to knit. "And now, I am afraid, I must ask you what financial interest these relatives have in your death."

Rachel Treherne met this question calmly, as one meets a long expected shock. She said,

"I knew you would ask me that, but it is not at all an easy question to answer. The circumstances are very unusual. I think I told you that my father had left me this money as a trust. He made no legal conditions as to how I was to dispose of it, but he told me what he wanted me to do, and I promised that I would carry out his wishes. Miss Silver, I do feel sure that I can trust you—you have really made me feel sure about that—but what I am going to tell you now concerns my father, and you won't ever speak of it to anyone, will you, or—or write it down?"

Miss Silver looked at her. Miss Silver said,

"I will not speak of it, and I will not write it down."

Rachel Treherne went on.

"My father ran away with my mother. She had a little money, and he had none. This is important, because it is what brings in my mother's relations. Without her money he couldn't have made a start, and so, in disposing of his fortune, he wished her relations to be considered on the same footing as his own. He took her to the United States, and they had a very hard struggle. They lost their first two children. It was ten years before Mabel was born, and I came five years later. Then my mother died. My father was only just getting along up till then, but the following year he began to make money. Everything he touched turned to gold. Oil was found on some land he had bought for a song. It made him an immensely wealthy man. He came back to this country and died here. The things he asked me to promise were these. It weighed on him that the man who had been his partner in buying the oilfield had not profited from it. There was some quarrel. The land was believed valueless. The partnership broke up, and Mr. Brent walked out. My father made a fortune, and it weighed on him that he ought to have shared it with Sterling Brent. He told me that he had always kept on the right side of the law, but that what mattered when you came to die was whether you had kept on the right side of your conscience. He had tried to find his old partner, but he hadn't been able to. He told me the sum that was due to him, and he said I was never to touch it, and I was to go on trying to find Mr. Brent or his heirs. That was the first thing."

"You have not been able to trace Mr. Brent?"

"No. It is so long ago that I think he must be dead. If he is not traced during my lifetime, the money is to endow a certain number of scholarships for Americans at Oxford and Cambridge, to be called the Brent Scholarships."

Miss Silver gave an approving nod.

"Mr. Treherne expressed more than one wish, I think you said."

"Yes. The other thing that I promised is much more difficult to carry out. He wished his money to come into the hands of those who would use it best. He considered that in the interval between his death and mine there would be changes in the characters and circumstances of the possible heirs. Children would be born, young people would grow up and marry. There might be deteriorations or improvements. There might be deaths. He did not feel able to decide on what was to happen to his money after another generation had passed, so he left the decision to me. That is not so unusual, though I was very young—too young. But what he asked me to promise was, I think, a very unusual thing. I was to make a new will every year. He said most people made their wills and forgot all about them. He wanted to ensure that I would keep mine up-to-date. I was to go through it once a year and adjust the legacies in the light of what had happened during that year."

Miss Silver's needles clicked and checked. She said,

"Dear me—a very onerous task to lay upon a young girl."

"I promised, and I have kept my promise. I don't know that I would make such a promise today. But I was very young. I loved my father, and I would have done anything he asked of me."

Miss Silver coughed.

"It did not occur to your father that you might marry?"

The colour came into Rachel Treherne's face. Not the brilliant flame of a little while back, but a faint, becoming flush.

"I don't believe he did. Men are like that."

Miss Silver was watching her.

"And you?"

Rachel Treherne laughed a little sadly.

"Oh, I thought about it—girls always do. But—well, since we are being so very frank, he thought I had too much money, and I thought he had too little courage. And after that I was much, much too busy."

"It would have made it all a great deal easier for you if you had had a husband and children. But since you have no natural and undisputed heirs, this arrangement of Mr. Treherne's must result in maintaining a continual state of excitement and uncertainty in the family—if it is known. Now, Miss Treherne, this is a very important question. *Is it known?*"

Rachel Treherne frowned. The frown made her look older. She said in a slow, vexed voice,

"I am afraid it is known."

"How? Who spoke of it? Your father? You? Surely not your legal adviser?"

"My father spoke of it to my sister. He was very ill. I'm sure he wouldn't have done so if he had been himself. It has always made things very difficult for me."

"Most unfortunate," said Miss Silver. "And does everyone in the family know of the arrangement?"

There was a momentary flash of humour in Rachel Treherne's dark eyes.

"I should think so. You see, it was a grievance, and when my sister and her husband have a grievance, well, they like to share it. I think it is quite safe to say that everyone in the family knows I revise my will once a year in January. Some of them are tactful about it, some of them resent it, the young ones treat it as rather a joke. If only they didn't know—"

Miss Silver took up her pencil and added a word to her

notes on Mabel Wadlow. The word was, "Indiscreet." She leaned back and said,

"Is it possible that the terms of your present will are known?"

"I don't know."

"You must know whether there is such a possibility."

Rachel was silent.

"Have you at any time had a draft of your will in the house?"

"Yes."

"You are not helping me, Miss Treherne. Would it have been possible for anyone to see that draft?"

"I suppose it would. Oh, one doesn't think about things like that!"

"I am sorry to distress you, but I am afraid we must think about them. You had the draft in an unlocked drawer?"

"No, locked. But I am careless about my keys."

"I see. And if I were to ask you who would chiefly benefit if you were to die before you could make this annual revision of your will, would you answer me?"

Rachel Treherne pushed back her chair and got up. She said,

"No, Miss Silver, I couldn't tell you that."

Miss Silver remained seated. She was knitting again.

"Do you wish me to take your case?"

Rachel Treherne looked at her. Her eyes said, "Help me." Her lips said,

"Please—if you will."

The needles clicked.

"I wonder if you will take my advice," said Miss Silver.

Rachel's lips parted in a sudden charming smile.

"If I can," she said.

"Go home and tell your sister that you took the opportunity of being in town to go through your will, and that you have made considerable changes in it this time. She will certainly inform your other relatives, and for the present there will be no more attempts upon your life."

All the colour went out of Rachel Treherne's face.

"No—I couldn't do that."

"It would be a safeguard."

"No, I won't do it! I won't tell lies—it's too degrading!"

"Make it true then. See your lawyer, alter your will, and let your relations know that you have done so."

Rachel stood there silently with her hands on the table edge. She seemed to lean on them. At last she said,

"I will think about it. Is there anything else?"

"Yes. I am thinking of taking a short holiday. Can you recommend me to cottage lodgings in your neighborhood? I should be an acquaintance who is friendly with the Cunninghams. It would then be quite natural for us to meet, and for you to invite me to the house."

"I can invite you to stay."

"Without exciting remark? It is very necessary that no one should imagine I am anything but a private visitor."

Rachel Treherne smiled again.

"Oh, but I am always asking people down—all sorts of people. It will be quite easy. I like having people who can't afford to go away, and—" She stopped short and coloured vividly.

But Miss Maud Silver was not at all offended.

"I shall do very well as a gentlewoman of restricted means," she observed. "Let me see—I can come down on Saturday. You can just mention Hilary Cunningham, but I should not stress the connection. And I think you had better call me a retired governess." Most unexpectedly her eyes twinkled. "And that need not trouble your conscience, because it is perfectly true. I was in the scholastic profession for twenty years." She got up and extended her hand. "I disliked it extremely. Good-bye, Miss Treherne."

CHAPTER 6

Miss Treherne was met at Ledlington by her extremely comfortable car. As she was driven through the dark lanes she
could not help thinking how secure she must appear. Nobody
who saw her drive away with a fur rug over her knees and the
steady, responsible Barlow at the wheel, could have believed
that under this appearance of safety there was a nightmare of
fear, an anguished struggle against suspicion. She looked at
Barlow's solid back, and could hardly believe it herself.

She was glad that the house would not be full—only Mabel
and Ernest, and Caroline, who was so much the child of the
house that she did not count. She supposed that Richard might
turn up, but she was always pleased to see Richard. She was
tired, but she would have a clear hour before dinner. The
thought of a hot bath was pleasant, and Louie brushing her hair.

She came into the hall, and found it full of people. Ernest,
Mabel, Richard, Caroline, and Maurice and Cherry who had
apparently just arrived and wished to dine but not to sleep,
because they had to get back to town.

"And this makes quite a good road-house, darling."
Cherry's light, fleeting laugh had no more warmth than the
term of endearment which she applied to everyone she met.
Her prettiness had something brittle about it—the very fair
hair with a sugar-loaf cap crammed on amongst its curls, the
very thin hands with their pointed blood-red nails, the
painted arch of the lips. As always when she saw them
together, Rachel's eyes went to Caroline, who came forward,
kissed her, and said in that slow, soft voice of hers,

"Are you quite frozen?"

"No, not quite. How many of you are sleeping here? I suppose Mrs. Evans knows. Cherry, you and Maurice had much better stay. Barlow says the roads will be dangerous in another hour—it's freezing on the melted snow."

Mabel Wadlow turned round with her hand on her son's arm. She was a small woman, and had once been as fair as Cherry, but her skin had gone lined and sallow, and her hair as colourless as dried grass. It had something of the same off-greenish tint. She had a high, fretful voice.

"That's what I've been saying," she complained. "And perhaps Maurice will listen to you. Of course what I say doesn't matter to anyone."

Maurice said, "Oh, come!" and slipped an arm about her waist. He had the same small, regular features as his sister, the same rather near-set eyes; but whereas Cherry had seen to it that her lashes were a good half dozen shades darker than her hair, his were still as sandy as nature had made them. He wore a small struggling moustache, and occasionally threatened the family with a beard. He was at the moment quite determined to throw up a legal career in favour of politics. He hoped to induce his aunt to finance this change of plan, but up to date he had found her very unresponsive. He said,

"Well, I would like to have a talk with you, Rachel."

Rachel Treherne said "Presently" in rather a weary voice.

"You've missed Cosmo," said Mabel Wadlow. "He was seeing someone in Ledlington. He came out here for tea. Oh, and Ella rang up and wanted to know if she could bring a friend over to lunch—you know, that Mrs. Barber she stays with. They came over in Mrs. Barber's car. I don't know how all these people afford cars, I'm sure." Mrs. Wadlow's tone suggested that this was a personal grievance.

Rachel felt a faint thankfulness at having missed Mrs. Barber—one of those people who are obsessed with the excellence of their own good works and are forever thrusting them down your throat. But it appeared that she had rejoiced too soon. Ella

Comperton proposed transferring herself from Mrs. Barber's cottage to Whincliff Edge in time for lunch next day, and Mrs. Barber would drive her over. She couldn't stay to lunch, but she would drive her over. Mrs. Barber therefore had not been completely avoided. One might perhaps be out shopping, or taking Neusel for a walk. And by the way, where was Neusel?

She had reached the staircase, when with a scurry and a rush a black and tan dachshund precipitated himself down the stairs, giving tongue as he came. When he actually reached her his screams became frantic. He nuzzled an adored ankle, shrieked on a high top note, took a fond bite at a restraining hand, moaned, screamed again, and snatching a glove, raced off with it ahead of her.

"I can't think how Rachel can bear that noisy dog," said Mabel Wadlow, with her hand to her head. "Oh dear—just listen to him! Now, Maurice, it's quite settled that you stay. No, Cherry, it is not the slightest use your making that sort of face. I know no one pays any attention to me, but perhaps you'll listen to your father. Ernest, tell Cherry that it is all settled, and that they are to stay. And now I really do think we should all go and dress."

Cherry Wadlow looked across to where Richard Treherne was reading a letter. She laughed and said,

"Richard isn't staying. Like to drive me up to town, Dicky? You're not one of the nervous ones."

Richard Treherne looked up—a dark, strongly built young man with glasses. His best friend could not have called him handsome, and when he frowned as he was doing now he looked formidable, but his voice when he spoke was a remarkably pleasant one.

"Cherry darling, when you call me Dicky I am liable to an attack of homicidal mania. Just as well I am staying here, because if you did it when we were alone together in a car, there might be a nasty accident."

"In fact I'm not Carrie."

"And if you call Caroline Carrie, I shan't wait till we're alone—I shall just get on with it and murder you here and now."

"Might be rather amusing," said Cherry. "Car-o-line, what would you do if a murderer offered you his heart and his blood-stained hand?"

Caroline smiled. She was one of the people who do everything with a kind of slow grace. Richard Treherne once said that she always suggested music off. She was not very tall, or very small, or very dark, or very fair. She had lovely brown eyes and very beautiful hands and feet. People who loved her loved her very much indeed. She smiled now and said,

"I should tell him to wash it." And went up the stairs without looking back.

At her own door Rachel Treherne was met by Louisa Barnet—and Louisa in not at all a good temper.

"You'll be frozen, Miss Rachel. What you wanted to go up to town for on a day like this, the dear knows, for I don't. And that Noisy's got one of your new gloves."

Miss Treherne called in a laughing, indulgent voice.

"Noisy! *Darling!* Not my new glove! Oh, Noisy—*please!*"

"A good smack is what he wants if you ask me!"

"But I don't, Louie dear. Noisy—wicked one—give it up—there's a darling!"

Neusel, thus wooed, advanced with prancing and tail-wagging to drop the glove. He leapt joyously and licked his mistress's face as she bent down to pick it up.

Louisa frowned severely.

"'Orrid creature!" she said. "It passes me how you can *let* him. And I wouldn't have him in your room if it was me, because he've just been sick."

Rachel gazed at the sparkling eyes and healthful aspect of the sinner.

"He looks all right."

"Oh, it didn't trouble *him*," said Louisa darkly.

"He'll only scream if we shut him out."

"Then he can scream where he won't be heard!" said Louisa, picking him up by the scruff of the neck and carrying him off.

CHAPTER 7

After dinner when they were all in the drawing-room, Ernest Wadlow piloted his sister-in-law to a sofa at some little distance from the group round the fire. The last thing on earth that Rachel desired was a *tête-à-tête* with Ernest, but in the twenty-five years of his marriage to Mabel she had learned the impossibility of deterring him from anything upon which he had set his mind. In his nervous, fidgety way he was quite indeflectable. She therefore resigned herself, and hoped that he would say what he wanted to say and get it over. This, however, was hoping against hope. Ernest sat down, straightened his *pince-nez*, coughed, remarked upon how cold it was, and then enquired whether she had been shopping.

Rachel leaned back, said "No," and awaited developments.

"A very cold day for shopping," said Mr. Wadlow.

He was a small man and precise in his dress, but for some reason he always wore collars which appeared to be at least one size too large for him, and which afforded the public an uninterrupted view of an unusually large Adam's apple. For the rest, he had the same near-set eyes as his son and daughter, but his hair and his small worried-looking moustache were quite dark.

Rachel said, "But I wasn't shopping."

Ernest Wadlow took off his *pince-nez* and began to polish the lenses.

"Ah—business," he remarked. "You have a great deal on your hands. Very capable hands they are too. But you mustn't

29

overdo it—you mustn't overdo it." He replaced the *pince-nez* and gazed at her solemnly. "You really do look very tired."

Rachel smiled.

"Thank you, Ernest. When a man says that to a woman, what he really means is that she is looking plain."

Mr. Wadlow appeared shocked.

"My dear Rachel—what an idea! The fact is, Mabel is worried about you."

"She needn't be."

"Ah, but she is. And it's not at all good for her to be worried, as you know. Only this afternoon she had a really alarming attack of palpitations. She said then 'Rachel is overdoing it'—I am quoting her exact words—'If she doesn't take care of herself she will have a breakdown.' I replied, 'My dear, you know perfectly well'—again I quote my actual words—'you know perfectly well, and your sister Rachel knows perfectly well, that if she finds the burden of her business affairs too much for her—she knows,' I said, 'that I shall be only too glad to give her any assistance in my power.'"

"I am sure of it," said Miss Treherne.

Mr. Wadlow straightened his *pince-nez*. The Adam's apple quivered.

"'But,' I said, 'I am not one to proffer assistance or—er—advice where it has not been asked for, or in circumstances which might expose me to a rebuff.'"

Rachel made a sudden movement.

"And was Mabel having palpitations all the time you were saying this?"

Ernest Wadlow stared without offence but with some slight surprise.

"I was relating the conversation which led up to the palpitations."

Rachel smiled. She disliked her brother-in-law, but it was seventeen years since she had admitted as much to anyone.

"My dear Ernest, all this is waste of time. I am tired tonight, but I am perfectly well. There is no need for Mabel to have palpitations on my account, and there is no need for you to offer me your very kind help with my business affairs. Now if that's all you wanted to say to me—"

She knew already that it was not. The purpose for which she had been isolated was still unfulfilled. From behind the glimmering, ever crooked *pince-nez* it maintained a steady pressure.

"Do not go, Rachel. We are a good deal concerned—I think I may say that we are even alarmed about Maurice. He has informed his mother and myself that he intends to join the Communist party. I believe he wishes to go to Russia for a year."

"I should encourage that. It will probably cure him."

"Mabel is distracted at the idea. She has been told that the sanitary conditions are far from satisfactory, even in Moscow and Leningrad."

"I don't see what I can do about it, Ernest."

Mr. Wadlow fidgeted. His Adam's apple slid up and down.

"If you were to see your way to assist the—er—scheme in which he was so desirous of joining—"

"You mean that Share-and-Share-Alike Colony?"

"Mabel thinks it would keep him in England."

What Miss Treherne would have liked to say was, "And why should anyone suppose that I have the slightest desire to keep Maurice in England?" But she curbed herself—she had had much useful practice in the art—and merely observed,

"A wild-cat scheme. I couldn't possibly have anything to do with it."

Mr. Wadlow put out a deprecating hand.

"Youth is always at extremes. Maurice will learn wisdom."

"I hope so."

There was real anxiety in Ernest Wadlow's voice as he said,

"But if he goes to Russia—Rachel, we can't feel easy about that."

"Perhaps he won't go."

"He will if this other scheme falls through. He is quite off reading for the Bar. He says all our legal machinery in this country is effete and ought to be liquidated. Mabel is more than uneasy. But if he had five thousand pounds to put into the Colony—"

A warm glow of anger brought the color to Miss Treherne's cheeks.

"Five thousand pounds? My dear Ernest!"

Mabel Wadlow had come up behind the sofa. She leaned between them and said in a low voice, but with surprising energy,

"Oh, Rachel! It wouldn't be anything to you, and it would keep my boy at home."

Rachel Treherne got up.

"I can't discuss it. I couldn't possibly put money into that sort of thing."

Mabel's voice began to flutter.

"Oh, Rachel—how unkind—my boy—your own nephew! And after all—it would only mean—advancing some of what will come to him—some day."

The glow rose to a white heat. Rachel Treherne said,

"You mean when I am dead. But who told you that Maurice would come in for five thousand pounds, or five thousand pence, if I were to die tomorrow?" She spoke quite low.

Someone had switched on the wireless at the other end of the room. There was talk and laughter. She looked at Mabel and Ernest, and she thought, "He was down for ten thousand in that draft . . . *And they know it.*"

She saw their faces change—Ernest just got to his feet, Mabel peeked and tearful, leaning a little forward with her hands on the padded back of the sofa. Her heart turned sick within her. She said quite low,

"Please don't let us talk of it any more," and turning, walked over to the group by the fire.

CHAPTER 8

They made room for her. Richard pulled up a chair. Caroline caught her hand as she passed and held it against her cheek.

"Oh, darling—you're still cold!"

"It's only my hands," said Rachel Treherne. Her face burned. She leaned back and screened it from the fire.

"What were the parents talking to you about?" said Cherry in an inquisitive voice.

They were still talking to each other at the far end of the room. Anger had loosened Rachel's tongue. With a trace of surprise she heard herself say,

"Something that I don't want to go on talking about."

Cherry's eyes sparkled maliciously.

"Oh, then it was Maurice. And I bet they wanted you to give him money—as usual. But if there's any going, I'm a much more deserving object."

"I said I didn't want to talk about it, Cherry."

Maurice was glaring at his sister. Richard Treherne struck in.

"I saw the most extraordinary thing when I was on my way over this afternoon. I came the cliff way, and as I passed Tollage's place, he'd got two men digging out a length of that old mixed hedge of his. A great pity, for it makes a good wind-break, but his wife wants to see the sea from her drawing-room windows. Well, the men called out to me as I passed and showed me half a dozen adders they'd dug out, laid up for the winter under the hedge. There was quite a crowd of village boys hanging round on the watch to see if any more would turn up."

Maurice laughed.

"Pity Cherry wasn't there," he said. "An adder would make just the right kind of pet for her."

Cherry rolled her eyes at Richard. She had changed into a pale green dress with no back, no sleeves, and very little front. Her skin was as white and as smooth as milk. She said in an affected voice,

"Oh, I should *love* a snake!"

Richard's eyes met hers with rather an odd look.

"Well, you had your chance. You must have come that way."

"Adders are rather dull," said Cherry. "What I should adore is one of those long, slinky, thin ones, bright emerald green, with a forked tongue. And it must be long enough to go three times round my arm and then do a sort of coil round the neck."

"I hate snakes," said Caroline in her soft voice.

She was wearing green too—a bright stuff patterned with silver. It had long sleeves, and a long skirt, and a high draped neck. Richard thought, "She looks like leaves coming out in the spring—with the sun on them—all warm and fresh. Oh, Caroline *darling!*" But on the surface he produced a slightly cynical smile and observed,

"Let us by all means get up a family subscription and present Cherry with a garter snake for her next birthday."

Cherry laughed her fleeting laugh.

"Oh, Dicky—how wizard! But why a garter? Do I know them?"

"I believe they are green—and—very poisonous."

"And that's what you get for calling him Dicky," said Maurice.

The Wadlows came back into the circle at what Rachel felt to be an opportune moment. What was the matter with Cherry that she must always be a disturbing element? . . . Jealous of Caroline? . . . Yes, undoubtedly. . . . Attracted by Richard? . . . Perhaps. . . . Oh dear—poor Cherry—what waste of time!

She came back to hear Richard say,

"You've met Gale Brandon, haven't you, Rachel?"

"Yes—quite a number of times. In fact I always seem to be meeting him. But I didn't know you knew him."

"Ah! He's a prospective client. Merrivale introduced us, and he wants me to build him a very odd kind of a house, as far as I can make out. We had rather a disconnected sort of conversation, because Merrivale was telling a long story about how he photographed a lion on the Zambesi. At least, it started by being a story about a lion, but a lot of other beasts seemed to crop up as it went along. Merrivale was holding forth in front of the fire like he always does, and this man Gale Brandon had me by the arm walking me up and down and telling me all about how to build a house, so that the whole thing got rather mixed up, and my idea that the house is going to be on the odd side may be due to the way Merrivale's lions and alligators and baboons and things kept bounding in and out of the conversation. It may all turn out rather less like the Zoo than it seems at present. By the way, a further complication was that the man Brandon kept breaking off to talk about Whincliff Edge. It appeared to be a good deal on his mind, but whether it was the house that he admired or you, Rachel, I couldn't quite make out."

Rachel smiled.

"He's an American, you know. I think he admires everything. He hasn't been over here very long, and he's full of enthusiasm. I believe he even admires the climate, but I expect today has shaken him there."

"I'll tell you something he doesn't admire," said Richard, "and that is our Louisa. He asked me in his ingenuous manner why you had had a vinegar plant installed."

Cherry giggled. Mabel Wadlow pursed her lips and murmured "Impertinent!" Ernest gazed judicially through his tilted lenses and pronounced,

"Really most offensive. He shouldn't have said that."

With the cold light of controversy in his eyes Maurice intervened.

"Nobody could possibly like Louisa—she's a thoroughly disagreeable woman. But that is not her fault—it's the fault of your damned capitalism. You take one person, and you give them money, power, position, authority. You take another—"

Caroline's eyes danced suddenly. She leaned to Richard and said at his very ear, "He's going to call Louisa a wage-slave—I feel it in my bones," and even as she said it, Maurice did.

"You make her a wage-slave, relying for her very bread upon a condition of servile dependency—"

Cherry's laugh rang out.

"Well, I shouldn't have called Louisa *servile*," she said, and for once everyone agreed with her.

"Louisa is dreadfully rude," said Caroline. "Even to Rachel. Even to Noisy—isn't she, adored angel?"

Neusel had the middle of the hearthrug. The upper and lower chests having been sufficiently toasted, he had just turned over. A pleasing warmth now played upon the spine. The melting note in Caroline's voice, and what he felt to be her very proper form of address, induced him to lift one eyelid slightly and give a very faint twitch to the end of the tail. He then relapsed into an ancestral dream in which he bearded a vast archaic badger in its lair and slew it.

Rachel Treherne laughed rather ruefully.

"Louisa can be rude," she said. "But she thinks it's good for us, and she is really devoted."

Caroline shook her head.

"To you, darling, but not to us—definitely. She simply hates us."

"Oh, Caroline!"

"She would like to take you away to a desert island and wait on you hand and foot—it sticks out all over her."

"And finish up by dying for you in some highly spectacular way," said Richard.

Rachel laughed, but there was a troubled look in her eyes.

She changed the subject, and the talk drifted away to winter sports and to a girl called Mildred that Cherry had met at Andermatt who was engaged to a fabulously rich young man called Bob. They were to be married some time early in December, and Cherry was to be a bridesmaid.

"And we shall have to give her a wedding present, I suppose," said Mabel Wadlow in her discontented voice. "She's got everything she wants, and she's marrying a man who's got more than he knows what to do with, but I suppose we shall have to try and think of something."

"I should love to give her a diamond spray from Woolworth's," said Cherry. "I should adore to see her face when she got it. I say, Maurice, let's do it anonymously. I've got an old case of Cartier's, and we could put it in that."

"And who's been giving you a brooch from Cartier's?" said Maurice. "And where is it anyhow?"

"Darling, I pawned it immediately—what do you think?"

"Cherry!" Mabel Wadlow fluttered with anxiety. "What is all this? I insist upon knowing."

Cherry laughed.

"Darling, if you're going to come over all maternal, I'm off."

"Cherry, answer your mother!" said Ernest.

She laughed again.

"What a fuss! Bob gave me a brooch, I pawned it, and that's all there is about it."

"But, Cherry—"

"And I'm not the only person who knows the way to a pop-shop—am I, Car-o-line? The bother is they always do you down. What did they give you on your diamond ring, Carrie?"

Caroline did not speak. She looked at Richard. He said,

"You haven't told us what you got for your brooch."

"About a quarter of what it was worth," said Cherry. "Quite a bit of luck my meeting Caroline—wasn't it? She

37

went out as I came in, and the man showed me her ring, but he wouldn't tell me what he'd given her for it."

Richard smiled agreeably.

"Nor will she," he said.

CHAPTER 9

Rachel Treherne went to her room with a tired and heavy heart. The thought of going to bed and forgetting all about the family for seven or eight hours was a pleasant one, but on the other side of the night there would be another day, in which she foresaw an interview with Ernest, several interviews with Mabel, a talk with Maurice, a talk with Cherry, a talk with Caroline. Ernest would press her to produce the capital for Maurice's anticapitalist crusade. Mabel would weep, flutter, reproach her, and probably have palpitations. Maurice would deliver a lecture on communism. And Cherry—no, she didn't really see herself talking to Cherry. Let Mabel deliver her own lecture on the impropriety of accepting valuable jewellery from a young man who was engaged to be married to somebody else.

Caroline—oh, Caroline was different. She must find out why the child should have pawned her mother's ring. All Rachel's thoughts softened as they dwelt on Caroline.

She found Louisa in a grimly silent humour. It was no use forbidding her to wait up, yet to be late was to incur a gloomy frown. Her dress was thrown upon a hanger and thrust fiercely into the wardrobe, but when Rachel said, "You seem tired, Louisa. Go to bed—I shan't want anything more," the words came out with a rush.

"Oh, I know you'd be glad enough to send me away, and there's those that 'ud be glad enough to see me go. Right down on their bended knees they'd be, and thanking the devil if I was out of the house and gone for good and no one to stand between you and them!"

Rachel, sitting at her dressing-table, saw the dark face work. She turned a little and said in a gentle, weary voice,

"Louie, I'm very tired. Not tonight—*please*."

Louisa caught her breath in something between a sob and a sniff.

"You won't be warned, Miss Rachel. You're angry with me because I see clear, and because I try to warn you. Not tonight—and tomorrow it'll be not today, and so it'll go on until they've got their way and it's too late, and then there'll be nothing left for me but to go and throw myself over the cliff."

"Oh, Louie!"

"Don't you think I'd do it? Don't you know I'd do it if harm was to come to you, Miss Rachel?"

Rachel Treherne got up.

"Louie, I really am too tired for this sort of thing tonight. Just go and call Neusel—Mr. Richard was letting him out for me. And then you had better go to bed."

To her relief, Louisa obeyed. She stalked to the door and opened it, but before she had time to go out there was a joyous rush of feet and Neusel arrived with all the delirious excitement of one who achieves reunion with the beloved object after incredible exertions. He tore about the room, uttered several ear-piercing barks, dragged all the bedding out of his basket, and finally flung himself down upon his back on the hearthrug, where he abandoned himself to an ecstasy of wriggling punctuated by short screams.

"Like as not he'll be sick in the night," said Louisa.

Rachel went down on her knees and gathered him up. Here at least was one who gave all and demanded nothing in return. At the moment she felt a great deal more warmly towards Neusel than she did towards Louisa. He laid his head upon her shoulder, gazed at her with melting brown eyes, and then with a sudden wriggle was out of her arms and sniffing eagerly.

"What is it, Noisy?" said Rachel.

He was standing quite still now about a yard away, tail and flanks quivering, ears pricked, and eyes intent. At the sound of her voice he threw her a rapid glance and whined.

"Noisy, what is it?"

He whined again, snuffed, and ran to the bed, where he stood on his hind legs and pulled at the bedclothes.

Rachel got up and began to collect his bedding.

"Certainly not!" she said. "You don't sleep on my bed, you little wretch. Come along, Noisy—you've got a lovely basket of your own." She patted it invitingly as she spoke.

But Neusel had begun to bark at the top of his voice. She turned, to see Louisa on the far side of the bed. She had an odd startled look on her face.

"There's something wrong, Miss Rachel."

Rachel said, "Nonsense!" But the dog was leaping, yelping, barking. As she spoke, he tore at the sheet with his teeth, and barked, and tore again.

Louisa Barnet took hold of the bedclothes in her strong bony hands and stripped them back—eiderdown, blankets, and upper sheet. They came down on the carpet with a soft thud. She let them fall, and sprang back with a scream, and a "Lord have mercy!"

Rachel did not scream, but she turned cold from head to foot. At the bottom of the stripped bed lay her new hot water bottle, green to match the furnishings of the room. But on either side of it there was a something—a coiled something that was not green, but brown. She looked with quite unbelieving eyes and saw one of the coils move and a flat head rise a little way and stay as if it hung on the air. Neusel with a run and a flying leap had landed at the pillow end of the bed. Louisa screamed again.

Neusel sprang in, bit savagely and sprang back—and in and back, and in and back again, teeth clicking, ears flapping, every movement swift and deadly as a snake's own. It was all over in the time it would take to draw half a dozen breaths, but Rachel did not breathe at all. At least she thought she had not breathed until Neusel jumped down and ran to her, head up and eyes sparkling with pride. Then she filled her lungs and went down on her knees to take him in her arms and look him over—because if he had been bitten—if he had been bitten—her dear little Noisy—

She looked up, to find Louisa standing over them ashy pale.

"He's not hurt, Louie. Oh, Louie—my clever, clever little boy! Are they dead?"

"The two of them," said Louisa. "Dead as door-nails. I'll say that for him, he was quick. In and out again before you could say Jack Robinson, and them teeth of his clicking!"

Rachel shuddered. She restrained the joyous pride with which Neusel frisked and barked about her, and got to her feet again. The brown coils lay inert and lifeless. Not a ripple stirred them. Louisa said in a sharp whisper,

"They're dead. And it might have been you! Who put them there, Miss Rachel?"

Rachel stood looking.

"I don't know."

"Someone that wished you dead, Miss Rachel—you can't get from it. Who is it that would like to see you dead, and have what's yours?"

Rachel did not turn her head. In an odd stiff voice she repeated the words she had just used.

"I don't know."

Louisa Barnet went over to the hearth and picked up the tongs. She said just over her breath,

"I could name some—but you wouldn't believe me."

Rachel shuddered again.

"How can I believe a thing like that?"

The dark, grim face worked.

"You'd best, Miss Rachel." She came over to the bed and

41

picked up one of the dead snakes with the tongs. "You can believe your own eyes, can't you? Someone brought these adders and put them in your bed—and that's no love-gift."

She went over to the fire, dropped the limp coil into the heart of it, and went back to pick up and dispose of the second snake.

Rachel watched her with a dazed look.

"Are they adders?" she said rather faintly. "They were talking about adders downstairs tonight. Richard said Mr. Tollage was digging out his hedge. The men found a lot of adders in the bank."

Louisa Barnet thrust at the fire with the tongs and dropped them back upon the hearth.

"Mr. Richard?" she said. "Oh, yes—he'd know, no doubt."

Strength came back to Rachel Treherne—strength, and anger.

"Louie!"

"Oh, no—you won't hear a word! Him and Miss Caroline can do no wrong by you—not if you was to see them with your own eyes." She came suddenly near and caught a fold of Rachel's maize-coloured dressing-gown between her hands. "Oh, my dear—you don't believe, and you won't believe, and I mustn't say a word. But what would you feel like if it was the one you loved best in all the world—if there was them that was creeping and crawling and going all ways to gain their own end, and you only a servant that nobody wouldn't listen to nor take any notice of whatever you said and whatever you did? Oh, my dear, wouldn't it wring your heart same as mine's been wrung? Oh, the Lord, he knows how it's been wrung, and he'll forgive me if you won't!"

Rachel put her hand on the woman's shoulder and spoke gently.

"Louie, we're both upset. Don't let us upset each other. There are things I can't listen to—there are things you mustn't say. But that doesn't mean I won't do something about this. I won't just shut my eyes and go on blindly. I promise you that—I promise you. And now I'd like clean sheets, so there's something you can do whilst I'm undressing."

When she was alone, Rachel Treherne sat a long time in the armchair by the fire. In his basket Neusel slept the sleep of the virtuous and victorious. The noise of water and the noise of wind came to her ears with their accustomed sound. Here, on the edge of the cliff, there were very few days or nights so still that this wind and water music was wholly absent. When she was away, she missed it. When she was here, it was the first thing she heard in the morning, and the last at night. It could weep with her when she wept, or charm her fears away. But tonight it had sombre undertones. The wind was a desolate voice. The sea dragged on the shingle under the cliff.

She got up at last and looked at the clock. The hands stood at midnight. She felt a momentary startled wonder that so little time should really have passed. She felt she had been far, and far. So far that it was hard to come back again. Yet it was only an hour since she had left the drawing-room—half an hour since she had sent Louie away.

She sat on the edge of her bed and lifted the receiver from the telephone beside it.

She got through very quickly. Miss Maud Silver's voice sounded most reassuringly awake and clear.

"Yes? What is it? . . . Oh, Miss Treherne? . . . Yes—what can I do for you? . . . You would like me to come down tomorrow instead of Saturday? . . . Yes, I will certainly do so. You need say no more—I quite understand. I will wire my train in the morning. Good-night."

Rachel hung up the receiver. She felt as if the burden were off her shoulders.

She got into bed, put out the light, and stopped thinking. She slept until Louisa came in with the tea at half past seven.

CHAPTER 10

Richard Treherne came through the hall on the way to breakfast. As he passed the study door, he heard voices. The door was ajar. He pushed it a little way, and then stopped because he heard Cherry say in a taunting voice,

"You should have done what you were told, Car-o-line. I said I'd tell on you if you didn't give me a rake-off."

Richard waited to hear what Caroline would say.

She said nothing.

He pushed the door a little wider, and saw her standing at the window with her back to him. Cherry, a little nearer, half turned from him, half turned to Caroline, showed him a malicious profile. Her pale hair caught the light.

"You'd much better pay up," she said. "I expect you got at least fifty pounds for that ring—they were whacking big stones—and if you got fifty you can easily spare me a tenner."

Caroline did not turn her head. She said, "Why should I?" in a tone of gentle scorn.

Cherry Wadlow laughed.

"Because you'd better. I warned you I'd tell about the ring, and I told. But there's something else I can tell about too if I don't get my little rake-off."

Richard came in, shut the door behind him, and crossed the floor.

"And that's about enough of that!" he said. "Cherry, in case you don't know it, blackmail is an indictable offence, and you can get quite a nice long stretch of penal servitude for it."

She put out her tongue at him like a child.

"And a nice time your darling Caroline would have in the

witness-box. You'd love it, wouldn't you, darling? It would be a perfect scream. 'You pawned a diamond ring, Miss Ponsonby. I believe it belonged to your mother. You must surely have had a very strong motive for parting with it. Oh, you wanted the money? Now perhaps you will tell us what you wanted the money for. Ah—you don't want to do that, I see. Very natural indeed. You wouldn't like to tell the Court what you wanted the money for, would you? No, I thought not—a most natural reluctance.' There, Dicky—that's how it would be. Do run me in. I think it would be simply wizard—don't you, Carrie? Shall I tell him what you wanted the money for? . . . No? All right, I'll let you off this time, because though revenge is sweet, I'd really rather have that tenner, so I'm giving you time to think it over." She slipped her arm through Richard's. "Wouldn't you like to kiss me good-morning, darling?"

Richard would have liked to strangle her, but as he was quite sure it would please her inordinately to think so, he curbed himself and said in a bored tone,

"Not amusing, Cherry. You're out of the schoolroom now, though it's a bit difficult to realize it."

He had the satisfaction of seeing her change colour. She gave his arm a vicious pinch, dropped it, and ran out of the room. The door banged.

Caroline said, "It's wicked to hate people, but I think I hate Cherry."

"What she wants is a daily dozen," said Richard—"laid on with a good stiff hair-brush. Maurice the same. The only comfort is they've got it coming to them one way or another. Now—what's all this about? Are you going to tell me?"

The colour came into Caroline's face. She said,

"No."

Richard took her hands in his own. He looked away from her face and down at her up-turned palms. He said,

"Better tell me, Caroline."

She said "No" again, but rather faintly.

"Silly to make mysteries, my dear—*really* silly, when it's you and me. Don't you know that you can tell me anything?"

She said "Yes," and caught her breath and said, "Anything about me. But this isn't anything about me, Richard."

"Thank the Lord for that! But I think you'd better tell me."

She tried to pull her hands away, and when he held them fast she threw him a piteous look which he found hard to bear.

"Please, Richard—I can't. Please, Richard, let me go."

He lifted her hands, kissed them, and let them go.

"Well, don't let Cherry bully you. And don't forget I'm here. What do you mean by letting her drag us all into a melodrama before breakfast? It's indecent. The emotions should never be excited before three o'clock in the afternoon—no constitution will stand it. Come and eat cold ham and scrambled eggs and kippers. Particularly kippers. They have a very stabilizing effect."

Breakfast was not a particularly tranquil meal. The Wadlows, Ernest and Mabel, had obviously cast themselves for the role of suffering martyrs, but they did not suffer in silence. They asked for coffee in tones of gloom, refused sugar as if it had been poison, and gazed upon Rachel at the head of the table with a steady reproach which she found extremely trying. Maurice sulked as openly as if he had been five years old, whilst Cherry advertized the fact that she was in a bad temper by jerking her chair up to the table, clattering with her knife and fork, and pushing away her cup of tea with so violent a shove as to send half of it into Caroline's lap.

For a moment Rachel saw them, not as part of her family, but as four singularly irritating and disagreeable people. It was like looking through a tiny hole in a dark curtain and seeing a room beyond and the people in it. A strange room, and strange people. A bright light beat on them and showed her just how odious they were. For that brilliant half minute she disliked them extremely, wondered why she had put up with them for so long, and made up her mind to send them packing. Then the hole in the curtain closed. The light was gone. The moment was over. The Wadlows were family again. You were fond of them, you put up with them, you could never, never, never be rid of them. Even more truly than in the marriage service they were yours till death did you part. It was not an enlivening thought.

Ernest ate fruit and cereal, Mabel cereal without fruit. Cherry crumbled toast and upset her tea. Caroline ate nothing at all. The telephone was active.

Maurice answered it the first time, and reported that Cosmo Frith was coming over bag and baggage before lunch.

"He might just as well live here and have done with it."

"So might any of us for the matter of that," snapped Cherry.

This was so undeniably true that no one attempted to deny it.

The telephone bell rang again. This time there was a telegram. Richard took it down, laid the message beside Rachel's plate, and saw her change colour. He wondered why, and then wondered whether he had been mistaken when she said,

"Miss Silver will be arriving this afternoon by the five-thirty. I shall have to send Barlow to meet her. It's my day for Nanny Capper."

"Who is Miss Silver?" said Cherry, staring.

Rachel hoped she wasn't sounding nervous. She said,

"I don't think any of you have met her. She's a retired governess. Not very exciting, I'm afraid, but I want to have her down here for a bit."

Cherry pushed back her chair rudely.

"Oh, why not turn the house into homes for the aged and have done with it!" She strolled towards the door with her hands in her pockets, whistling. She was wearing mustard-coloured tweeds and a large emerald-green scarf. She stopped just as she was going out of the room, because Maurice was taking another call. He turned with the receiver in his hand.

"Oi! It's for you. The faithful, or shall we say the unfaithful, Bob."

Cherry said "Damn!", cast a comprehensive glare at the breakfast table, and snatched the receiver. With her father and mother watching her, ears pricked and eyes intent, she had to keep her own face sulkily indifferent while Mr. Robert Hedderwick said in a voice of violent passion,

"Cherry, you're driving me mad!"

The Wadlows saw her eyebrows lift a little. They heard her say,

"Why?"

The line quivered under the energy with which Mr. Hedderwick told her why. Cherry found it very difficult to go on looking sulky, because this was all most exciting. And gratifying. The fact that Bob Hedderwick was within a few weeks of his marriage to Mildred Ross contributed an added thrill.

"Cherry, I've got to see you!"

She said, "All right."

"Tonight—at the usual place."

Cherry said, "Well, I don't know," and was rewarded by another outburst.

"I tell you I'm going clean off my head! I've got to see you and talk it out! You've got to come! Say you will!"

Cherry said, "Perhaps," and rang off.

This was heady stuff for the breakfast table. She had the utmost difficulty in not looking as pleased as she felt. She poured herself out another cup of tea and sipped at it to hide a lurking smile. Meanwhile the telephone bell was ringing again. Richard spoke over his shoulder, his palm against the mouthpiece.

"Personal, private and particular for you, Rachel. G.B. on the line."

The young people's complaint about having the telephone in the dining-room came home with force to Rachel as she took the receiver and heard Mr. Gale Brandon say with his agreeable American accent,

"Miss Treherne?"

Of course there was an extension in her bedroom, but it would look so marked if she switched over. The family would think—Mr. Brandon would think. . . . She was particularly anxious to avoid anything that looked as if she were making a mystery. No, it wouldn't do at all. She said,

"Miss Treherne speaking."

Gale Brandon's voice became eager.

"Oh, now, Miss Treherne—I wonder if you would do me a favour. I don't really like to ask you, but I know you've got a very kind heart, and if you'll think that here I am on the wrong side of the Atlantic for getting help from any of my own women folk, well I think that kind heart of yours will urge you very strongly to step into the breach and help me choose my Christmas presents."

Rachel heard the pleased note in her own voice as she said,

"But it's much too early. I haven't even begun to think about mine."

Gale Brandon's voice sounded pleased too. She thought, "He's pleased with himself," and tried to bang the door on that other thought, "He's pleased with me."

He laughed and said, "If I don't start early I don't at all. I just stall and quit. Now if you will come into Ledlington with me this morning—I don't know how much we could do there but we can make a start."

"Well, I don't know."

His voice took a pleading tone.

"I shall be just lost if you won't. You know, I do lose my head in a store, and I am liable to send a pair of skates to my bedridden Uncle Jacob, or the latest thing in lipsticks to my Aunt Hephzibah. What I need is guidance, and that's a fact. And if I

49

wait for a day when you're not busy, Christmas will be gone and the next one coming along, so won't you just cut out all those things you were going to do and let me come along and call for you in half an hour's time?"

Several bright thoughts arrived in Rachel's mind simultaneously and made quite a cheerful explosion there. If she went out with Gale Brandon, Ernest and Mabel would not be able to talk to her. Maurice would not be able to talk to her, and she could put off talking to Caroline. She would also avoid Louisa, who was looking like a thunder-cloud. And she could make quite certain of being out when Mrs. Barber brought Ella Comperton over.

She said with alacrity, "Well, I oughtn't to, but I will," and hung up.

CHAPTER 11

Gale Brandon drove a fast car very fast indeed. He said he had come to live at Whincliff because it offered the best selection of roads without any speed limit which he had so far been able to discover. There was no limit between Whincliff and Ledlington, yet on this particular morning he showed a disposition to dally.

"How many presents do you want to get, and what sort of people are they for? Have you really got an Uncle Jacob and an Aunt Hephzibah?"

He turned his head to smile at her. A big, good-looking man in the early forties, with a ruddy tan on his skin and a bright dancing something in his eye—zest and humour always, anger sometimes. He said,

"I certainly have, and they've got to have presents. Uncle Jacob likes a good crime story, so he's easy—seven murders

50

in the first chapter, and a good average kept up all through. But Aunt Hephzibah has me beat. She don't read, she don't drink, and she don't smoke. I once gave her a bottle of scent, and it was a near thing whether she cut me out of her will. It's just a relaxation for her altering her will, so I have to be very careful. Now, Miss Treherne, what makes you look like that?"

She had thought his eye was on the road.

"I think I hate talking about wills," she said.

"Then we won't talk about them. Would you say it would be safe to send Aunt Hephzibah a handbag?"

"She'll have to pay duty on it, won't she?"

Mr. Brandon looked a good deal cast down.

"Well—if I hadn't forgot all about the duty! And would she be mad! Didn't I say I needed guidance? Look what you've saved me from already."

Rachel laughed.

"That's my horrid practical mind. I've had to learn to be practical, you know—it didn't come naturally. But if you can't get your presents, why are we going on?"

"Oh, I've got friends this side of the Atlantic too. I'll have to let a cousin of mine see about the old folks at home, but there'll be plenty we can be getting along with this morning. To start off with, there'll be chocolates and toys for about a dozen children. . . ."

They did the toys and chocolates very successfully, and then sat down and took stock of their purchases over a cup of coffee. Mr. Brandon produced a list.

Gloves for Peggy and Moira. $6\,^1/_2$.

Silk stockings for Jane. Half a dozen pairs. $9\,^1/_2$.

Handkerchiefs for Irene. Sheer linen. One dozen.

Handbag for Hermione. Dark blue. Initials.

He handed the list over. It continued on the same lines to the bottom of the page, where there was a large question-mark on a line by itself.

"Now that," said Mr. Brandon, "is what I wanted to ask

you about. All these other things, they're for the wives and daughters of very good friends of mine over here. I've known most of them a long time, and I know just what sort of things they'll like, and just what sort of things it would be all right for me to give them. They're what I should call friends-of-the-family presents—the kind of thing that means 'I wish you a happy Christmas, and I hope you'll have a good time.' But there's another present I want to give that I'm not so sure about. It's for a woman, and it's for a woman I've known all her life. I'd like to give her something that's really worth while—something she can wear. But I don't want to offend her or have her think I'm presuming."

Rachel Treherne felt a sort of cold shock which she could not account for. She had the momentary feeling that if she could account for it she would be rather horrified. She said at once,

"You've known her all her life?"

"Something like that."

"And how well do you know her?"

His eyes danced.

"Pretty well. Better than she knows me."

"But—are you friends? You see, I can't say what you can give her unless I know just how friendly you are." She felt as if she were excusing herself, and changed colour. "Do you know, you are making me sound inquisitive. I don't really think I can advise you at all."

He leaned to her across the little table.

"Now look here, Miss Treherne, you couldn't sound inquisitive to me whatever you said. But this is rather a delicate matter."

Rachel felt her cheeks burn.

"After all, we're almost strangers," she said.

If she had expected Gale Brandon to be rebuffed, she was disappointed. He said in an earnest voice,

"Oh, I don't feel that way at all, and I'd appreciate your

advice. You see, I have a very great affection and respect for this lady—in fact I love her."

Rachel said, "Does she love you?"

"I don't think so. I've never asked her."

"Are you going to ask her?"

"Oh, yes, when the right time comes."

She smiled, and wondered why her lips felt stiff.

"Well, Mr. Brandon, if you want my advice, I should say wait till you have told her how you feel. Then you will know whether you can give her this present."

He took some time to think about that. Then he said,

"Well, I had a kind of idea that I would like the present to tell her. Do you get what I mean? I thought I'd make it something she wouldn't take unless she meant to take me with it. Then if she did take it, I'd know."

Rachel laughed a little.

"That might be very dangerous, Mr. Brandon. I'm afraid there are women who would take your present and think no more about it."

He shook his head.

"She wouldn't do that."

They bought the friends-of-the-family presents first. Rachel could not help a quick surface amusement over the very definite likes and dislikes which Mr. Brandon exhibited. So far from needing her help, he knew exactly what he wanted, and made it quite plain that he must have it. The shade of the stockings, the stitching on the gloves, the initials for bag and handkerchiefs—he had his mind made up at a glance, and though he deferred to her charmingly he always took his own way. But when they crossed the Market Place to Mr. Enderby's old dark shop his manner changed, lost its certainty. He dropped back a good twenty years and showed her the anxious, eager boy he must have been then.

The Market Square is the center of Ledlington, and in the center of the Market Square stands the statue of Sir Albert Dawnish of which the townsfolk are so justly proud. They have a well-founded belief that it can give points and a beating to any other statue in any other market town in England, both for its own size and for that of the cheque which paid for it. From a highly ornate pedestal Sir Albert in rigid marble trousers gazes down upon the cradle of his enormous fortune—or, shall we say, upon the spot where once that cradle stood. The first of the long line of Quick Cash Stores which have made the name of Dawnish a household word was pulled down some years ago, but the statue of Sir Albert is good to last as long as the Market Square.

Mr. Enderby's old shop is behind Sir Albert's back. He would not in any case think it worth looking at. It has, indeed, a somewhat rickety air, as if its four hundred years had at last begun to tell upon its constitution, but the oak beams are still staunch, and the brickwork holds. About a hundred and fifty years ago Josiah Enderby the third threw out a bow window the better to exhibit his goods. This solitary concession to the modern spirit of display remains as Josiah left it. Nothing else has emerged from the fifteenth century. The shop is still very nearly as dark, stuffy, and inconvenient as it must have been when Elizabeth was on the throne. The old oak boards are bare to the customer's foot. There is no electric light and no counter. A long trestle table black with age serves Mr. Thomas Enderby as it served his forebears. In spite of these drawbacks, or perhaps because of them, the shop is a famous one. The Enderbys have always had two assets, absolute probity and a most astonishing flair for stones. Thirty years ago Tobias Enderby was considered the finest judge of pearls in Europe. His son Thomas runs him close. People with great names and deep purses have sat at that trestle table and watched an Enderby—Josiah, Tobias, Thomas—bring out his treasures for their inspection. Not always easy to buy from, the Enderbys. A few years before the war a Personage who has since lost the throne which he then adorned made the mistake of speaking rudely to Tobias. He wished to buy the Gonzalez ruby, once the property of

Philip II of Spain, and come by devious ways to the Market Place in Ledlington. The Personage offered a fabulous price. He offered to double any other offer which the Enderbys might receive. But he also offered them some discourtesy. Nobody seems to know quite what it was, but old Tobias gazed past him with an abstracted air and murmured, "No, sir, it is not for sale."

Rachel told Gale Brandon the story as they were crossing the Square.

"It's rather nice to feel that there are some things money won't buy."

He stood still under the very shadow of Sir Albert Dawnish.

"Now, Miss Treherne, I don't like to hear you say that. And why? Because it sounds to me as if you were letting money get you down. You know, you're all right as long as you're on top of it, but the minute you let it get on top of you you're done. It's a servant, and like all servants you've got to look out it doesn't get the upper hand. Use it, work it, don't let it drive you, don't let yourself think you can't do without it, don't let yourself believe for a single moment that it can give you any value you haven't got already. It's the other way round. It's you who give money its value by the way you spend it." He laughed suddenly and came down on a schoolboy joke. "It isn't the money that makes the man, it's the man that makes the money."

"I didn't make mine," said Rachel.

"Then somebody made it for you."

He laughed again, and took her across the line of traffic. With her hand on the latch of Mr. Enderby's door, Rachel said with all her heart,

"I wish they hadn't."

CHAPTER 12

Thomas Enderby was exactly like an old grey mouse, except that a mouse's eyes are bright and dark, and his were veiled and of no colour at all.

There was an interchange of courtesies reminding Rachel of an old lady she had known as a child who was wont to say with an approving nod of the head, "Compliments pass when gentlefolk meet."

The compliments having passed, Mr. Brandon said something in a low voice, from which Rachel inferred that their visit had not been without preliminaries. With a bow Mr. Enderby disappeared through a door in the back of the shop, returning immediately with a square of black velvet which he laid before Miss Treherne. He then disappeared again, and this time for longer.

As she sat waiting, Rachel was aware of the romantic atmosphere. This old house, this old room; the very chair she sat in, with its high back and straight arms; the floor, black with age, uneven from the passing of the generations—all made a setting for the man who had brought her here to choose a lovegift for another woman. She was conscious of him as she had never been conscious of a man before. His look stirred her as if it had been a touch, and his touch. . . . She steadied her thought to face what this might mean—the folly of a lonely woman who had had no time for love and had let it pass her by; the terror of a frightened woman groping for a hand that she might trust to; or something deeper, saner, more steadfast. . . . Whichever it was, it meant pain. It meant that she must brace herself to meet pain, to endure it, to tread it down.

The change in her feelings dazed her. She had found pleasure in Gale Brandon's society, in the vigour and freshness
which he brought into the family atmosphere, and in his obvious admiration for herself, but she had never dreamed that
she would feel like this because he told her that he loved
another woman.

Thomas Enderby came back with an old-fashioned box of
Tonbridge ware in his hand. It was, of course, an anachronism,
but an anachronism whose age conferred a certain respectabil-
ity. He sat down at the table, pushed his spectacles up amongst
the hair which strayed across his brow, opened the box,
removed a layer of cotton wool, and took out three packages
done up in tissue paper. He had very thin, pale fingers and
bloodless nails. His hands moved in a delicate and leisurely
manner as he unfolded the paper. In the end he sat back and
contemplated the three ornaments which he had disposed upon
the square of black velvet, his eyes no longer hooded and dim,
but bright with the discerning admiration of the connoisseur.

Rachel looked too.

The oak spray came out of its wrappings first. She found it
hard to take her eyes from it—two diamond oakleaves and
three acorns, the cups shining with brilliants, and each acorn
a pearl, two white and one black.

She said, "Oh, how lovely!" and Mr. Thomas Enderby
agreed.

"It was my father's design. It was commissioned by the
Duchess of Southshire, but she died before it was completed.
It took my father some years to satisfy himself over the pearls.
He never really wished to sell his favourite pieces, so that I
am afraid her Grace's decease was rather a relief to him. Now
this chain came to us from abroad—Italian work, made to a
Russian order."

The chain was about twenty-five inches in length. It had pale
gold links, most exquisitely fine, between alternate sapphires
and emeralds, each stone beautifully cut and set with diamond
sparks, the whole effect one of lightness, brilliance, and grace.

"This of course is the finest stone," said Mr. Enderby. He touched the third ornament caressingly. "There is nothing like a ruby after all, and this is one of the best we have had. Look at the colour!"

The ruby burned between two diamond wings—the lifted arch of an eagle's wings. Between the flash of them the stone seemed alive.

"I am not, unfortunately, at liberty to give you the particular history of this piece," pursued Thomas Enderby. "My father designed it for a member of a royal house, and it has recently come back to us." He turned to Gale Brandon. "Those, sir, are our three best pieces."

Rachel felt rather dazzled. The jewels were most beautiful. They were also most costly. She admired the romance of the gesture which would offer one of these exquisite things as a declaration of love without any certainty of its acceptance. But quick on this came the thought, "It spoils it all to let another woman choose."

It was at this moment that he leaned to her and said,

"Which do you like best?"

The words struck a spark of resentment from her. She said, a thought quickly,

"But it isn't what I like. I can't choose for a woman I've never seen. I don't know what she's like, or what she likes. Pearls are for one sort of woman, rubies for another, and emeralds and sapphires for another still. You'll have to choose for yourself, Mr. Brandon—I can't help you."

Gale Brandon's eyes danced with a teasing light. He looked most extraordinarily alive in the little dark room.

"Isn't that too bad!" he said. "But I wasn't asking you to choose for me. I just felt very interested to know which of Mr. Enderby's pretty things you liked best. Because, you see, I've figured it out this way. Say there's one that I like best. Well, if you choose it too, then there are two votes for that. Do you see what I mean?"

"But it isn't my vote that ought to count, because I'm quite in the dark. Why, I don't even know the colour of her hair."

A smile flickered over his face.

"Well, we'll all be getting grey hair some day. I hope she's going to wear it a good long time, so it would be better to choose something that's going to go on looking good when she's got those silver threads among the gold."

So she had golden hair. . . . It didn't go a good grey as a rule. . . . She said in the friendliest tone she could compass,

"If she is fair, the emerald and sapphire chain would suit her."

"But I didn't say she was fair, Miss Treherne."

"I thought you did. You quoted the song about silver threads among the gold."

"That was a figure of speech. I certainly shouldn't call her fair—except in the romantic sense—and I can't see that there is one of these jewels that wouldn't be mighty becoming to her. But I really would appreciate it if you would tell me which one appeals to you, Miss Treherne. You see, it's the woman's point of view I'd like to get."

She found herself laughing a little scornfully.

"Do you really think all women are alike?"

He laughed too.

"It would certainly be dull if they were. But I would really like to know which of these pretty things you do like the best. I'm interested in your point of view. And then I'd like to know whether you like the one that I like, and when we've settled that we'll ask Mr. Enderby which is the one he'd save if his shop was burning."

Thomas Enderby's hand went out a little way and drew back.

An irrational gust of gaiety blew into Rachel's mind. She put out her own hand and touched the oak spray with its pearl acorns.

"Oh, that's my one. I lost my heart to it at once. But I don't believe Mr. Enderby can bear to let it go. He's lost his heart to it too."

"And I've lost mine," said Gale Brandon—"so there are three of us. Well, Mr. Enderby—what about it? Will you let me have it—for the loveliest and kindest lady in the world?"

"It's not everyone I'd let it go to," said Thomas Enderby.

CHAPTER 13

Rachel got back to find that she had missed Mrs. Barber by a comfortable margin. Ella, meeting her in the hall, remarked on how unfortunate this was.

"Away yesterday, out today. I only hope, Rachel, that she won't think you want to avoid her. Of course quite ridiculous, because she is such an exceptionally interesting and charming person, and I know she particularly wanted to talk to you about slum clearance."

Cosmo Frith, emerging from the study, demanded why any human being should imagine that any other human being should want to talk about slums. He slipped his arm through Rachel's and kissed her on the cheek.

"Well, my dear, I needn't ask how you are. You look fine. And who was the cavalier? Wouldn't he stay to lunch—or didn't you ask him? I thought he looked pretty well pleased with himself as he drove away."

Rachel laughed. Her colour was bright.

"Oh, I asked him, but he had to get back. It was Mr. Brandon, the American who has taken the Halketts' house for the winter. I thought you had met."

"No. Fancies himself, doesn't he?"

Rachel laughed again.

"I think he fancies everything, and that includes himself. I've never met anyone who enjoys things so much. We've been shopping for Christmas presents."

Cosmo looked exactly like a child who hears another child praised. He was a handsome man of forty-five. His grey hair set off a fresh complexion and a pair of fine dark eyes with well marked brows. His waist measurement was rather larger than it had been a year or two ago, and there were moments when he feared a double chin. He withdrew his arm and said with a lift of the eyebrows.

"Christmas presents—in November? What a nauseating idea!"

"And why nauseating?" enquired Ella Comperton. "I think this modern fashion of laughing at Christmas is a terrible sign of the times. My dear mother always used to say, 'Ah, it isn't the gift—it's the loving preparation that counts,' and we used to be set down to our Christmas presents as soon as the summer holidays were over."

"Horrible!" said Cosmo. "But I suppose that the Society for the Prevention of Cruelty to Children hadn't been invented then." He turned to Rachel. "And what were you and Mr. Brandon lovingly preparing?"

"Chocolates, and toys, and gloves, and handbags and stockings for a lot of young people. He didn't really need me at all. He knew exactly what he wanted."

They went in to lunch. Cosmo as usual monopolized the conversation, a good deal to the annoyance of the Wadlows and Miss Comperton. Maurice and Cherry having departed, their parents wished to talk about them. Ella wished to talk about slums. She had come primed from Mrs. Barber, and she wished to pose as an expert. But there was no talking against Cosmo. He told anecdotes, and laughed at them heartily in a deep, rollicking voice. He retailed the news which they had already read in the morning papers. He narrated the inner history of the Guffington divorce. He gave them the reasons which had led the ultra-particular Lady Walbrook to give her consent to her daughter's marriage to a very notorious gentleman, Mr. Demosthenes Ryland. He had inside information as to the exact circumstances in which that rising star Seraphine had broken her Hollywood contract. Not that he neglected the excellent food with which he was served. He appeared to be able to eat and talk at the same time.

Rachel was quite pleased to listen. She could laugh at Cosmo, but she was very fond of him, and she was very glad to have an alternative to the Wadlows and their young, or Ella on slums.

The evil hour was, however, only postponed. As soon as lunch was over Mabel demanded an interview, and a very long, tearful and trying interview it proved to be, under such headings as a Mother's Love, a Mother's Anxieties, a Sister's Heart, and, by implication, a Sister's Purse.

Rachel did her best to endure the Mother's Love, to soothe the Mother's Anxieties, and to display the Sister's Heart, whilst keeping a reasonably firm hand upon the Sister's Purse. It was all very difficult and very, very exhausting.

When Mabel had at last been induced to lie down, there was Ernest, with a Father's Anxieties and a Father's Responsibilities.

Retiring to her room after this encounter, Rachel found herself pursued by her cousin Ella, tall, raw-boned, and purposeful, with a small attaché-case full of pamphlets and photographs.

"Most disappointing that you should have missed Mrs. Barber. I am a very poor substitute, but I promised her faithfully that I would do my very best to interest you."

She was still there when Louisa Barnet came in to draw the curtains. She rose regretfully and began to pack the attaché-case.

"The time has simply flown—hasn't it? I must go and wash my hands for tea, but I'll leave you those pamphlets. Dear me, Rachel, you look quite tired. I hope you didn't do too much this morning. Most inconsiderate of Mr. Brandon, I call it." The door closed behind her.

Louisa rattled the curtain rings.

"Fair wore out is what you look, Miss Rachel. And it's not what you did this morning that's to blame neither."

She got rather a wan smile as she turned.

"Well, I don't think it is, Louie. You know what Miss Ella is. She'd got those papers on her mind, and she was bound to show them to me."

Louisa looked angrily at the pamphlets.

"What's it now? She doesn't stick to nothing, does she? Last time it was lepers, and the time before it was something to do with circuses, and the time before that it was naked heathen cannibals. And what I say is, if they was made that way, then it was for some good purpose, and it's not for us nor yet for Miss Ella to go flying in the face of Providence. Interferingness—that's what it is, and you can't get from it!"

Rachel bit her lip.

"But, Louie, Providence didn't make lepers or cannibals, and He certainly didn't make slums."

Louisa gloomed.

"That's what you say, Miss Rachel. I've got my own ideas, and I'm not the only one. And it's no good talking about lepers and cannibals to me when I see you looking as white as a sheet, and saucers under your eyes for all the world as if they were full of ink. You'll never be going over to see Mrs. Capper tonight?"

"Oh, yes—she counts on it. And I like going, you know. She'll be a pleasant change, because she always tells me what a nice little girl I used to be, and when we've finished with me we go over all the other children she nursed. I feel I know them all quite well though I've never seen most of them. I sometimes think how odd it would be if we could all meet."

Louisa took no interest in Mrs. Capper's charges. It annoyed her to think that there had been a time when Mrs. Capper had brushed Miss Rachel's hair and turned down her bed. Rachel's visits to her old nurse were a source of irritation, and she never let slip an opportunity of suggesting that it was too wet or too cold, or that Rachel was too busy or too tired.

"That Miss Silver is coming at half past five, Miss Rachel. You'll want to be in."

Rachel couldn't help laughing.

"Her train gets in at half past five—she won't be here before six. I shall be back quite soon after that. Put my torch in the hall and hang out the lantern. Barlow can drop me before he goes to the station, and I'll come back by the cliff."

CHAPTER 14

Cosmo seemed to think it was his turn for a *tête-à-tête* with Rachel after tea. He had a portfolio full of sketches to show her, and he made it clear that he had no intention of showing them to the whole family. He was quite as annoyed as Louisa had been when Rachel reminded him that it was her day for Mrs. Capper. He said "Stuff and nonsense!" several times in a loud voice, and walked up and down jingling the keys in his trouser pocket and lecturing her about running herself off her legs, and when he had finished lecturing her he started in to scold the family for allowing her to wear herself out.

"It's all very well, my dear, but good people are scarce, and if no one else will stand up to you and tell you you're doing too much, well I will. I'm not afraid of you, and I'm not afraid to speak my mind. You're looking fagged out. What you want is a holiday. Why don't you go right away from telephones, and begging letters, and neighbours who want you to do their shopping for them, and the whole boiling of us? Unless—" He stopped and bent affectionately over her chair, one hand on the arm and the other on her shoulder. "Unless . . . Come, Rachel, here's an idea. What about letting me show you Morocco? We'll take Caroline to chaperone us, and you shall pay all the bills." He laughed heartily and dropped a kiss on her hair. "Think it over my dear, think it over."

Rachel laughed too and got up.

"I think I should make a better chaperone than Caroline. And now I'm going to see Nanny, so you must look after yourselves."

It was an astonishing relief to get away. At Whincliff Edge everyone was so busy grinding axes that the noise quite deafened her. Louisa with her jealous devotion, Mabel and Ernest with their grievances, Cosmo with his possessive affection, Ella with her deserving causes—they pressed about her, exhausting the very air she breathed, always asking, always demanding, always wanting more. And under all this surface clamour and pressure there were depths in which something dark and stealthy moved, and waited to pull her down. In Nanny Capper's neat kitchen she was in another world—a much older, simpler, kinder world where Nanny herself played Providence and nobody else was more than seven years old.

"Up in the night he got in his bare feet and nothing on over his night things, and that's how I caught him, standing a-tiptoe in your father's dressing-room and tugging at the little top drawer to get it open. Two in the morning it was, and the noise of the drawer that waked me. And 'Master Sonny,' I said, 'for goodness gracious sake, whatever are you doing?' And you should have heard how he spoke up. 'I want a handkerchief,' he says, and 'Oh, Master Sonny,' I said, 'there's aplenty in your own drawer, and one under your pillow, for I put it there myself.' And what do you think he said? Never flinched, but looked me straight in the eye. 'They're too little,' he said. 'They're not men's handkerchiefs. I want a real man's handkerchief to blow my nose with. And please will you open the drawer, because I can't reach it, Nanny.'"

"And what did you do?" asked Rachel, who knew the answer.

Nanny Capper was a very fat old woman in a white cashmere shawl over a black cashmere dress, and large shapeless slippers trimmed with fur on her large shapeless feet. She never got out of her chair except to go to bed, but she enjoyed life hugely. When she had anyone to talk to she talked, and when she hadn't anyone to talk to she turned the wireless on. A stout niece looked after her, and she saw her beloved Miss Rachel once a week. She asked no more. She had four chins, and they all shook when she laughed as she did now.

"Oh, I gave him one—opened the drawer, and gave him the largest handkerchief I could find. I knew Mr. Treherne wouldn't mind, seeing he was a visitor and Mr. Brent's son that was his partner. A very nice gentleman Mr. Brent was, but they had some sort of a quarrel, him and your father, very soon after that, so Master Sonny never came back again. A couple of months we had him that time, and him and Miss Mabel sparred something dreadful. Always one to whine and whine she was, and he couldn't abide it. But you was only four months old, and he was mortal taken with you. You'd think he'd never seen a baby before, and I don't suppose he had, not close to. There—I often wonder what's come to him. He promised to be a fine man. But first there was the quarrel, and then Mr. Brent went away, and it was after that your father made all the money and we come back to England. Did you never find out anything about them?"

Rachel shook her head.

"No. Father wanted me to try, so I tried, and I've gone on trying, but it doesn't seem to be any use."

"Well, I liked Master Sonny, and if ever he does turn up, you'll know it's him right enough, because there was a man in the place where we were that did tattooing—and if Mr. Brent didn't have that poor child's name pricked out on his arm! The left arm it was, and just above the elbow. A downright shame, and so I told him. But he only laughed, and Master Sonny stuck up his chin and said, 'I didn't cry—did I?' And no more he hadn't, and it must have hurt him cruel. And how Mr. Brent could have stood by to see that poor child maltreated like that—well it passes me. And that reminds me of little Miss Rosemary Marsh. She used to come visiting to Mr. Frith's when I had Mr. Cosmo. Half a crown a time her mother used to give her when she had to go to the dentist, and Mrs. Frith, she was wonderful taken with the idea, and I said to her, 'No, ma'am, *if* you please. If Master Cosmo don't learn to bear pain now he never will.' And with one thing and another that's how I come to leave and go out to your dear mother that had Miss Mabel on her hands five years old and expecting you every minute. And I took you from the month. But Mr. Cosmo's grown a fine man, and I'm pleased to think I had him in my nursery, if it was only six months. Often drops in he does when he's this way. And the stories he's got to tell, why you wouldn't believe there was such goings on—now would you? But he ought to get himself a good wife to settle him down, for he's not as young as he was, and so I told him last time he was here. None of us are, more's the pity. And 'Nanny,' he says, 'what can a poor fellow do if the one he wants won't have him?' and he looked at me as pleading as if I'd just locked the cake in the nursery cupboard. 'Go on asking her,' I said. And he looks at me very solemn and says, 'What have I got to offer her, Nanny? A parcel of debts, a tongue that wags too fast as you've often told me, a roomful of pictures that nobody cares to buy, and a heartful of love that she don't want. She could have had me any time these twenty years, and she knows it.' And I took and patted him on the shoulder and told him that faint heart never won fair lady."

Rachel got up. Cosmo had been proposing to her at intervals ever since she grew up. It was a habit, and she had come to take it as no more than his rather tiresome way of expressing the cousinly affection which she valued. But just at this moment to feel that a proposal from Cosmo was lurking among the water-colours which he would certainly insist on showing her either tonight or in the very near future was really the very, very last straw. And Nanny to be coming over all sentimental and trying to plead his cause with a bit of a squeezed-out tear in the eye and a made-up quaver in the voice! Anger put colour into her cheek and crispness into her tone as she said,

"It's a mistake to go on when people don't want you to, Nanny. Tell him to look for somebody else before it's too late. And now I must go."

"Oh, Miss Rachel, it's early yet."

Mrs. Capper knew when she had gone too far. Her tone was a propitiatory one. It promised, "Sit down and talk, and I won't say another word about Mr. Cosmo." But Rachel shook her head.

"No, I must go. I've got someone arriving by the five-thirty—they'll be up at the house before I am now."

"The clock's fast, Miss Rachel. Did you hear about Mr. Tollage digging out his hedge, and the adders that was in it? Gave me the creeps it did to hear about them." She kept hold of Rachel's hand and talked fast to beguile her into staying. "I said to Ellen, 'I don't thank Mr. Tollage for nothing, turning all them snakes out to find new lodgings. I'm not letting any,' I said. 'And you keep a sharp look out that they don't come worming themselves in.' And what do you think she told me she'd seen with her own eyes? You'd never credit it, but those young rascals of boys was selling adders a penny apiece to anyone that was fool enough to buy. They say old Betty Martin bought a good few—and if she isn't a witch, there's never been no such thing. And Ellen says two of the boys spoke up and told her they'd sold a couple of live ones—caught them in a shrimping-net and tied it up with string. Though what in the world anyone 'ud want live adders for passes me."

Rachel got her hand away, but she was no longer in a hurry

to go. Her knees felt weak. She managed enough voice to say,

"What boys? Who bought the snakes?"

"They were strangers to Ellen. All they said was a lady in a green scarf had bought the two live adders, shrimping-net and all. She gave them a good half-crown too. That was a funny thing, wasn't it, when you come to think of it?"

"Yes," said Rachel. She wondered if her voice sounded as strange to Nanny as it did to herself.

Mrs. Capper shook her head with its neatly plaited hair and its little lace cap.

"Because what would anyone want a pair of live adders for?"

"I can't think," said Rachel. "Goodnight, Nanny—I really must go."

CHAPTER 15

Rachel stood in the dark by the gate of Mrs. Capper's cottage and tried to pull herself together. Cherry had gone away that morning in a bright green scarf—a flaring emerald scarf which even in the dusk might catch a child's eye and be remembered. But anyone could have a green scarf. Caroline had one—jade green, very bright—too bright. Mabel had given it to her for her birthday only a week ago.

A trembling took Rachel—a sick trembling. Not Caroline. No, no, no—not Caroline! There are things you can't believe.

She stood quite still. The air was very cold. The trembling passed. She got out her torch and switched it on. The beam was so faint that it hardly showed her the gate against which she leaned. She could scarcely believe her eyes, for the battery was a new one put in that morning. She hesitated as to whether she would take the cliff path after all, or whether it would be safer to go the long way round by the road. But the road was a very long way round, the cliff path safe enough for anyone who knew it. Her eyes had already accustomed themselves sufficiently to the darkness for her to be able to distinguish the outline of the cottage against the sky, and the lighter surface of the road.

She put out the torch, walked a little way, and found that she could see well enough. It was quite easy to make out the path, and that was all that really mattered. There was just one place where it ran for about twenty yards right on the edge of the cliff with a long drop to the beach. She thought she would save the torch and use it there. This was the one dangerous spot, for the low parapet which guarded it was under reconstruction, most of it having collapsed in the heavy storms of a month ago.

She had just switched the torch on, and was finding it more confusing than helpful, when she thought she heard a footstep behind her. She stood still to listen, the torch swinging in her hand, making a dancing pattern on the path. There was both relief and warmth at her heart. Twice out of the last three times that she had been to see Nanny, Gale Brandon had appeared from nowhere to walk home with her along the cliffs. She had left early tonight. She did not doubt for a moment that he had found her gone and was following her now. Without appearing to wait for him, she thought that she might dally a little and give him a chance to catch her up. The idea of company was pleasant. She had no wish to listen to her own thoughts.

She walked a few paces and stood at the edge of the path looking out over the sea. It was a high tide and far in, but only the very highest tide with a winter gale behind it ever reached the foot of the cliffs. Black ridges of rock ran down into black water. There were scarcely visible, darker shadows in a general gloom, but she knew that they were there. Over them and over the cliff the wind blew cold. It had voice enough to drown the sound of the oncoming footsteps. There had been a lull, and there would be a lull again. She waited for it and listened, looking out over the water.

And then there was the sound, right behind her. She made to turn, received a violent blow between the shoulders, dropped her torch, and stumbled forward over the edge of the cliff. That half turn saved her life. She fell sideways instead of headlong, her right arm flung out, the hand grasping at emptiness, but all her left side in contact with the shelving cliff. Her left leg rasped against rock, her left hand caught at a sod, a tussock. Her foot checked the descent for a moment, and in that moment she had both hands fast in the twigs and branches of some small shrubby bush. She hung there, not dazed but sharply, horribly aware of the rocks below. But she knew that she could not hang there long. The bush would give, or her frantic grasp.

And then her left foot found a hold again, a little jutting shelf of rock, narrow, oh, so narrow, but firm as the cliff itself. She got the toe of her other foot upon it, and the worst of the strain was off her hands. The bush and her hold of it were enough to steady her.

For a moment the relief was as sweet as if she had been saved, but on the heels of that came the realization of her position. She could just make out the edge of the cliff. It seemed to be about eight feet above her. She could maintain herself here for a time—but for how long? It was very cold. Her hands were bare—she never wore gloves if she could help it—and this had helped to save her. But if her numbed fingers could hold no longer, if she were to turn faint—the rocks were waiting. The only living soul within call was the one who had pushed her over the cliff. She did not dare cry out.

As she looked up, there was a sound from above—a kind of grunt and the scrape of stone on stone. Something blacker than the darkness came over the verge and rushed past her. She heard the crash of its fall far down below. The wind of it sang in her ears—and her own cry—and the wind that came in from the sea. Her body shook, and her heart. If she had not remembered the rocks she would have let go.

She looked up at the place from which the big stone had

come and waited for another. There were plenty there, great lumps of rock from the ruined wall—loose too, and not hard to push over. The next would stun her, carry her away. . . . None came. She thought, "I cried out. He thinks I fell."

Then she was aware that someone was looking at her—looking down at her as she looked up. She could see nothing that could be called a shape, but there was a place where the darkness was solid. It was the same place from which the stone had come. Someone who hated her was there—someone who wanted her to die—someone who wanted to make sure that she was dead before he went on his way. She said "he," but she did not know that it was a man. There was someone there who desired her death. That was all. It might have been a woman. That scrutiny was worse than anything that had gone before. It seemed to last a long time. Then the blackness moved. She did not know which way it went, but it was gone. The worst horror left her. She shut her eyes and tried to pray.

She never knew quite how long it was before she saw the light. She must have been aware of it through her closed lids, because she stopped in the middle of a verse from a psalm and opened her eyes. And there, not a dozen feet away on her left, was the dancing ray of a torch. It was not on the same level as she was, but four or five feet above the path, swinging easily in a man's hand. Through the sound of the wind Gale Brandon's voice came to her, singing a snatch of a negro spiritual:

> "Look down, look down that lonesome road
> Before you travel on—"

She called with the strength of agony,
"Help, Mr. Brandon—help!"
He stopped, and she heard her name spoken roughly.
She called again, the strength going out of her.
He said, "Rachel!" with a sort of angry shout, and the beam came down and struck her upturned face and open eyes.

He said, "My God!" and then, "Can you hold on?"

"I don't know. Not very long."

"You can. I won't be long."

And that was all. The light swung back to the path, and she heard his running feet.

She tried to think how far it was to Nanny's cottage. Not very far, but there was no one there who could help. Ellen wouldn't be back till seven.

The wind was chilling her, and she was getting stiff. There was only just room for the fore part of her feet on the narrow ledge. From the arch of the instep outwards they had no support. She could not move at all. Her left palm was cut from its desperate clutchings at the rock when she fell. Her head began to feel dizzy. She shut her eyes.

And then a lull, and the sound of running feet again, only this time they were coming nearer, and she heard Gale Brandon shout, "Hold on! I'm coming! It's all right!"

He was above her now, with the torch cunningly tilted to show him her position without dazzling her. He had a white bundle in his arm and he began paying it out.

"Nanny hadn't any rope—I had to tear up her sheets. That's why I've been so long."

The linen fell dangling beside her against the face of the cliff.

"Now, Rachel, can you let go at all with either hand?"

She said, "No."

Gale Brandon said, "You must!" The light slipped to and fro across her hands. He said in an encouraging voice, "You've got quite a good bunch of stuff in that right hand. Does it feel firm?"

She couldn't really feel anything at all, but she said "Yes."

"What sort of foothold have you got?"

"Rock—but I've only got my toes on it."

"That's fine. Now I'm going to swing the sheet close up to you on your left. It's knotted into a sling at the end. I'll try and pull the sling up under your elbow. The minute you feel it there let go the bush with your left hand, push your arm through the loop, and catch the sheet above it. That'll bring the sling under your armpit. Now do that quick, and then I'll tell you what to do next."

Rachel did it, she never quite knew how. She found herself holding to the linen rope and feeling it cut in under her armpit as her weight came on the sling.

Gale Brandon said, "That's fine." The light slid over her again. "Now you've got to put your head through. It's quite easy. And then your right arm, so that the sling will be under both armpits."

Rachel said, "I don't think I can."

She heard the sharpest tone of command that had ever been used to her.

"Do what you're told, and do it at once!"

She did it.

She was holding the linen now with both hands, and the sling was round her body.

He said, "Now we're all right. I'm going to pull you up, but you must help yourself as much as you can. It's nothing like sheer—there's a good bit of slope in our favour. Take advantage of every bit you can. And don't be frightened I'll let you go, because I won't. You're quite safe now."

Safe! The next few moments were the most terrifying she had ever known. If she had been less afraid she might have fainted. It was a very poignancy of terror which kept her conscious. It would have been much easier if she could have swooned. No use thinking about what would be easier—she had got to help Gale.

But at first there was nothing she could do. The linen strip tautened and took her off her feet. A pause while she swung there, and then the bush scratching her face, her hands, as she was drawn up through it, a few inches at a time. Now the twigs were rasping against her stockings, and now she got a knee on a projecting tussock and eased the weight. Then on again, but less difficult now. The cliff sloped to the path, and she was dragged up, half leaning, half scrambling, until she reached the edge and Gale took her under the arms and pulled her up beside him.

They reeled back together across the whole width of the path to a place where there was rough grass under their feet. And stood so clasped they made one shadow there. And neither spoke. She could feel the labouring of his breath and the strong, measured beating of his heart. She had never been so close to another human being. The cold went out of her, and the fear.

And then all of a sudden he loosed her and sang out, "Who's there?"

Rachel, holding to his arm, turned round and saw a lantern bobbing along the track, coming from Whincliff Edge. It spilled its circle of light about a long skirt and a pair of feet which she would have known anywhere. She said weakly, "It's Louisa," and sat down upon the grass.

And then there was Louisa, crying over her and fussing, and being told not to fuss with a good deal of energy by Gale. Most of it went over Rachel's head, for she was really faint now, but neither Gale's commands nor her own dizziness could entirely arrest the flow of Louisa's lamentations.

"Oh, my dear Miss Rachel!" She said that several times. And, "I had to come—I was that anxious. Oh, my dear—that it should come to this! And I'd die for you—cheerful and willing—but I can't stop them—"

"Will you be quiet!" said Gale Brandon. "I want to get your mistress home. Put that lantern down and help me to take the rope off her!"

She had not realized that it was partly the linen strip cutting in under her arms and across her chest that was making her faint, but when it was gone and she could take a deep, full breath again her senses cleared.

Gale lifted her up.

"Can you stand?"

"Oh, yes."

"Walk?"

His arm was round her, the arm to whose strength she owed her life. It felt very strong.

She said, "Oh, yes," again.

"That's fine. Then we'll be going. Louisa, you go on ahead with the lantern. No, not that way. I've got my car up at Nanny's cottage. I don't want her to walk farther than she need. Pick up that torch and come along!"

Actually, the movement did Rachel good. Her shoulders and arms had been numb, but the feeling came back to them. She was sore and bruised, but had no real hurt. She had not yet begun to think.

But when they came to the car and he had sent Louisa in to tell Nanny she was safe, she clung to his arm as if it was all she had to trust to.

"I'd like to sit in front with you."

"I'd like to have you, but I thought you'd be more comfortable at the back—you can lean right into the corner."

"No—I don't want to—I want to stay with you."

He frowned at the fear in her voice. He said,

"Why are you afraid? There's nothing to be frightened of now." He put his arm round her and said insistently, "Is there?"

Before she had time to answer Louisa came out of the cottage.

He was frowning in the dark beside her all the way to Whincliff Edge.

CHAPTER 16

In her room Rachel reviewed the damage, and decided that it might have been much worse. She was bruised and she was scratched, but that was the worst of it.

"And you'll go straight to your bed, Miss Rachel, and not see no one," said Louisa tearfully.

Rachel considered. She could say that she had had a fall, and either go to bed or sit comfortably here by the fire. But she wondered if it would be humanly possible to keep Mabel out of her room, because if it meant a *tête-à-tête* with Mabel, she would rather confront the whole family and have done with it. Also she wanted to see Miss Silver.

She stood warm and relaxed from her bath and looked thoughtfully at Louisa.

"What I'd like to do, Louie, would be to have my dinner here quietly by the fire in my dressing-gown with Noisy. I don't want to go to bed a bit, but I don't feel like bothering to dress—or talk. That's the thing—do you think you can keep the family out?"

Louisa nodded fiercely.

"Indeed I can, my dear, if I have to lock the door on you and take away the key." She came close, picked up one of Rachel's hands, and held it against her cheek. "Oh, my dear, there's nothing I wouldn't do for you—you know that."

Rachel drew her hand away with a little shiver.

"I know, Louie." She sank into the big chair and leaned back gratefully.

But Louisa stood her ground.

"Aren't you going to tell me what happened, Miss Rachel?"

Rachel steeled herself. A scene with Louie now—oh, no!

"I had a fall," she said. "I went over the edge of the cliff, and Mr. Brandon pulled me up. It was horrid, but it's over. I'm not hurt, and I don't want to go on talking about it."

Louisa did not speak. She wasn't crying any longer. She said harshly,

"You're shutting yourself up from me. Do you think I don't know the devil's work when I see it? How did you get over the cliff—will you tell me that? You that know every foot of that path like this room! Mr. Brandon pulled you up. Did he push you over?"

Rachel laughed. It was lovely to be able to laugh.

"Don't be stupid, Louie!"

"Oh, yes, I'm stupid, Miss Rachel—stupid to care like I do. But *someone* pushed you—you'd not have fallen else. And you think it couldn't be Mr. Brandon, because he's made you believe he's fond of you."

Rachel lifted her head.

"That will do, Louie. You had better not go too far. Now bring me my block and a pencil. I want to write a note."

The note was to Miss Silver. It said:

"Make an excuse and come to my room as soon after dinner as you think wise. Louisa will show you where it is."

Presently Caroline came tapping at the door. Rachel let her in for five minutes, and told her not to tell Mabel. She thought the girl looked pale and troubled.

"Is anything the matter, Caroline?"

Her hand was taken and kissed.

"Just you, darling. You mustn't go falling about on the cliffs—you might fall over. I got a frightened feeling. Are you sure you're all right?"

Rachel said suddenly, "What have you done with the green scarf Mabel gave you?"

Caroline drew back, startled.

"Darling—why?"

"Did you wear it yesterday? Yesterday afternoon—on the cliffs?"

Caroline stared.

"I walked up to meet Richard. I didn't wear the scarf. I don't like it very much—it's too bright. Why, darling?"

"Someone saw a girl in a green scarf, and I wondered if it was you."

Caroline looked puzzled.

"Anyone can have a green scarf."

Miss Silver arrived at a little after nine o'clock. By the time she came Rachel was wishing that she need not see her until the morning. She had been sitting there by the fire in a curious atmosphere of safety and contentment, because she was quite sure now that Gale Brandon loved her. There wasn't any other woman. He loved her, Rachel Treherne, and no one else. And she loved him. She had no doubt, either about his feeling or her own. Without a spoken word, with no more than a rough, insistent clasp, he had made her sure. All that she had put aside nearly twenty years ago was being given back to her, good measure, pressed down and running over. Her heart was bright with a steady flame of happiness. No wonder the thought of talking to Miss Silver struck a jarring note.

But even as she crossed the room with Noisy frisking beside her and unlocked the door, her mood changed, because it was not just her life that was being attacked, it was this new happiness. And it was worth fighting for.

She meant to fight.

Miss Silver came into the room in the kind of garment affected by elderly ladies who frequent boarding-houses. It was quite obviously a summer dress that had been dyed black. Some jet trimming now adorned the neck and wrists. A long, old-fashioned gold chain descended into her lap as she took the chair on the other side of the fire. Her neat, abundant hair was tightly controlled by an unusually firm net. She wore black cashmere stockings and *glacé* shoes with beaded toes. A broad old-fashioned gold bracelet set with a carbuncle encircled her left wrist, and a formidable brooch with a design of Prince of Wales' feathers carried out in hair and seed pearls and surrounded by a plaited border of black enamel also picked out with pearls hung like a targe upon her bosom. She carried a black satin work-bag turned back with bright rose-pink. Rachel felt it would be quite impossible that anyone should suspect her of being a detective. She had almost to close her eyes before she could believe it herself.

Such politenesses passed as would be usual between any

hostess and any guest. There were also salutations from Noisy, who appeared very much pleased with the visitor. Then Miss Silver said briskly,

"I see you have a good deal to tell me, but before you begin—are we perfectly private here? Those two doors?"

"One leads to my bathroom, the other to my own sitting-room. There is no other way into the bathroom, but it might be best to lock the door leading from the sitting-room into the passage."

She was about to rise, but was prevented. Miss Silver said, "Allow me," and trotted over to the sitting-room door. Rachel heard her open the second door. Then the click of the key informed her that it was being locked.

Miss Silver came back, but she did not immediately sit down. She went first to the bathroom and looked in, after which she resumed her chair, opened the black satin bag, and drew out her knitting, a mass of pale blue wool which, unfolded, declared itself as one of those rambling wraps or scarves in which invalids are invited to entangle themselves. Miss Silver herself called it a cloud.

"For dear Hilary. Such a sweet girl, and the pale blue should be most becoming. And now, Miss Treherne, why did you ring me up in the middle of the night? And what has been happening today?"

CHAPTER 17

Rachel answered both questions as briefly as possible. She told her about Neusel finding the adders in her bed, and thought how long ago it seemed. Then she told her about being pushed over the cliff.

Except for a single "My dear Miss Treherne!" Miss Silver listened in complete silence. She had ceased to knit. Her hands rested idle on the pale blue wool, and her eyes never left Rachel's face. At the end she said quickly,

"You are not hurt?"

"No—only bruised."

"You have been providentially preserved. May I ask you one or two questions? This visit to your old nurse—how many people knew of it?"

Rachel lifted the hand on her knee and let it fall again.

"Everyone. You see, I go every week."

"And this Mr. Brandon—did he know?"

Rachel felt her colour rise.

"Yes, he knew. Lately he has been walking back with me. I have found him waiting when I came out."

"But he was not waiting for you this evening?"

"I think he came at the usual time. I had left early."

"Yes? Why did you do that?" The small, nondescript eyes were very keen.

"Nanny said something which upset me."

"Will you tell me what it was?"

Rachel hesitated. Then she told Miss Silver the story which Ellen had brought home about the woman in the green scarf who bought two live adders in a shrimping-net. But she could not bring herself to repeat all the nonsense old Nanny had talked about Cosmo Frith.

"I see. And what member of your household has a green scarf?"

All the colour went out of Rachel's face.

"My two young cousins, Cherry Wadlow and Caroline Ponsonby. That is what upset me—but it's quite, quite impossible."

"And they were both here at the time?"

"Cherry went away this morning." The restraint she had put upon her voice broke suddenly. "Miss Silver—"

Miss Silver looked at her very kindly.

81

"My dear Miss Treherne, I do beg that you will not distress yourself. You are very fond of Miss Caroline, are you not?"

Rachel closed her eyes.

"It is quite, quite impossible," she said in a tone of intense feeling.

Miss Silver picked up her knitting.

"Let us revert to the events of this afternoon. You did not take your clever little dog with you?"

"No. Nanny doesn't like him, and I'm afraid he doesn't like her. He sits on the other side of the room and growls. In fact they're better apart."

"Ah—a pity. And that would be known too, I suppose. A great pity. He would probably have given you some warning—but it cannot be helped. Miss Treherne, are you sure that you were pushed?"

Rachel lifted steady eyes.

"Quite sure, Miss Silver."

"Was it a man or a woman who pushed you?"

"I don't know."

"Try and think. A man's hand is larger, harder—there would be more force. Try and remember what sort of a blow it was. Were you struck with a hard impact? Was there much weight behind it? Or was it more of a push? You said that you were pushed."

A faint shudder passed over Rachel.

"It was a very hard push."

"So that it might have been a man or a woman."

"I think so."

"It wasn't the kind of blow that a very strong man would strike—Mr. Brandon for instance?"

Rachel began to laugh.

"How do you know that Mr. Brandon is so strong?"

"Only a very strong man could have pulled you up."

Rachel went on laughing. It was a relief to laugh.

"My dear Miss Silver, if Mr. Brandon had knocked me over the cliff, I should never have had a chance to catch hold of my bush. I should have gone flying right out to sea."

Miss Silver's eyes twinkled pleasantly.

"And that is just what I wanted to know," she said. "It comes to this, you see—the person who pushed you over did not use any very great force. You were taken unawares, and you were thrown off your balance. It may quite easily have been a woman."

Rachel winced sharply. All the laughter went out of her.

Miss Silver leaned forward.

"I am sorry to pain you, but I am bound to ask these questions. However, for the present I have done. I spent quite a profitable time before coming up to you. I had some conversation with all your relatives. I find that the manner in which people behave to someone whom they consider quite unimportant is often highly illuminating."

Rachel had no illusions about her family. She quailed a little. She hoped for the best as she said,

"And were you illuminated?"

Miss Silver stabbed her pale blue wool with a yellow needle like a long, thin stick of barley-sugar. She said in a dry little voice,

"Oh, considerably."

Rachel said, "Well?"

Miss Silver coughed.

"Each of them has something on his or her mind. With most of them it is, I think, money."

"Yes?"

"Mrs. Wadlow talks very freely. It does not matter to her whether the person she talks to is a stranger or not. All that matters is that she should be able to talk about her dearest Maurice, and her fears for his health if he should go to Russia, and her hopes that you will make it possible for him to engage in some much safer enterprise in this country. She also talks, but with less feeling, about her daughter, whom she seems to suspect of being financially embarrassed and possibly on the brink of an elopement."

"Mabel said all that?"

Miss Silver nodded.

"In about twenty minutes—on the sofa—after dinner. I had not much talk with Miss Caroline, but I observed her. She is deeply troubled, and uncertain what she ought to do. Mr. Richard is, of course, in love with her, and her trouble may merely be that the course of true love does not run quite smooth. Are there financial obstacles to their marriage?"

Rachel said, "I don't know. Richard won't take anything from me. I helped him with his training, and he has paid me back. I don't know whether he is in a position to marry or not. Caroline ought to have about three hundred a year, but I think she must have had losses. She's been doing without things, and I know she sold a ring. I haven't liked to say anything—she's sensitive."

Miss Silver's needles clicked again.

"Mr. Wadlow has a worried manner. Small things appear important to him. This kind of character is confusing even to the trained observer. Trifles are so much in evidence that one is tempted to assume that there is nothing behind them. This may be the case—or not. I reserve judgment about Mr. Wadlow."

"And Cosmo?"

"Mr. Frith is a very charming person. I was particularly struck with the fact that he took the trouble to be charming to me."

Rachel's heart warmed to Cosmo, all the more because she had felt a little nervous. He didn't always take the trouble to make himself agreeable to a dull visitor. She had known him to read a book in a corner all the evening—and yawn over it too if he felt bored. She said,

"I'm glad you like Cosmo. He's a bit of a spoilt child, but he has the kindest heart in the world."

Miss Silver smiled brightly.

"Kind hearts are indeed more than coronets, as dear Lord Tennyson says."

Rachel felt a wild desire to finish the quotation, but she restrained herself.

"How did you get on with Ella Comperton?" she asked.

"She seems very much interested in slum clearance."

Rachel laughed.

"She is always very much interested in something. It is never the same thing for very long. All very worthy objects, but she rather does them to death."

Miss Silver looked up shrewdly.

"She collects for them?"

"Most zealously. Did she collect from you?"

"A mere half-crown. And from you?"

Rachel laughed again.

"I'm afraid I don't get off with half-a-crown."

Miss Silver laid down her knitting and produced notebook and pencil from the black satin bag.

"Forgive me, Miss Treherne, but I should be glad to have the name of any society or charitable institution to which you have contributed through Miss Comperton during the past year, together with the amount contributed."

Rachel bit her lip.

"Miss Silver, I hardly think—"

Miss Silver's eyes brightened.

"An attempt has been made on your life. I suspect no one— yet. But until I suspect someone it is my business to suspect everyone and to check up on everyone. If they are innocent, no harm is done. On the contrary. Confidence is re-established. If one of them is guilty—are you a religious woman, Miss Treherne?"

Rachel said, "Yes."

Miss Silver nodded approvingly.

"Then you will agree with me that the best thing that can happen to anyone who is doing wrong is to be found out. If he is not found out he will do more wrong and earn a heavier punishment. And now—those particulars if you please."

Rachel gave them.

CHAPTER 18

When Miss Silver reached her own room she sat down on a small upright chair and plunged into thought for the space of about ten minutes. Then she glanced at her own little clock, a loudly ticking contraption of Swiss origin in a wooden case freely decorated with carved edelweiss, which she had placed in the exact centre of the mantelpiece, and observing that it was still not quite ten o'clock, rose up and rang the bell.

She was just thinking of ringing it again, when a plump, rosy-faced girl arrived in a hurry.

"Now I wonder," said Miss Silver, "whether I might speak to Louisa. That is her name, is it not—Miss Treherne's maid?"

"Oh, yes, miss. But if there's anything I can do—"

"Not at the moment, thank you. Was it you who unpacked for me? . . . And your name? . . . Ivy? Thank you very much, Ivy. Now if you will just ask Louisa to look in for a few moments on her way upstairs. I suppose her room is somewhere near Miss Treherne's. . . . Oh, the door beyond Miss Treherne's sitting-room? Then I shall only be taking her a step out of her way."

When Ivy had departed, Miss Silver retraced her steps. She passed the doors of Rachel Treherne's bedroom and sitting-room, and then stood listening for a moment before tapping lightly on what she now knew to be Louisa Barnet's door. Receiving no answer, she turned the handle and went in.

About ten minutes later she was back in her own room saying, "Come in!" to Louisa's knock. But Louisa was by no means anxious to enter. She remained upon the threshold.

"Were you wanting anything, miss?"

Miss Silver said "Yes," and added in a tone of authority, "Please come in and shut the door."

Louisa complied ungraciously. Her manner made it plain that it was not her place to wait upon the bedrooms.

Miss Silver indicated a chair at a slight distance from her own.

"Will you sit down. I want to talk to you."

"It's getting late, miss."

"Sit down please. I am a private enquiry agent, and I am here in that capacity. I want to talk to you about your mistress—about the attempts which are being made upon her life."

Louisa took the chair and sat down upon it. The action did not so much suggest compliance as an inability to continue in a standing position. She had a horrified look, and her face twitched. After a moment she said in a stumbling voice,

"Miss Rachel has told you—"

"She told me about a number of attempts, and I would like to go over them with you, because I am sure there is no one who can help me as much as you can."

Louisa's eyes dwelt on her. They were dark with feeling.

"If you can help Miss Rachel, I'll help you. It's time someone did."

Miss Silver nodded.

"Very well put. You shall help me, and together we will help Miss Treherne." She produced a shiny exercise-book. "Now, Louisa—this first attempt—the slippery stairs. Do you remember that?"

Louisa nodded.

"I shan't never forget it. She might have been killed."

"Well, Louisa, I don't want to worry Miss Treherne, but I would like to know who else was in the house, and what rooms they were occupying."

"Same as they always do. And they was all here, the whole

87

lot of them. Mr. and Mrs. Wadlow, they have Mr. Treherne's suite on the ground floor because of Miss Mabel having palpitations. Bedroom, dressing-room, bathroom and sitting-room they've got, and right underneath Miss Rachel—the same rooms as you might say, only on the ground floor. Then Mr. Frith and Mr. Maurice, they're in the bachelors' quarters when they're here—on the ground floor too, and their own entrance next the garage. Miss Caroline, she has the room opposite Miss Rachel, and Miss Cherry Wadlow next door. And Miss Comperton is next door to you here. And Mr. Richard, he's got the two over Mr. Frith and Mr. Maurice because of having a lot of office work to do with his architecting."

Miss Silver nodded.

"And where were all these people when Miss Treherne was washing her dog?"

Louisa tossed her head.

"I know where one of them was," she said, "for she was coming out of her room as I went by, and that was Miss Caroline Ponsonby. She shut the door quick, but I'll take my Bible oath I saw her—and she'd been crying too."

"Did you see anyone else in the neighbourhood of the stairs that afternoon?"

"Mr. Richard come up a half hour later, and he was knocking at Miss Caroline's door wanting her to come out, but she wouldn't, and maybe she'd her own reasons."

"You didn't see anyone else?" enquired Miss Silver.

She got a look.

"No, I didn't. I'd something else to do than watch the stairs."

Miss Silver turned a page in the shiny notebook.

"In the matter of the burning curtains—what time of day was it, and who discovered them to be alight?"

"Round about seven o'clock in the evening, and I found them myself. All alight they were and blazing. I come up to put out Miss Rachel's things, and who should come out of the sitting-room but Miss Caroline and Mr. Richard? And when I went through into the bedroom, there were the curtains all alight and blazing."

"Very suspicious indeed," said Miss Silver. "Fortunately Miss Treherne was in no real danger. I am sure you were most prompt." She turned another leaf. "And now we come to something a good deal more serious—the affair of the chocolates."

Louisa's mouth twitched.

"If I hadn't been here—" she said. Her hand went to her lips. "Miss Rachel that's so good to them—"

"You were with her when she bought the chocolates?"

"Yes, I was. And so was Miss Caroline. Did she tell you that?"

Miss Silver gazed mildly.

"I do not think so. Now can you tell me about how long the box was in the house before dinner, and where it was during that time?"

"It was in Miss Rachel's sitting-room from five till half past seven, and that's when it was got at. Miss Rachel, she was in her bedroom, and the chocolates were in the sitting-room. Anyone could have got at them, and someone did."

"Do you know who it was, Louisa?"

"I've got my own ideas, miss—how can I help having them? But Miss Rachel, she won't listen to a word. She won't let herself believe—that's what it is."

"Ah, yes, there are none so blind as those who will not see. Well, that is very helpful." She turned another page. "We now come to the very curious affairs of the snakes." She gazed with an air of prim intelligence. "What put such an idea into your head, Louisa?"

There was just a moment when nothing happened. Then a faintly startled look touched Louisa Barnet's eyes, to be immediately displaced by a flash of almost insane anger. She said on a rising note,

"What's that you said?"

Miss Silver did not raise her voice at all.

"I asked you what made you think of putting those snakes in your mistress's bed."

Louisa half got up out of her chair and dropped back again with a hand at her side. The flush of fury faded from her face and left it damp and yellow. She choked and said thickly,

"Me? Why, I'd die for Miss Rachel. She knows it, and you know it!"

"But you put the snakes in her bed, didn't you? Please don't think you can lie to me, because I know you did. I can even tell you why. You wanted to make Miss Treherne believe that one of the relations was trying to injure her. You would like to make her believe that it was Miss Caroline, so when you heard that a lot of adders had been found in Mr. Tollage's hedge you took Miss Caroline's green scarf out of her room and you went off up in the dusk to see whether you could get hold of one of these snakes. And you had very good luck, because you were able to buy two live ones in a shrimping-net from some boys who didn't know you. You paid them half-a-crown, and they remembered the green scarf, as you hoped they would. It was very foolish of you to keep the shrimping-net in your room. I found it in the wardrobe, hanging behind your coat. People who are trying to commit murder have to be a great deal more careful than that, Louisa Barnet—if they don't want to be found out."

Louisa gave a dreadful gasp. Her head went back against the wall and her eyes stared. For a moment Miss Silver thought that she was going to faint, but she recovered herself. Her head came up with a jerk and her eyes blazed. She said in a high, shaking voice,

"You come here prying, and you think you've found something out, and you think how clever you've been, but it's not you nor no one else'll make my Miss Rachel believe I'd harm her! She knows right enough I'd die for her and willing Miss Rachel does! So you're not so clever after all!"

There was the slightest of taps upon the door, so faint a sound that it was strange to see how it halted Louisa.

Miss Silver said, "Come in," and the door was opened. It was Rachel Treherne who stood on the threshold in her maize-coloured dressing-gown. She stood looking gravely in upon them. Then, as Louisa got to her feet, she came forward and shut the door.

"What is happening?" she said in a cool and quiet voice.

Louisa began to sob.

"What's brought you here out of your bed, which is where you ought to be? And you'll only hear lies about me if you listen to her. Are you going to stand there and take a stranger's word against me that's loved you these twenty years?"

"What does this mean?" said Rachel. She looked at Miss Silver, and it was Miss Silver who answered.

"It is true that you ought to be in bed. Is it too late to suggest that you go back to your room and allow me to give you an explanation in the morning?"

Rachel shook her head.

"Much too late. There was something I wanted to say to you, but it doesn't matter. I am afraid I must ask for your explanation now."

Miss Silver looked at her kindly.

"I would rather have waited, but I see that you must know. Will you not sit down? I will be brief, but I feel obliged to explain myself."

"Are you going to listen to her lies?" said Louisa roughly.

Rachel rested her hand on the back of the proffered chair.

"I am certainly going to listen," she said. "You will please not interrupt, Louisa." She drew her wrap about her and sat down. "Now, Miss Silver."

Miss Silver sat down too. Louisa put out a hand and took hold of the brass rail at the head of the bed. She was a little behind Rachel and facing Miss Silver, at whom she stared with hard and angry eyes.

Miss Silver addressed herself to Rachel, sitting very composed and upright with her hands folded in her lap.

"When you came to see me in London, Miss Treherne, I derived certain very definite impressions from what you told me. I could see that you believed yourself to have been the victim of three murderous attempts, but I did not feel entirely able to take that view myself—not on the evidence you then laid before me. To me it pointed, not necessarily to attempted murder, but rather to the presence in your household of some neurotic person who wished to make you believe that you were in danger, or who was actuated by what, I understand, is now termed exhibitionism. It used to be called showing off."

"The Lord's my witness!" Louisa Barnet's voice shook passionately.

Rachel put up a hand without looking round.

"If you want to stay, Louie, you must be quiet."

Miss Silver went on as if there had been no interruption.

"It was the second attempt which made me suspect that we had a neurotic to deal with. I do not know why nervously disturbed persons should so commonly set fire to window curtains, but it is quite a constant occurrence. It makes a lot of show and does very little harm. When I discovered from Louisa herself that the fire in this instance occurred at a time when any member of the household would know that it was bound to be discovered by your maid, who would naturally be in attendance to help you dress for dinner—well, if I had needed convincing I should then have been convinced. But I had already made up my mind. I arrived down here to find in Louisa Barnet the very type I was looking for."

Louisa flung up her hand.

"Miss Rachel—are you going to listen to this?"

"I think we will both listen," said Rachel.

Miss Silver went on speaking.

"After I had left you, Miss Treherne, I went to Louisa Barnet's room, and there I found two things which I had expected to find. One of them was a shrimping-net."

Rachel became so pale that there was no colour left in her face at all. She put out a hand as if to ward something off, and said in a whisper,

"Oh, no, no—not Louie!"

"Miss Rachel—"

"It was Louisa Barnet who put the snakes in your bed, Miss Treherne."

Rachel turned. She moved her chair, and turned in it so that she could see Louisa's face. She said,

"Did you, Louie?"

Louisa came with a rush and fell at her knees.

"It wasn't to do you no harm—oh, my dear, it wasn't! They'll make you think it was, but it wasn't. No, she won't make you think it, because you know my heart. You know— oh, my dear, you *know!*"

"Why did you do it, Louie?"

Louisa sat back on her heels with the tears running down her face.

"You wouldn't listen to nothing, and you wouldn't believe nothing. What could I do?"

"So you put adders in my bed. Get up, Louie, and sit down!" She turned to Miss Silver. "Did she do the other things too?"

"Yes, Miss Treherne, but I do not think she meant you to be hurt. She wanted to frighten you—about your relations, to make you believe they were trying to injure you. She began by writing you anonymous letters. Then she made the stairs slippery, but she was there to warn you not to step on them. She set your curtains on fire, but she put them out again. She made you believe that your chocolates had been poisoned, but I think it was only ammoniated quinine—I found the bottle on the washstand. It is a great pity that you did not have the chocolates analysed, but she was, of course, quite sure that you would not do so."

"Ammoniated quinine—was that the second thing you found?"

"Yes, Miss Treherne. I had expected it. A very bitter taste, and quite harmless. Louisa did not wish to poison your body—she merely wished to poison your mind. Against your relations. Chiefly, I think, against Miss Caroline, of whom she is jealous."

There was a silence. Then Rachel said in a mere ghost of a voice,

"Oh, Louie!"

Louisa stood up. Her tears were dry, and her eyes burned. She stood up, tall and fierce, and all at once she dominated the room. She said in a hard, even voice,

"You don't ask me if it's true."

"Is it true, Louie?"

She threw up her head.

"I'm going to tell you what's true." She turned as if she was looking for something and snatched up a square old-fashioned Bible from the table beside the bed. "I'll tell you the truth, and the whole truth, and nothing but the truth, so help me God— and I'll swear it on that woman's Bible. But I can't make you believe me if so be she've stopped your ears with her lies."

"Are they lies, Louie?"

"It's a lie for anyone to say I'd hurt you! I've never wanted nothing but to see you happy, and I've never done nothing but to keep you safe. But I couldn't get you to believe me."

"Tell me what you did and why you did it, Louie."

Louisa sat down on the side of the bed again. She clasped her hands over the Bible and said,

"If she can read anyone like a book, then she'll know I'm speaking true. I've heard of such, but how she does it passes me. And if she can read everyone so clever, why don't she tell you who it is doing the devil's work in this house? For this is what I'll tell you, and it's true. There was someone polished the step before ever I did it. And it wasn't that day—it was the Sunday evening, and Miss Rachel come in late.

Everyone knew it, and knew she was bound to be late for dinner. So there they all were, waiting for Miss Rachel to come hurrying down so as not to keep them. And one of them knew that when she come hurrying she'd be bound to fall because the top step was polished like glass. But, Miss Rachel, you sent me down to tell them not to wait, and I wasn't hurrying myself for them, so I'd time to take hold of the banisters and save myself. And I took hot water and washed the stuff off and never said nothing because it wasn't no use. But in the night it come to me that I'd got to show you. I thought if you saw it with your own eyes, maybe you'd believe me, so I did the three stairs when you were washing Noisy the next Saturday, but you wouldn't take no heed. And I did the curtains like she says, and the chocolates, and the adders. But don't you never think I'd have let you step into that there bed, my dear. Adders is stupid in the winter, and I reckoned they'd stay in the warmth by the hot water bottle. And what I was going to do was turn the bed right back and see something. And call out, like I did, and strip the bed. But I got a fright, for I didn't reckon on their being so lively. It must have been the heat. They were like dead things when I bought them."

Rachel leaned her head on her hand.

"Noisy killed them clever enough, and I put them on the fire with a good heart. I thought now you'd believe there was someone trying to do you a mischief."

"And it was you all the time! Only you, Louie!"

Louisa leaned forward, gripping the Bible.

"You're not going to believe that, my dear!" She turned to Miss Silver. "Are you going to let her believe that? If you can't tell lies from truth, what's the good of you? I'm telling you the truth. I didn't mean to do nothing to those chocolates—it never came into my head. But whilst Miss Rachel was in her bath I went in and had a look at them. The soft ones was in a bag separate, and I thought I'd see if I couldn't get them into the box. I'd about finished, when one of them rolled over, and there, underneath, you could see it had been meddled with. I put it straight in the fire before I stopped to think, and then it come to me I'd thrown away my chance to make Miss Rachel believe. So I looked to see if that was the only one, and it was. I looked quick and careful, but there wasn't any more. So then I thought what I could do, and I done it with the ammoniated quinine, like she says."

Miss Silver's eyes brightened, sharpened.

"One of the chocolates had been tampered with? You're quite sure of that?"

The defiant dark eyes met hers. The defiance went out of them.

"I'm sure," said Louisa—"certain, certain sure—and I've got the Book in my hand that I've sworn on to tell the truth. And I'll say more than that. If there's any plague in this Book, from the plagues that come on the Egyptians to what come on Judas that was a traitor, let them be nothing to what I'm willing to have come on me if I've taken anything away from the truth or put anything to it."

Rachel looked at her and looked away. She lifted her head from her hand and said in a low, steady voice,

"Who pushed me over the cliff?"

CHAPTER 19

Louisa moved with the Bible in her clasp. When she had laid it down on the little table beside the bed she came back and put a hand on Rachel's shoulder.

"Do you think I pushed you, my dear?" The voice was deep and gentle, the words simply spoken as to a child.

Rachel looked up at her and then down again. She said,

"No, Louie. You do love me." Then, after a pause, "But someone pushed me."

"I think you should go to bed now," said Miss Silver. "We will talk about it in the morning."

Rachel got wearily to her feet.

"Yes—I can't think—I can't talk about it any more tonight. Louie, I can't talk to you. You must go to your room."

"Miss Rachel—"

"Not tonight. I can't. Please go."

She turned back at the door herself because Miss Silver beckoned her.

"I won't keep you, Miss Treherne, but—will you change rooms with me tonight?"

Rachel smiled faintly.

"No, I won't do that."

"Then will you lock the doors—the two on the corridor and the communicating door from the sitting-room?"

"Yes—I was going to."

"Your little dog sleeps in your room? Would he bark if anyone came in?"

"Yes, I think he would. At least he growled horribly when Ella Comperton put her head in one night."

"Why did she do that?"

"She wanted to know if I had any aspirin."

"And had you?"

"No. I never take things like that. She ought to have known."

"And when was this?"

"About a fortnight ago. So I think that Noisy would live up to his name."

Back in her own room, Rachel thought again how peaceful it looked. Noisy had opened one eye when she came in, but he was now fast asleep again with his blanket thrown off and one ear flapped back. Rachel put it straight, felt him move against her hand, and thought, "How simple to be a dog. You love someone very much, and they love you."

She slipped off her dressing-gown, turned out the light, and lay down in bed. She sank through a kind of mist of fatigue into drowning depths of sleep and stayed there.

Much later in the night she rose to the surface, and was visited by dreams which changed continually. In one she saw herself walking like a prisoner across a waste of snow. Her wrists and ankles were chained with heavy links of gold, and she was quite alone. Then Gale Brandon came rushing over the snow in a sleigh and caught her up in the wind of his flight and swept her on. His arms were warm and strong.

Then she was running from something she could not see. She ran right up the Milky Way, and the stars flashed in her eyes and dazzled her, until they changed into cars with burning headlights, and the Milky Way into a concrete road. Someone blew a horn right in her ear, and she began to run again. Gale Brandon said, "You're quite safe now," but she couldn't find him because all the lights went out. Miss Silver said, "Simple faith is a great deal more uncommon than Norman blood." But it was Louisa who was crying as if her heart would break. The sound of her sobs turned into the noise of waves. Rachel hung on the cliff again, but it was daylight now. If she could look up she would see who it was that had pushed her over. But she couldn't look up. She had to look down at the rocks which were waiting for her. She heard Gale Brandon call her name, and woke.

It was still dark. The fire was dead. There was no light in the room. But she thought she heard a sound. She thought that there was someone outside her door—an ear against the panel—a hand upon the latch. Noisy's basket creaked. She heard him move, stand up, go pattering over the floor. And then she heard him growl. It was the faintest sound, a mere thrum in the throat. She called him, and he came running, to jump on the bed and flounce joyously in under the eiderdown. Rachel let him stay.

Presently she slept again.

Louisa brought her tea with an air of tragedy which was daunting in the extreme. Rachel's heart sank, but years of practice had given her a certain technique; she managed to postpone the impending scene.

The next thing that happened was more cheerful. The telephone bell rang beside the bed, and there was Gale Brandon to say good-morning and ask how she felt.

"Stiff," said Rachel.

"Are you getting up?" He sounded eager.

"Not at the moment, but I'm going to."

"I'd like to come over and see you if I may."

"Of course you may. I haven't thanked you for saving my life."

"You don't want to do that."

"But I do."

"I mean, you don't need to. I've been doing the thanking. Well, I'll be over. Is eleven o'clock too early? . . . All right, I'll make it half past." He rang off.

As she hung the receiver up, there came a gentle tapping on the door and Caroline Ponsonby came into the room in a green dressing-gown. Perhaps it was the colour that made her look so pale. She came and leaned on the foot of the bed, and Noisy pushed his nose out from under the eiderdown and made a little snuffling sound of welcome. Caroline said, "Bad spoilt one!" and stretched a hand to pull his ear. After a moment she straightened herself and looked at Rachel.

"Are you all right, darling? I worried about you in the night."

Rachel thought, "She looks as if she had seen a ghost. What is it?" She said,

"Was it you who came to my door?"

Caroline flushed.

"I did—once—when it was nearly morning. Did you hear me? I didn't mean to wake you. I couldn't sleep."

Rachel put out her hand.

"Come here and tell me why you couldn't sleep."

But Caroline stood where she was.

"I was frightened—about you—about the fall you had. I was afraid to go to sleep. You know how it is when you feel as if a horrid dream was waiting for you." She gave a pretence of a laugh. "I thought I wouldn't give it a chance, that's all. But you are all right?"

"Perfectly all right."

Caroline opened her mouth as if she was going to say something, and then shut it again and ran out of the room. Her eyes were full of tears.

CHAPTER 20

Rachel went down to breakfast as the lesser of two evils. If she shared the family meal she would get all the family questions over at once, whereas to stay upstairs was to invite separate visits from Ernest, Mabel, Ella, Cosmo, and Richard, with the same solicitous enquiries from each visitor in turn. She put a little colour in her cheeks and hoped for the best.

Everyone certainly did ask an inordinate number of questions. Ernest Wadlow's chief preoccupation appeared to be a desire to establish the exact spot where she had fallen. He arranged spoons and forks to represent the line of the cliff, with a breakfast cup for Nanny's cottage, and lumps of sugar to simulate the broken wall.

"If you came out here you would switch on your torch at the gate—I suppose you did switch on your torch?"

"The battery had run down," said Rachel.

Ella Comperton coughed.

"Well, Rachel, I should have thought you would have

made sure of having a good battery before attempting that dangerous path."

Ernest transferred his attention to Ella.

"I do not think one can fairly describe the path as dangerous—not with a good torch."

"But it wasn't a good torch, and nothing would induce me to attempt it, Ernest."

"I can't imagine why you didn't let the car fetch you," said Mabel Wadlow in her fretful voice. "It could perfectly well have met Miss Silver's train and then picked you up."

Rachel felt her colour rise.

"But I like walking," she said, and wondered how many of them would guess that she liked walking because Gale Brandon sometimes walked with her.

"But without a proper torch!" said Ernest. "Do you mean to say that the battery was quite run down?"

"It wasn't much use."

Richard looked over the top of the *Daily Mail*.

"But I put a new battery in for you yesterday morning."

Rachel said, "Yes."

Cosmo Frith lowered the *Times* and observed genially,

"In that case, my dear, you must have taken the wrong torch."

One of those arguments peculiar to families developed. The condition of the battery became the subject of a heated debate which culminated in Cosmo bursting out laughing and declaring that the culprit should be allowed to give evidence on its own behalf. He went out into the hall for the torch, and came in switching it on and off.

"Nothing much wrong with it, my dear, to my mind. A good thing you didn't lose it when you fell. Of course it's not so easy to tell in daylight, but the battery seems pretty hearty to me. I'll try it inside the china-cupboard."

A moment later he was calling from behind a half closed door.

"Here, Richard, come and see! Rachel, I'd like you to take a look. I'll swear there's nothing wrong with this battery."

Rachel looked, and saw a bright beam and a brilliant ring of light. Over her shoulder Miss Silver saw them too.

"Nothing wrong with it—eh, my dear?"

Rachel said in a puzzled voice,

"It wasn't like that last night."

She drew away from the cupboard door and back to her place, to be immediately pounced on by Ernest.

"Now let us suppose that you had walked as far as this— the first lump of sugar represents the beginning of the wall— how much farther had you gone before you fell? I am allowing a yard to each lump of sugar."

"I really don't know, Ernest."

He gazed reproachfully over the top of the crooked *pince-nez*.

"But, my dear Rachel, you must have some idea. I do not expect complete accuracy—we are not in a court of law—but you must surely be able to hazard a guess."

"I don't know that I want to, Ernest. I would really so much rather not have to go on thinking about it."

"Or talking about it," said Cosmo Frith. "And you shall not, my dear. We're all much too thankful you weren't hurt to worry about might-have-beens."

Ella Comperton pushed back her chair.

"Well, it all seems to me to be a good deal of fuss about nothing. I'm sure I had a nasty tumble myself the other day, and nobody made any fuss about it. I don't know what everyone is going to do, but I am going to write letters, and then later on I shall take a little constitutional. Caroline, you look as if you would be none the worse for some fresh air and exercise."

"Caroline is coming into Ledlington with me," said Richard.

But if there was relief on Caroline's face, there was no gratitude. The defenceless look which had brought Richard to her rescue sank a little deeper into her eyes, but it was still there.

He spoke to her for a moment as they came out of the dining-room together.

"You needn't come, but—I won't worry you—"

She took a quick breath.

"It's not that. I've got to pack."

She walked off towards the stairs, but he caught her up.

"How do you mean, you've got to pack?"

She took hold of the banisters and stood half turned from him.

"I think—I've got—to go away—"

"What do you mean? You needn't—I'll go."

She said "No" in a heart-broken voice, and ran from him up the stairs.

When Rachel came up after seeing the housekeeper she found Richard in her sitting-room. He turned from the window as she came in and said without any preamble,

"Why is Caroline going away?"

Rachel felt an acute distress. It seemed to flow to her from Richard. It took hold upon her heart. She said quickly,

"But I didn't know she was going. Have you quarrelled?"

He was very pale.

"Listen, Rachel. You must have known—what I feel—about Caroline. Everyone must have known. I've never tried to hide it—never wanted to. She's been everything to me as long as I can remember. I was only waiting—till I was in a position—"

"I know. What has gone wrong?"

"I don't know—I tell you I don't know. I asked her to marry me—yesterday—after tea. We went out for a walk on the cliffs—it was dark. I didn't mean to do it, but I found myself telling her—asking her. And she said 'No.'"

"Richard!"

"It was damnable. I don't know what made me choose an idiotic place like that. I couldn't see her face. I couldn't get any sense out of her. She was all frozen up, and when I tried to take hold of her she ran away. I tell you I don't know what to make of her. And this morning—she's just told me—she's going to pack—"

Rachel took him by the arm.

"Wait a minute—I want to ask you something. You say you were on the cliffs. What time were you there, and what part of the cliff were you on?"

He said impatiently, "I don't know! Does it matter? I got back about six. We went by the upper path, and after Caroline left me I came back along the edge. I must have just missed you, I suppose."

He felt her grasp tighten.

"Did you see anyone—meet anyone?"

"No, I don't think so. Why?"

"And you're sure you did change the battery in my torch yesterday morning?"

"Quite sure. Rachel, what is all this about?"

She said in a low, steady voice, "Richard—" and before she could say any more the door opened and Miss Silver came into the room with her head a little on one side and a pleasant if somewhat foolish smile upon her face.

"I do hope I don't intrude, but you did say in a quarter of an hour's time, and I make it exactly the quarter. My watch keeps excellent time. A twenty-first birthday gift from my parents, and I do not think it has ever been out of order—but that was before the days of cheap watches. Dear me—what a charming room this is. And what a delightful view. It reminds me of a picture which I remember seeing in the Royal Academy—well now, it would be quite twenty years ago. That headland, and the rocks, and the peculiar greenish grey colour of the sea—"

As she tripped to the window for a nearer view, Richard turned a face of barely suppressed fury upon Rachel. It enquired, "Is she going to stay?" and a flicker of Rachel's eyelids replied, "She is."

She went with him to the door and squeezed his arm.

"I won't let her go if I can help it," she said in a whisper.

They were both looking across at Caroline's door.

Richard said "Thank you" in a stifled voice and made off.

Rachel went back into her sitting-room and shut the door.

CHAPTER 21

Miss Silver turned round from admiring the view. Her hand was raised and her lips primmed in reproof.

"Oh, dear, dear, dear! That was very bad," she said. "Very bad indeed, Miss Treherne. If I had not come in when I did—oh, dear me! You were, I am afraid, about to commit a very grave imprudence."

Rachel had the oddest sense of guilt. Amusement contended with offence.

Miss Silver came nearer.

"Shall I tell you what you were about to say when I came into the room? You said, 'Richard—' and what you were going to say was, 'I didn't fall over the cliff—I was pushed.' Is that not correct?"

Rachel's eyes sparkled a little.

"Quite correct. And why shouldn't I have said it?"

Miss Silver shook her head.

"Most, most imprudent. But there—we will say no more about it. Shall we sit down?"

When they were seated she resumed with a good deal of briskness in her voice.

"As far as it is possible, I have verified the movements of every member of this household between the hour of five and ten minutes past six yesterday evening. That covers the time you were out, does it not?"

"I left here just before five—about ten minutes to, I think.

And I got up to say good-bye to Nanny at a quarter to six, but she kept me for a little while after that. It must have been about five minutes to six when I—fell." Her voice dropped to the word.

Miss Silver nodded.

"Yes—I have a little margin. Now, if you will listen—"

She opened a shiny notebook and began to read from it in a quick, matter-of-fact voice:

"Miss Comperton:—Seen going upstairs when tea was being cleared—say 5.15. Not seen again until Ivy took her water at half past seven. She was then in her dressing-gown.

"Miss Caroline and Mr. Richard:—Went out together at five o'clock. Mr. Richard returned alone at ten minutes past six. I had just arrived myself, and I saw him come in. No one seems to know when Miss Caroline came in."

"Have you been questioning the servants?" said Rachel in a tone of distaste.

Miss Silver shook her head.

"It was not necessary. Louisa has supplied me with those details which did not come under my own observation. It was quite easy for her to do so."

"And you trust her?" There was a faint trace of bitterness in Rachel's tone.

"In a matter of this kind—yes, implicitly. And she knows how to hold her tongue. Let me resume.

"Mr. Frith:—Retired to the study after tea. He had a portfolio of sketches and appeared to be sorting them when the maid called Gladys answered the bell at half past five. He gave her a letter for the post in case anyone should be going out. She said he seemed to be very busy with his paintings, and he had the wireless on. The wireless was still on when I entered the hall at nine minutes past six, and about a minute later Mr. Frith opened the study, looked out into the hall, and, seeing a stranger, drew back again.

"Mr. and Mrs. Wadlow:—Were not seen by anyone between a quarter past five when tea was cleared and half past seven when Gladys took them their hot water. Mrs. Wadlow was then in her bedroom lying down on the bed, and Mr. Wadlow was in the adjoining sitting-room. The communicating door being wide open, Gladys was able to see him as she crossed to the washstand.

"As to the members of the domestic staff, I find that from half past five until my arrival at nine minutes past six they were in the servants' hall listening to a wireless programme from Luxembourg—with three exceptions. These were the girl Gladys, Louisa, and the chauffeur. Gladys says she went up to her room after answering the study bell at half past five. She had a pair of stockings that she wanted to darn and a letter to write. She stayed up there until she heard the car. The chauffeur was in Ledlington meeting my train.

"Louisa's account of her own movements is as follows:—She let Noisy out for a run, and had some difficulty in getting him in again. She says he was out for a quarter of an hour. She then put on her outdoor things, lighted the stable lantern, which she tells me she prefers to a torch, and started out along the cliff to meet you. According to this it must have been quite six or seven minutes past six before she left the house. It was probably a little later, or she would have met Mr. Richard. How long would it take her to reach the place where you went over?"

"About ten minutes."

"That would put her arrival with the lantern at about twenty-five minutes past six. Does that fit in?"

Rachel said, "I think so. Everything happened much more quickly than it seemed. It was only a quarter to seven when I got back to my room. I know I looked at the clock and couldn't believe my eyes. Saying good-bye to Nanny seemed like hours and hours ago."

Miss Silver nodded.

"I once met a very clever man who maintained that time did not exist. I never could understand what he said, but I

107

knew quite well what he meant. Well now, Miss Treherne, we must be practical. From these notes you will realize that it would have been possible for any one of the following persons to have pushed you over the cliff—Mr. Wadlow, Mrs. Wadlow—"

Rachel Treherne burst out laughing.

"My dear Miss Silver, my sister Mabel would literally die of fright if she found herself alone on the cliff path after dark. And as for pushing me over, I can assure you that it was a much stronger hand that did that."

Miss Silver smiled.

"I will agree that it does not seem probable that Mrs. Wadlow was actively concerned in the attempt. I am merely covering the time between half past five and ten minutes past six, and for that period neither Mr. nor Mrs. Wadlow has any effective alibi. That is to say, they can probably speak for each other, but no one else can speak for them. The other persons without alibis are Mr. Frith, Miss Comperton, Louisa Barnet, the girl Gladys—and lastly, Miss Caroline and Mr. Richard. It is true they left the house together, but they returned separately. I deduce a quarrel, but we have no means of knowing how long they were together before they separated, or what they did after that. Now that covers the people who were in the house, but there are some others who cannot be excluded from an enquiry. Maurice Wadlow and his sister Cherry left Whincliff Edge after breakfast yesterday morning. I should like some evidence as to their subsequent movements. It would not have been difficult for them to have returned either singly or together. From what Mrs. Wadlow has told me it would seem likely that Miss Cherry was fully occupied with her own affairs, but this requires corroboration. We have next to consider Mr. Gale Brandon, but in view of the fact that he went to considerable trouble to pull you up we may perhaps assume provisionally that he did not push you down. There remains one other person as to whose movements we have no evidence at all, and that is your old nurse's niece, the young woman Ellen."

Rachel could not help laughing again.

"Ellen!"

Miss Silver nodded.

"Yes, Ellen. I should like to hear a little more about her, but first there is the question of motive. You make your old nurse an allowance?"

"Yes, she has two pounds a week and the cottage."

"And what would happen if you died?"

"She would go on getting it as long as she lived."

"And Ellen?"

Rachel hesitated.

"Miss Silver—it's absurd!"

Miss Silver coughed.

"Abnormal certainly. That is the way with crime. But you have not answered my question. Would Ellen Capper profit by your death?"

Rachel said with an effort,

"I have left her a hundred pounds."

"And does she know this?"

"Nanny knows. She was worrying about Ellen's future, so I told her."

"Then of course Ellen knew. And knew just when you visited her aunt, and when you would be coming away."

"Yes, but I was early yesterday evening. I usually stay till six."

"Ten minutes—" said Miss Silver. "Well, Miss Treherne, I think Ellen must account for her movements. And that brings me to what I have to say to you. Miss Treherne, this is no longer a case for a private enquiry agent. A serious attempt has been made upon your life, and it is my duty to point out to you that you ought to call in the police."

Rachel got up. Her face was very pale and her eyes bright.

"No, I won't have the police brought into it," she said.

"Miss Treherne, the attempt was a very dangerous one. If it had not been for Mr. Brandon's presence of mind it would

109

have been successful, and I should now be waiting here to give evidence at an inquest. I urge you to inform the police without delay."

Rachel walked to the window and stood there.

"I won't do it." After a short silence she turned round. "Miss Silver, how can I? If there were nothing else, think of the talk—local at first, then spreading until it got into the papers. Haven't you enough imagination to see the headlines? I have. Everyone would be brought into it, everyone's affairs ferreted out—Cherry's flirtations—Maurice's crazy politics—any stupidity which any of us may have tumbled into—any debt—any folly however light, however irrelevant. You know as well as I do they'd all be whipped to a froth and served up to tickle the taste for scandal. That's what we'd get if we called in the police. And there would be worse than that, because all those other things would come out, and they would arrest Louisa—they'd have to. You must see that I can't possibly have the police brought into this."

"Miss Treherne—"

Rachel was no longer pale. Her cheeks flamed.

"Miss Silver, I give you fair warning—if the police are brought in, I shall deny the whole thing! I shall say that I fell. No one will be in a position to contradict me except—except the person who pushed me over, and—and—that's not a very likely thing to happen, is it?"

Miss Silver said "No—" in a meditative tone. After a slight pause she continued briskly. "Well, I have done my duty. I would like further to urge upon you that you should immediately protect yourself by destroying your existing will and making a new one, the provisions of which you would keep to yourself. This accomplished, and an announcement made to that effect, your life would, I think, be safe, because the person who has attempted it could not be sure of having escaped suspicion, and would be unlikely to incur a fresh risk until the terms of the new will had transpired."

"That is what you said before—in London—when I came to see you."

"And I say it again. It is good advice."

Rachel crossed the room. When she came to the door which led into her bedroom she leaned against it. It was as if she could not go any farther. She kept hold of the half turned handle and breathed deeply. Then she said,

"I can't take it—I can't. I told you why. They're my people. They're all I've got. I love some of them—very much. I owe something to all of them—because we are a family. I can't just—save myself and leave them all—under suspicion. If I took your—good advice, there would never be any love or confidence again—there couldn't be. I don't feel as if I could live like that. I want to live—very much. But it's too big a price—I can't pay it. I must know the truth. I must know whom I can trust and whom I can love. I'll take any risk to find that out."

She straightened up and looked blindly and piteously at Miss Silver.

"Find out," she said.

CHAPTER 22

About a quarter of an hour later Miss Silver emerged from her own room and descended the stairs. There was no one in the hall, but just as she arrived on the bottom step Gladys ran out of the study.

"Oh, miss," she said, "you're wanted on the telephone. It's a London call."

Miss Silver did not hurry. She said, "Oh, thank you," and then, "Will you just show me—" And when they were both in the study and she found that it was empty, she said in the voice which was so exactly that of a retired governess, "The call will not keep me for more than three minutes. There is something I want to ask you about. I wonder if you would be so kind as to go to my room and wait for me there."

The call took its allotted three minutes and no more. Miss Silver's remarks were few and cryptic. She said, "Speaking," and then, "You have asked them all?" And at the end, "Yes, it is what I expected. Thank you. Good-bye." After which she hung up the receiver and went upstairs again.

She found Gladys standing by the window, a pretty, serious-looking girl with a bright colour and rather a nervous manner. She turned round now, fingering her apron.

"It's Ivy does these upstair rooms."

Miss Silver smiled agreeably.

"And very nicely, I am sure. But it was you that I wanted to speak to. I have Miss Treherne's permission to ask you one or two questions. The fact is, someone played a stupid trick on her last night—a very stupid, startling trick—and I am wondering whether you can help us to find out who it was."

"Me, miss?"

"Yes, Gladys. Just answer me quite truthfully, and no one will blame you if you did slip out with Mr. Frith's letter."

The bright color became a number of shades brighter.

"Oh, miss!"

Miss Silver nodded gently.

"You did, didn't you? Mr. Frith rang the study bell at half past five and gave you a letter for the post in case anyone was going out, and I expect you thought, 'Now why shouldn't I go out?' That was it, was it not?"

"There wasn't any harm—not when he asked me."

"And I daresay you have a friend who comes up on the chance of your being able to slip out."

The colour faded.

"I don't know who's been telling tales. I'm sure I've done no harm."

"I am sure you have not. You see, I want you to help me.

112

Miss Treherne would like to know who played this trick on her, and I thought if you were out you might have noticed if there was anyone about. What time was it when you went out?"

"It was half past five when Mr. Frith rang. I just went up for my coat and slipped out through the garage so as no one would see me. Not that there was any harm, but some of them—well, they tease me about Tom."

"How long were you out?"

"The garage clock struck six as I come in."

"Did you see anyone—meet anyone?"

"I went down to the post-box—it's just outside the gate— and, well, Tom happened to be there, and we were talking for a bit, and then he said he was pushed for time and couldn't come up to the house with me, so he went off on his motor-bike. He works in a garage in Ledlington."

"Now, Gladys, where does the cliff path come in? Because that's what I want to know about."

"Well, the real path comes in just a bit down the road from the gate, but anyone that was coming to the house, they wouldn't come down on to the road at all. They'd take the garden gate up by the garage and come in that way right off the cliff."

Miss Silver said, "I see—" And then, "You haven't told me whether you saw anyone. Did you?"

Gladys looked down and fidgeted with her apron.

"It was a lot too dark to see anyone."

"But you met someone?"

"Not to say met."

Miss Silver looked at her sharply.

"You did not see anyone, and you did not meet anyone. But there *was* someone all the same."

"Only Miss Caroline."

"What was she doing?"

"Coming in off the cliff."

"Did you speak to her?"

"No, I didn't."

113

"Then how do you know it was Miss Caroline?"

Gladys stood looking down at the hands that were twisting her apron.

"Come now, it was dark—you couldn't tell one person from another. You couldn't be sure that it was Miss Caroline."

Gladys's head came up. Her eyes were wet and angry.

"Well then, I could! It was Miss Caroline all right, because I could hear her talking."

"Talking? To whom?"

"To herself. There wasn't no one else—only Miss Caroline. And I wouldn't have told anyone, but she was crying and carrying on like you do when something's upset you, and seeing I heard her as plain as what I hear you—well, it was Miss Caroline all right. But it wouldn't be her playing any practical jokes, because for one thing she was too upset, and for another everyone knows what a lot she thinks of Miss Treherne."

"Yes, yes," said Miss Silver. "And now will you tell me what Miss Caroline was saying?"

Gladys stared.

"It wasn't anything to make sense. She was all upset."

"Well, I would like you to tell me exactly what you heard."

Gladys sniffed.

"When anyone's upset like that they don't think what they're saying—it don't mean anything. You could tell she didn't hardly know what she was saying."

"Miss Caroline may have had a fright as well as Miss Treherne. You see, Gladys, we want to get to the bottom of this. Will you tell me just what Miss Caroline said."

Gladys sniffed again.

"She was crying something shocking. Just the other side of the garden gate she was, and she come through it a little way and stood there crying and talking to herself. And I stood still where I was because of not letting her know I was there, and the first thing I heard her say was, 'I can't—I can't!' and she was crying fit to break her heart. So then she said, 'I can't do it!' and she stood a bit and went back to the gate, and she said, 'She's always been so good to us.' And she said, 'I can't!' and she went out through the gate again, and I come in by the garage."

Miss Silver had a puzzled look on her face.

"And it was six o'clock when you came in?"

"No—it wasn't any more than ten minutes to, or maybe a quarter."

Miss Silver coughed.

"But you said the garage clock was striking six as you came in."

"Oh, yes, it was. But it strikes fast that clock does. Barlow, he likes it that way. He says it's as good as an alarm."

"So you had only been out a quarter of an hour?"

"Yes, miss. And I went up to my room and did some mending till I heard the car come back."

"Thank you, Gladys," said Miss Silver. She crossed to the door and opened it. "I think Miss Treherne would rather you did not speak about this."

Gladys gave a final sniff.

"I'm not one to talk," she said.

CHAPTER 23

I don't know what girls are coming to," said Mabel Wadlow in her complaining voice. "You may think yourself very lucky not to have any. What with feeling they're a failure if they don't marry, and not knowing who they'll take it into their heads to marry if they do marry, and out all night at dances, and off for the week-end without so much as telling you where they're going—well, it isn't any wonder that my health is such a constant anxiety to Ernest."

Mrs. Wadlow was reclining upon a couch in the drawing-room. Miss Maud Silver sat in a small armless chair at a convenient angle for conversation and knitted. The expression upon her face was one of almost reverential attention. Seldom if ever had Mabel encountered a more congenial companion. She felt that, for once, here was someone who was really interested in the state of her digestion, the number of hours that she had slept or had not slept the night before, the condition of her heart and pulse, her anxieties about Maurice, and, last but not least, the very troublesome and inconsiderate way that Cherry was behaving.

"I'm sure when I was a girl I would never have dreamt of making myself conspicuous with a man who was engaged to another girl, but Cherry doesn't seem to care. And she is supposed to be going to be a bridesmaid. Mildred Ross *asked* her, but of course that was before she had made herself so conspicuous. And now I wonder if the marriage will ever really take place, because of course he can't be in love with Mildred, and the worst of it is that Cherry isn't a bit in love with him—she says so herself. Girls are so frank now, aren't they? They will say anything, even to a total stranger. And Cherry says quite openly that she doesn't care for Bob—it's just the money. He is so fearfully rich, and Cherry says she must have money and she doesn't care how she gets it. Now what would you have said if you had heard a girl talk like that when you were a girl, Miss Silver?"

A reply rose readily to Miss Silver's lips, but she did not allow it to pass them. She permitted a faintly shocked expression to appear on her face, and remarked in a vaguely sympathetic tone,

"Ah—what indeed?"

Mabel Wadlow thought this a most suitable reply. There was an unwonted colour in her cheeks and an unwonted animation in her manner as she said,

"Of course it isn't all her fault. It is very hard indeed to be brought up with money all round you and not to have any of your own." She dropped her voice to a confidential tone. "My father made the most extraordinary will. I wouldn't speak of it to everyone, but I know that you are safe. You will hardly believe it, but except for a very, very moderate settlement made at the time of my marriage I did not receive a single penny from his estate. You may well look astonished. He left everything to my sister Rachel—my younger sister. Not by very much of course, and people often express surprise at hearing that she is younger than I am. But then an unmarried woman tends to age more quickly—don't you agree? You would think, wouldn't you, that she would have been glad not to have the responsibility of managing so much money. I think everyone was surprised that she did not hand my proper share over to me immediately. It would have saved us all a great deal of trouble and anxiety, and, as Ernest has always said, what is the good of piling up an immense fortune which is bound to go to somebody else when you die? You see, it isn't as if she had children of her own, or was likely to have them now even if she were to marry, which is extremely improbable. Rachel is thirty-eight."

Miss Silver's needles clicked.

"I knew a woman of forty-eight who married and had twins," she observed in an artless, gossiping voice.

"Well, I can't think how she did it," said Mabel Wadlow. "And it would be most unusual. No one in our family has ever had twins. And why anyone should *want* to have children? I'm sure they wouldn't if they knew. Night after night I lie awake worrying about Maurice, because when you have only one boy it's no use anyone saying 'Don't worry.' I'm sure the last book Ernest got out of the library about Russia was too, too dreadful. The sanitary arrangements! I don't know how they printed some of the things. But of course they don't mind now, do they? I mean they don't mind what they print. But naturally after that I couldn't sleep a wink, and Ernest insisted, positively *insisted* on my taking a sleeping draught. As a rule I would endure *anything*, but my pulse was so rapid that he insisted. It is marvellous stuff, you know, and I am very careful, because when it is finished I shan't be able to get any more. It was that very clever Dr. Levitas whom we met when we were travelling in Eastern Europe who gave me the powders. I had the most alarming attack, and he treated me, and he told Ernest it was one of the most interesting cases he had ever known. He said he had never had a patient who was so highly strung, and he told Ernest that I must never be worried, or thwarted, or allowed to excite myself in any way. But we have only three or four of the powders left now, and we never had the prescription, so we have to be very careful of them. They last a long time of course, because they are very strong and I only take a quarter of a powder at a time."

Mabel Wadlow went on talking about her powders, and her pulse, and what she felt like when she woke up in the night, and what Dr. Levitas had said about her constitution, and how terribly bad it was for her to be worried, and wasn't it quite inconceivable that one's own sister should allow one to have financial embarrassments when she could so easily remove them by simply writing a cheque. She continued until Miss Silver rolled up her knitting and rose.

"Do you know, I have knitted up all my wool. How kind of you to spare me so much time. I must go up and wind another skein."

But she did not go to her own room. She knocked instead on Miss Treherne's door, and found her just putting the telephone receiver back upon its hook.

Rachel turned round with a lost look.

"Gale Brandon was coming over. I've told him not to."

"Why did you do that?" said Miss Silver.

"He cares for me—I think he cares a lot. I've never had—that. I don't want it spoilt. I don't want it—mixed up with all this. I've told him not to come."

"Have you told him why?"

Rachel said "No." And then, as simply as a child, "He's angry."

Miss Silver said, "He will get over that, my dear." Her voice was brisk and kind. "I think you are quite right. I do not really want Mr. Brandon here at present, though I think we may be very glad of him later on. In their own way men can be quite useful. But just now I wish to talk to you. There are some things which I think you ought to know. Let us sit down."

Rachel took a chair.

"When anyone says that, it always means something unpleasant," she said rather wearily.

"I am afraid so," said Miss Silver.

She was wearing her snuff-coloured dress, with thick brown stockings and rather shabby black *glacé* shoes trimmed with ribbon bows. Her high stuff collar was fastened by a mosaic brooch which represented a pink and yellow temple against a bright blue sky. The eyes with which she contemplated Rachel were full of a keen intelligence tempered by kindness. She said,

"I have been talking to Gladys. I thought it most improbable that she would have stayed in her room mending stockings while the rest of the staff were listening to the wireless. As soon as I heard that Mr. Frith had given her a letter in case anyone should be going to the post I was convinced that Gladys herself had gone out with it, which proved to be the case."

"It was really very clever of you."

Miss Silver coughed in a deprecating manner.

"Oh dear, no, not at all. But I am afraid I have to tell you something which may distress you. On her way back she heard Miss Caroline weeping and talking to herself in the dark. The time—which she fixes by the striking of the garage clock—was a quarter to six. Miss Caroline came in through the gate from the cliff path in a state of considerable distress. Gladys heard her say, 'I can't do it—I can't!' And then she said, 'She has always been so kind to us,' and she ran out on to the path again, and Gladys came into the house."

119

Rachel smiled with stiff lips. She hoped with all her shrinking heart that Miss Silver did not know how stiff they were.

"And do you ask me to believe that Caroline—*Caroline* pushed me over the cliff?"

"I don't ask you to believe anything. I have told you what Gladys told me, because it is one of the things I think you ought to know."

"One of them?"

"Yes, there are others."

"Go on."

"I have also been having a conversation with Mrs. Wadlow. She talked a good deal about her daughter. She said that Cherry would do anything for money. She conveyed to me the picture of a completely ruthless young woman who would take what she wanted whether it belonged to someone else or not. I would be glad to have your opinion as to whether this picture is a true one."

Rachel's hand lifted for a moment and then fell again.

"Yes—Cherry is like that."

"Mrs. Wadlow also spoke about her son. She seems to resent the fact that you are not inclined to provide a sum of money which would keep him in England. May I ask whether Mr. Maurice shares this resentment?"

A gleam of rather bitter humour sparkled in Rachel's eyes.

"I have no doubt of it. I am a wicked capitalist, and it would be a highly ethical action to relieve me of as much of this wicked capital as possible. 'Liquidate it' is, I believe, the expression which he would use. To be really logical, of course, I ought to be liquidated too—" She stopped short on a quick breath, and slowly, very slowly, her hand went up to her throat.

"We will not stress that point," said Miss Silver, "but I think we will bear it in mind. Now with regard to Miss Comperton—I have some extremely unpleasant information for you. I have here particulars of various sums which you have from time to time entrusted to Miss Comperton for the benefit of certain charitable institutions. I have ascertained through an assistant who has made the necessary enquiries on my behalf that none of these charities has at any time received a larger donation from Miss Comperton than half-a-crown."

Rachel leaned forward, resting her weight on the arms of her chair. That was what she was chiefly conscious of—weight. Feet cold and heavy as stone, limbs like lead, and a heart as heavy as grief itself.

"*Ella?*" she said.

Miss Silver said, "I am afraid so. The manner in which she immediately pressed me for a subscription made an unfavourable impression. Greed is a quality which it is very hard to dissemble. I discerned it plainly, and it suggested the advisability of making enquiries."

"Is there anything else?" said Rachel.

"No—no—I think I may say not. But I would suggest that the time has come when you should inform your family of the fact that a murderous attempt was made upon you last night. I should like you to call them all together and tell them exactly what happened, and I should wish to be present."

Rachel turned extremely pale.

"Just now—when I was going to tell Richard—you stopped me."

"Certainly, Miss Treherne. It would have been giving him an advantage over the others. You were about to give him this advantage. You were, in point of fact, assuming his innocence. Now I want to say to you with the utmost gravity that you cannot afford to assume anyone's innocence in this matter. I do not ask you to assume anyone's guilt, but I do ask you in every case to adopt the same caution as if you were dealing with a person whom you knew to be guilty."

"But that is horrible!"

"Murder is horrible," said Miss Silver.

CHAPTER 24

Upon one pretext or another the family had been assembled in the drawing-room. Outside the day was dark and lowering. Within, though a bright fire burned on the hearth, there was a chill, a feeling of uneasiness.

Richard Treherne was the last to appear. They had waited for him in a silence which no one except Mabel seemed inclined to break. Cosmo Frith picked up the clock from the mantelpiece, remarked that it needed regulating, and busied himself with it.

"Cosmo can't keep his hands off a clock," Mabel complained. "I believe he winds his own every time he goes near it." To which Miss Maud Silver replied that in her opinion clocks should be wound once a week and never touched in between.

Mabel Wadlow, who still reclined amongst her cushions and had apparently neither moved nor attempted to occupy herself, had welcomed her return with effusion. But before resuming her chair Miss Silver drew it back into line with the couch in such a manner as to command a view of Miss Comperton in the armchair on the right of the fire, Mr. Frith now standing fair and square in the middle of the hearthrug with the *Times* held out at arms length before him, and Rachel Treherne leaning back in the armchair on the left.

Caroline Ponsonby had pulled a low stool close to Rachel. She sat forward with an elbow propped on her knee and her chin in her hand. She had so pale a look that no one could have called her pretty now. Miss Silver thought her very near the breaking-point, and permitted herself to wonder what would happen when it came.

Richard Treherne sat on the arm of Rachel's chair. Miss Silver saw him stoop down and say a word in her ear, and she saw the answer too, a shake of the head.

Caroline looked round once, and then went on staring past Cosmo at the fire.

Ernest Wadlow, who had come in last, brought a chair up to the sofa and leaned over his wife, asking her solicitously how she felt, and whether she had remembered to take her drops.

Miss Silver coughed, and, as if it had been a signal, Rachel Treherne spoke. She turned to Richard and said,

"Will you find yourself a chair? I have something rather serious to say."

Richard did not start, but he was certainly startled. And there was nothing in that, for, apart from the words, neither Rachel's voice nor her manner were natural. She was plainly putting a force upon herself. Perhaps even now she had Miss Silver's words in her mind. Perhaps, instead of assuming Richard's innocence, she had for a horrible moment feared his guilt. Miss Silver saw the hand which lay upon her knee contract upon itself until the knuckles whitened. Then, as Richard moved to a chair on the other side of the hearth, she saw the hand relax.

The *Times* rustled as Cosmo turned a page. He said rather abstractedly,

"Well, my dear, here we are. Do you know—a most extraordinary thing—here's a man Ferguson who was at school with me marrying a film star. Never heard of her, but they call her a star. The man must be off his head. I beg your pardon, Rachel—what were you going to say?"

"Something serious?" said Ernest Wadlow. He rumpled his hair and looked sideways over the tilted *pince-nez*. "I hope it is nothing—er—that is to say—nothing—" His voice trailed off without finishing the sentence.

Mabel raised herself on both hands until she was clear of her cushions and said in agitated accents,

"Something has happened to Maurice—I felt sure of it! Oh! Tell me quickly—is it an accident?"

"It's nothing to do with Maurice," said Rachel, and in the middle of saying it a shiver took her, because how did she know that it wasn't Maurice's hand that had pushed her over the cliff?

Mabel sank back, half sketched a palpitation, and then decided to postpone it until she knew what Rachel had really got to say.

Miss Silver looked at Ella Comperton, and found her nervous—oh dear, yes, decidedly nervous. She was picking at a little bag and missing the clasp, and when she found it, fumbling with it. When she did get it open, all the contents came tumbling out into her lap. The hand with which she extricated a handkerchief and pressed it to her nose was by no means steady. The nose twitched, the handkerchief twitched, the hand twitched. Miss Silver reflected, not for the first time in her career, that it must be very uncomfortable indeed to have a guilty conscience. She looked at Richard Treherne, and Richard said,

"What's the matter, Rachel? I hope you don't mean anything really serious."

"I'm afraid I do." Rachel was sitting up now with her hands clasped tightly in her lap. "I thought you ought to know—all of you—that something very serious did happen yesterday. I thought you ought to know."

Miss Silver saw all the faces—all except Caroline's, and Caroline's face was turned away from her and turned towards Rachel. Miss Silver could see nothing of it. But the other faces showed her, surprise—that was Cosmo Frith; a grave attention—that was Richard; fear—yes, certainly fear—that was Ella Comperton; and a deepening of the lines of habitual worry—that was Ernest Wadlow. Mabel Wadlow's expression remained a blend of fretful enquiry and her recent relief. If it wasn't Maurice it didn't really matter.

It was Richard who spoke again. He said,

"What ought we to know?"

Rachel looked round at them all. Then she said,

"Something happened—when I was coming back from Nanny's. I said I had had a fall, and that was true. But it wasn't all that happened. I didn't fall on the path—I fell over the cliff. And I fell over the cliff because someone pushed me."

Once more Miss Silver watched the faces and, more revealing still, the hands.

Ella Comperton said "Nonsense!" but her hands shook. Cosmo Frith crumpled up the *Times* and turned with astonishment in every line of his features. Mabel and Ernest Wadlow did exactly the same thing. They both said "Oh!" and their mouths dropped open. Richard Treherne made a sharp movement and said, frowning deeply, "Rachel! Good God— you don't mean that!" Caroline made no movement and no sound. Her eyes were fixed on Rachel's face, and only Rachel herself could see what was in them.

Rachel said quite firmly, "Yes, I do mean it. Someone came up behind me in the dark and pushed me over the cliff."

There was some sound from everyone in the room—a catch of the breath, a sharp release, something very near a gasp— and from Miss Silver herself a fluttered "Dear, dear me!"

"But, my dear—" said Cosmo Frith. He let the paper fall and came close. "Rachel, my dear, you can't mean it! Why didn't you tell us at once? There must be some madman about—that is, if you really do mean—My dear, the police should have been informed."

Miss Silver said in her prim, cool voice,

"Perhaps the police were informed. Did you inform them, Miss Treherne?"

She received a protesting look which left her quite unmoved. Rachel said,

"No."

"But, my dear," said Cosmo, "they ought to be communicated with at once. Tell me everything you can, and I'll ring them up—"

Rachel stopped him.

"No—I won't call in the police—" She paused, and added, "this time."

If there was anyone in the room who realized the significance of those added words, no sign betrayed it.

"Won't you tell us exactly what happened?" said Richard Treherne.

"It's all nonsense!" said Mabel querulously. "Because if you went over that cliff, why weren't you killed? It really is nonsense."

Ernest put a hand on her arm.

"Now, now—don't excite yourself, Mabel. I don't really think you should have been subjected to a shock like this. But what you say is, of course, perfectly correct."

Ella Comperton joined the chorus.

"There is surely some exaggeration. You have, I believe, some bruises and a scratch or two, but you cannot expect us to believe that you fell off the cliff on to the rocks and got off with no more than that."

Rachel sat up a little straighter.

"If I had gone down on to the rocks, you would all be attending an inquest instead of sitting here and telling me I don't know what I'm talking about."

Cosmo's hand came down on her shoulder.

"My dear, I think we hardly do know what we're talking about—any of us. This has been a great shock. Speaking for myself, I—my dear, it's a terrible shock." His hand pressed down for a moment, and was withdrawn. He got out a handkerchief and blew his nose. "I don't mind saying that it's knocked me over."

"Rachel, please tell us exactly what happened," said Richard.

She told them without emotion.

"If I had gone down on to the rocks—as I said just now—I shouldn't be here. I didn't go down. I caught at a bush, and it held me."

"Dear me," said Miss Silver—"most providential!"

"But you couldn't have been pushed," said Ella Comperton. "It's really quite impossible. Besides, who would push you? It is absurd."

Ernest Wadlow plucked off his glasses with a nervous gesture and set them back upon his nose at a different angle.

"As Ella says—"

"And how did you get up again?" said Mabel in an accusing voice.

Caroline leaned forward and caught a fold of Rachel's skirt. They heard her whisper something. Richard thought it was "You're *here.*"

Rachel's eyes went from one to another before she said,

"I was certainly pushed. I went over the cliff because I was pushed. The hand that pushed me rolled a stone down over the edge—afterwards—while I was hanging there—to make sure—at least I suppose it was to make sure. One of those big stones—it just missed me. I was able to hold on till Gale Brandon came by. He ran to Nanny's cottage—and tore up her sheets to make a rope—and got me up. He saved my life."

Cosmo blew his nose again, and pushed the handkerchief back into his pocket.

"My dear—this is really—I don't know when I've been so shocked. You will forgive me—you must know what we all feel about you. It seems quite incredible that anyone should try to harm you. But we've got to be practical. The police should be called in at once."

"I have nothing to say to the police."

"Dear me," said Miss Silver, "I should suppose—of course I am very ignorant about such matters, but surely you must have some idea as to the identity of the person who attacked you." She looked about her as she spoke, in a manner at once artless and inquisitive. "You must have some idea, surely?"

The room was suddenly silent. It was just as if all the small, usual, unnoticed sounds had ceased, and because they had ceased you noticed them. They left that strained, waiting silence.

Rachel broke it. She said, "None," and all the sounds began again.

Ella Comperton let go the arms of her chair and sat back. Richard got up in a hurry. Caroline Ponsonby dropped her hand from Rachel's skirt and pitched sideways off her stool in a dead faint.

CHAPTER 25

"How is Caroline?" said Cosmo Frith.

His knock had brought Rachel to her sitting-room door. He stood there just beyond the threshold looking more perturbed than she had ever seen him, his usual genial expression quite overcast, his voice uncertain.

"She's better. She ought to be quiet. We've left her lying down. She really oughtn't to talk."

Rachel went on saying these things to stop herself thinking, to stop Cosmo asking her why Caroline had fainted. If only everyone would go away and leave her alone.

But Cosmo was coming in. He took her arm, closed the door, and led her to a chair. He then seated himself in a purposeful manner. Nothing could be more certain than what that purpose was. Conversation—and conversation of the most serious character. He said without any of his usual poise,

"My dear, I expect you'd rather be alone, but after what you told us just now I felt—well, I won't worry you with what I felt, but there are things which I am bound to say to you."

Rachel looked across at him, and her heart warmed a little. She had always been fond of Cosmo, and without taking his proposals too seriously had been assured of his affection; but to see him so visibly shaken by her danger, this did thaw some of the ice about her heart. She was touched and melted. Her eyes thanked him as she said,

"It's over. Don't let us think about it."

"But, my dear, we must. Do you really mean that you won't call in the police?"

She nodded.

"But, my dear—why? Do let me beg of you—"

She shook her head.

"No, Cosmo."

"Why?"

"I can't tell you why."

He leaned forward. "My dear, I had better tell you that your story is being—how shall I put it—questioned. Ernest and Mabel seem to have made up their minds that the shock of your fall has led you to imagine that you were pushed. Ella agrees with them. When I came away they were exchanging stories about people who had suffered from hallucinations and loss of memory after a shock."

Rachel's eyes brightened becomingly.

"I am sorry to disappoint everybody, but I really did go over the cliff. Unfortunately for Ella's theory of hallucination—I feel quite sure that it was Ella—I have a witness, a perfectly credible witness, in Gale Brandon."

Cosmo Frith's eyebrows drew together.

"Ah, yes—he saved your life. But it wasn't the fall they were questioning, my dear. Honestly, Rachel, can you be absolutely certain that you were pushed?"

She said "Yes" with stiff lips. Then her composure broke. "Do you think I want to believe it? Do you think I wouldn't thank God with all my heart if I could make myself believe that I had slipped? But I can't, Cosmo, I can't. I was pushed, and that stone was rolled down on me, and though I couldn't see who did it, I felt—I felt—" Her voice stopped.

Cosmo repeated the last word.

"You felt? What did you feel?"

She covered her eyes with her hand and spoke in a whisper.

"Hatred. Someone wanting to kill me—wanting it terribly—"

His shocked voice brought back her self-control.

"Rachel! My dear, do you know what you're saying?"

"I think so."

"That it was someone who knows you—whom you know?"

"Yes—I think so. I felt the hatred. You don't hate someone—you—don't—know."

"Rachel! Rachel!" He got to his feet with a single abrupt movement and went past her to the window. Standing there with his back to her, he said in a shocked voice, "That's not like you. I can't believe it. Rachel, I *can't* believe it."

"I thought I couldn't either. That's the horrible part—I've come to believe that someone wants to kill me."

There was a silence. Then Cosmo turned round.

"You mean that soberly?"

Rachel said, "It's true."

"Then there's something I ought to tell you."

He came back and sat down again. "You know, my dear, I'm not a busybody, and I wasn't going to say anything, because after all it isn't any of my business, and you might have thought—well, to be quite frank, I didn't want to meddle."

Rachel lifted her head from her hand.

"What is all this about, Cosmo?"

His genial ruddiness was still under eclipse. She had never seen him with such a look of distress, and more than distress—embarrassment.

"Cosmo—what is it?"

He hesitated, and then said with an effort,

"My dear, you mustn't be vexed with me. This fellow Brandon—if anyone pushed you over the cliff, well, it seems to me that no one had a better opportunity."

"Cosmo!"

"Rachel, I beg of you to listen. You can be angry with me afterwards. Did the fellow know that you were going to see Nanny yesterday afternoon?"

"Yes, he knew."

"And that you would take the cliff path back?"

She was silent.

"Rachel—did he know that?"

She said, "Yes."

"He knew it. And he drove up to the cottage in his car. Louisa says that his car was there, and that he drove you home, and—"

Rachel interrupted him.

"This is nonsense. Gale Brandon saved my life."

He looked at her with compassion.

"You don't know very much about him, do you? You haven't known him very long. Are you sure you even know his real name?"

"His name is Brandon."

"Or Brent," said Cosmo Frith. And then, as Rachel stared, "Your father had a partner of the name of Brent, hadn't he?"

"Cosmo!"

"You have been trying to find this partner or his son, haven't you, ever since my uncle died? The father's name was Sterling Brent. The son was only a child when his father was your father's partner—about five or six years old, I believe, and everyone called him Sonny, but his name was Gale—Gale Brent—Gale Brandon."

"How do you know?" said Rachel. "Father looked for the Brents, and I've looked for them. We made sure that Sterling Brent was dead, but we went on looking for the child. How do you know that his name was Gale? Because that has been one of the difficulties—no one knew his name. My father,

Nanny, Mabel—they only knew him as Sonny. And you never knew him at all. Why do you say his name was Gale?"

There was a fluctuating colour in her cheek. Her eyes were bright and restless.

Cosmo nodded.

"Must seem odd. But odd things happen, my dear. I'll tell you how this one happened. Only a month or two ago I was digging into an old trunk that I've had stored since the year one, and there was a packet of letters from your mother to mine. They were very fond of each other, you know. Well, I was going to consign them to the flames. No use keeping old letters. When I saw my own name—and you know how it is, that's a thing you can't pass—at least I can't. So I looked to see what Aunt Emily had got to say about me, and this is what it was: 'Mr. Brent's little boy is with us on a visit. They call him Sonny, which I think a great pity, because it is sure to stick. His own name is Gale, which is unusual and nice. He is the same age as your Cosmo, and just about the same height.' There, my dear—are you convinced?"

"Did you keep the letter?"

He shook his head.

"I'm afraid not, but that's what was in it. You may depend upon it this fellow Gale Brandon is Gale Brent all right. Nanny swears he is."

"Nanny?" Rachel was really startled.

"Oh, he's been in to see her once or twice, wanting to know when you came, and how long you would stay, and she says she could swear to him. Anyway it's easily proved, because if he was Sonny Brent, she says his father had him tattooed—name, or initials, I'm not sure which, up on the forearm somewhere."

Rachel sat back in her chair.

"You seem to have gone well into it with Nanny," she said.

"Now you're vexed," said Cosmo in a rueful voice. "But that doesn't matter—you can be as angry as you like. Only, my dear, you needn't be, because it all just came out when we

132

were talking. You know what Nanny is. And I was going to tell you, and then I thought, 'Better not—you don't want her to think you've been meddling.' But now, my dear—now, when it's a question of your life being in danger—now I'm bound to speak, and you're bound to listen. Your father quarrelled with Sterling Brent, and then made a fortune out of the enterprise in which they had been partners. Don't you think it's possible that the man who didn't have his share in that fortune should have felt a bitter resentment, and perhaps have handed it on to his son? You say you were aware of a bitter hatred. I can imagine that Gale Brent might hate you if he thought your father had ruined his."

Rachel said, "He doesn't hate me."

"Does he tell you that? Do you believe him? Listen to me, my dear. Who knew you were going to Nanny's, and when you would be coming away? Who was there on the cliff path when you fell?"

Rachel's eyes brightened.

"Gale Brandon. And he pushed me over? So far, so good. But why did he pull me up again?"

Cosmo put up a deprecating hand.

"Oh, my dear, can't you find an answer to that? I'm afraid I can. You had gone over the cliff, but you hadn't gone the whole way down. You were still alive, and a potential danger to him. He tries to dislodge you by rolling down one of the stones from the broken wall, but it's so dark he can't see where you are. And then perhaps something startles him—a footstep, or a light. He may have seen Louisa's lantern. She says she stood for a time at the top of the path to see whether you were in sight. He may have seen her. He may—I don't know, but I suppose he may have had a return to sanity. Hatred isn't sane, you know. It carries a man off his balance, and he does what he does, and then—my dear, I don't know, but perhaps the sight of Louisa's lantern may have brought him back. He begins to realize what he has done, he begins to think. Anyone may have seen his car outside the cottage. If you are going to speak and say that you were pushed, he is bound to be suspected. What is he to do? Just what he does do, my dear—be the first to find you, and put himself beyond suspicion by staging a gallant rescue."

Rachel felt a cold horror which seeped into her mind and numbed it. Amongst all the dreadful things which she had thought of, and to which she had in some horrible way become accustomed, this new thing loomed up and dwarfed them all in horror. Always afterwards she knew how there had come into being that phrase—his heart was wrung. She did actually feel as if a hand had been laid on her heart—had closed upon it—twisted it.

She did not know that every vestige of colour had left her face. But Cosmo Frith showed his alarm by coming to her side. He bent over her at first with a hand upon her shoulder. Then, still holding her, he went down upon his knees by the chair.

"My dear, dear Rachel—don't take it like that! Has he stolen so much of you that you can't bear to know what he is? You've only known him for a few weeks—I've loved you all my life. I've told you so often and often—perhaps I've told you too often. That's the way of the faithful lover—he's always there, and so—well, everyone gets used to him. But now, my dear, now—now, when there's a chance that I can do something for you at last—won't you let me do it? Won't you trust me and let me take you out of all this? There are wonderful things that we could do together, wonderful places to see. Forget I'm the cousin you've known all your life, or only remember it to think how long I've loved you, and to think I'm your lover now and always will be, and that if you will let me I'll teach you—oh, my dear, I know I can teach you—to love me too."

Rachel was very deeply moved. This was not the Cosmo with whom she had shared a cousinly past. There was a warmth and an emotion which he had never shown her before. The thought that it was her danger which had evoked it could not fail to call up her own warmest feelings. After the long strain, the imminent terror, the chill of inevitable suspicion, this sense of kinship, kindness and protection was astonishingly grateful. If there had been no Gale Brandon, the moment might have brought Cosmo all he dreamed of. Even twenty-four hours ago he might have had his chance, but the water had gone down stream under yesterday's bridge since then, and that flow once past returns no more.

Rachel let herself rest against his arm for a moment. Then she drew back and said very kindly indeed,

"Oh, Cosmo dear, I never knew you cared—like that. But—" She felt the jerk of his arm at the word.

"Rachel!"

"Oh, Cosmo dear, I can't. It isn't any good. You're like my brother—you always have been—and I just can't think of you in any other way."

He drew back, got up, and walked away.

"Is that your last word?"

"I'm afraid so."

There was a horrid strained pause. Then the telephone bell rang. Rachel had never been so glad to hear it in all her life. As she went to the writing-table and took up the receiver, Cosmo stopped for a moment beside her and laid his hand upon her arm. He said quite low,

"It's all right, my dear."

She felt his lips just touch her wrist. Then he went quickly out of the room and shut the door.

With mingled sadness and relief Rachel turned to listen to what her bank manager had to say.

CHAPTER 26

Miss Silver came along the passage from her room and stopped at Caroline Ponsonby's door. She turned the handle noiselessly, and was aware of a curtained dusk, and silence. These were expected. She pushed the door an inch or two and listened for the sound of measured breathing. But it was a very different sound which broke the silence. Miss Silver's hand closed hard upon the knob, for what she heard was Richard Treherne speaking in a tone of agony.

"Caroline! Caroline! Caroline!"

Miss Silver stood where she was for a moment. Then she pushed the door a little wider and looked round it. Caroline lay on her bed with her face half hidden in the pillow, whilst Richard, on his knees beside her, buried his face in his hands and groaned.

As a gentlewoman, the thought of eavesdropping was extremely repugnant to Miss Silver. As a detective engaged upon a case of attempted murder, she treated her scruples with exemplary firmness. She heard Caroline give a heartbroken sob, and hoped very much that she would be permitted to hear something rather more articulate.

Her hope was fulfilled. Richard's head came up with a jerk.

"Oh, my darling—don't! You're tearing my heart out. I tell you I can't bear it. You turn away from me, you refuse me, you look at me as if I was a stranger, you faint—and you won't tell me why. Do you think it's any use pretending with me? Oh, my darling, you know it isn't. What is it all about? You've got to tell me. You can't go on like this. You're breaking your heart, and you won't say why."

Caroline spoke in a muffled voice against her pillow.

"I can't go on. I can't say why. I don't need to—you know."

"I know?"

"You know—I know—I can't go on." She raised her head suddenly. "Richard, will you go away—right away and never come back? Will you swear that you will never come back?"

"Caroline!"

She caught his wrist and pulled herself up.

"You must! I tell you I know. You've got to go away. It's killing me."

"Caroline!"

She pushed back the hair from her eyes, and staring over his shoulder, she saw Miss Silver peering round the door. The neatly netted front disappeared a fraction of a second too late. There was a discreet knock.

When Miss Silver entered, Caroline's face was hidden again. Mr. Richard Treherne was on his feet. If anyone was embarrassed, it was not the visitor.

"I thought I heard voices," she said brightly. She addressed a glowering young man. "I hope Miss Caroline is feeling better—but I only came to enquire, not to disturb her. I feel sure she needs quiet and should on no account be disturbed, but I thought I might just enquire."

Richard strode to the door and out of the room. For a moment Miss Silver looked after him with a peculiar expression on her face. Then she approached the bed.

"Miss Caroline," she said, "I am a stranger, but my business in this house is to help Miss Treherne who brought me here. I think you need help too. You are in great trouble—you know something which you are afraid to tell. Believe me, the truth is always best. Sometimes it is easier to speak to a stranger than to someone in the same family. If you will tell me what is troubling you, I will do my best to help you. I have no connection with the police, and this affair is not as yet in their hands. It is still possible for me to help you. But if you will not speak to me, let me urge you very strongly to cross that passage and go to Miss Treherne. She loves you dearly. There is nothing that you could not tell her. If you remain silent, great harm may come of it."

There was a pause. Then Caroline raised herself upon her elbow. Her eyes were wide and blank with misery, her features pinched and drawn, her colour ghastly. Miss Silver looked at her with compassion. She spoke in a gentle voice.

"I heard what you said just now. You told Mr. Richard that you knew. What is it that you know? It would be better for everyone if you would say."

Caroline stared at her. She said rather wildly,

"I can't think—I'm ill—I want to *think*. Oh, won't you please go away?"

Miss Silver nodded.

"Very well, I will go away and leave you to think over what I have said. I do not wish to hurry you, but it will be better for everyone if you will make up your mind as quickly as possible."

She went out of the room and shut the door. As she did so she saw the girl sink back again and hide her face.

CHAPTER 27

Rachel Treherne's door opened. Miss Silver was beckoned in.

"Will you please come here. I must speak to you. Something has happened."

Miss Silver looked at her with interest. It was quite obvious that something had happened. This was a Rachel Treherne she had not met before, alert, businesslike, angry—yes, certainly very angry.

Rachel shut the door and walked away from it, but remained standing.

"Miss Silver, my bank manager has just rung me up. A cheque bearing my signature had been presented, and as it was for a very large sum, he thought it best to refer to me before cashing it."

"Yes?" said Miss Silver.

"The cheque was made out to my brother-in-law Ernest Wadlow, and was endorsed by him in favour of his son Maurice. It was not crossed."

"Did you write this cheque, Miss Treherne?"

Rachel's head lifted. She said in a perfectly level voice,

"I gave my brother-in-law a cheque for a hundred pounds three days ago. He asked me not to cross it."

"Did he say why?"

"I understood that he wanted the money for Maurice, and that he thought the uncrossed cheque would be more convenient."

"And it is this cheque which is in question?"

Anger made a very handsome woman of Rachel Treherne.

"I don't recognize the amount. I gave Ernest a cheque for a hundred. The cheque presented was for ten thousand."

Miss Silver looked very grave.

"I do not understand," she said. "The figure would be altered easily enough, but the words—Miss Treherne, it would be impossible to change one hundred into ten thousand, unless the forger took the risk of simply making the alterations and initialling them—and with so large a sum there would be no chance of that succeeding. The drawer would inevitably be referred to."

Rachel shook her head.

"The words were not altered—they were forged. The number of the cheque is not the same as the one I drew—it is the next one. And that cheque is missing from my book. Either Ernest or Maurice must have torn it out and copied the cheque I drew—with a difference. I felt bound to tell you about it."

Miss Silver said "Yes—" in rather an abstracted tone.

Rachel's foot tapped the floor.

"Either my brother-in-law or his son had planned to rob me of this money—they may both have been concerned. Ernest and Mabel are quite besotted about Maurice. They had been pestering me to give them just this sum, and I had refused. So somebody forged that cheque. Now I want you to think what bearing this may have on what happened yester-day."

Miss Silver gazed at her mildly.

"A person who had just forged your signature to a cheque for ten thousand pounds would be the last person on earth to push you over a cliff before that cheque had been cleared. Your death would have rendered it quite valueless."

"I know that. But think of it this way. You forge a cheque, you let it go out of your hands, and then you begin to think what a frightful risk you have run. Even if it goes through, even if you get the money, there's bound to be a day of reck-oning. You may not be prosecuted, but you are bound to be exposed and ostracized. You won't be a part of the family any more. Don't you think you might cast about you for some way out?" Her voice hardened. "Maurice would have come in for just that ten thousand pounds if I had been killed last night."

"And your brother-in-law?"

"Five thousand. But Mabel would have thirty thousand."

"Under your present will?"

"Yes—that was my father's wish."

"Destroy that will, Miss Treherne, and inform your family that you have destroyed it."

"I have told you that I won't do that. I would rather die than not get to the bottom of all this."

Miss Silver nodded.

"And you could bear to find Mr. Ernest or Mr. Maurice there. It would lift a load off your heart, would it not?"

"Miss Silver!"

Miss Silver looked at her steadily.

"Now you are vexed. But it is true. If I could prove to your satisfaction that the attempt on your life had been made by your brother-in-law or his son, you would be very grateful to me."

Rachel lifted her eyes. Anger flamed and went out. A look of direct simplicity took its place.

"Yes, that is true. You see I don't love them—really. So it wouldn't hurt that way—I could bear it. It's not like thinking that someone you love—has been hating you—all the time." She made an abrupt movement. "I must see Ernest at once. I should like you to be here. I don't think we can go on pretending that you are a governess."

Miss Silver said, "No."

Rachel rang the bell, and Ivy was despatched to ask Mr. Wadlow if he would come upstairs to Miss Treherne's sitting-room. They waited for him in silence, Rachel at her writing-table, Miss Silver seated unobtrusively in a low chair at the fire. She had, for once, no knitting to occupy her hands. They rested idly in her lap. The expression on her face was stern and thoughtful.

Ernest Wadlow came in after his usual hurried manner—always a little short of time, always a little inclined to consider himself aggrieved. Neusel, stretched out at full length upon the hearthrug, twitched an ear, opened an eye, and growled softly in his throat. Mr. Wadlow looked at him with distaste.

"Did you want me, Rachel? Of course if you did—if there is anything I can do. I was looking up my Pyrenean notes. I am thinking of *Pyrenean Pilgrimage* as a title. I must say alliteration appeals to me. Or, alternatively, *Pyrenean Pilgrims*, or *Pyrenean Peregrination*. Which do you prefer?"

"I'm afraid I can't give my mind to it just now. I want to speak to you about a very serious matter."

Ernest's eyebrows went up fantastically high. They indicated that his sister-in-law had obviously forgotten the presence of a stranger. One does not discuss a serious matter

141

with a stranger sitting by the fire obviously prepared to listen.

Rachel had no difficulty in interpreting the eyebrows. She said,

"Please sit down, Ernest. Miss Silver is acting as my adviser in this matter."

It took so little to make Ernest Wadlow look worried that the immediate puckering of the lines about his eyes and mouth could not be considered as indicative of an uneasy conscience. The frown which drew his brows together gave him a puzzled look. He said,

"My dear Rachel—" And then, "I really cannot see—"

"Please do sit down," said Rachel. "Now Ernest—you remember my giving you a cheque for a hundred pounds three days ago?"

Mr. Wadlow appeared pained.

"I had thought it a private matter. But it does not signify— you are naturally quite at liberty. The circumstance is, of course, within my recollection."

"Ernest—what did you do with that cheque?"

"My dear Rachel, surely that is my affair."

Rachel said, "No." And then, "I'm afraid I must press the question. Did you send it to your bank?"

"No, I did not."

"Did you endorse it in someone else's favour?"

"*Really*, Rachel!"

"Did you?"

"Er—no."

"Did you cash it yourself?"

"You know perfectly well that I have had no opportunity of doing so."

"Then have you still got it?"

"No, I have not."

"Then, Ernest, will you tell me what you did do with it?"

Mr. Wadlow straightened his *pince-nez*.

"I find all these questions very hard to understand. They

appear to me to have a—a tendency which I would rather not particularize, but if I were forced to do so—"

Rachel leaned forward with her elbow on the table.

"What's the good of talking like that, Ernest? Something has gone wrong about that cheque, and I naturally want to know what you did with it. The bank has just rung me up."

Ernest Wadlow gave a sigh of relief.

"I suppose she forgot to sign her name. She has not your experience in business matters. But that is scarcely her fault. If the terms of your father's will had been different—"

"Ernest, what are you talking about? *She?* Did you give the cheque to Cherry?"

Mr. Wadlow registered indignation and surprise.

"Cherry? Certainly not! She has her dress allowance."

"Then it was Mabel—you gave the cheque to Mabel?"

"I did."

Rachel bit her lip. She repeated her sister's name.

"You gave it to Mabel? I never thought of that. Do you know what she did with it?"

Ernest fidgeted. The *pince-nez* dropped, and he had to stoop down to retrieve them. Once more in an upright position, he was seen to be slightly flushed.

"Had you not better ask her?"

"You endorsed that cheque to Mabel and gave it to her?"

"And I suppose she was not aware that the bank would require her signature. But to speak of an omission of that sort as a serious matter—" He gave a slight offended laugh.

Rachel opened a drawer, drew out a cheque-book, and handed it across the table.

"Will you look at the last two counterfoils, Ernest. The last but one belongs to the cheque I gave you. The one next to it has never been filled in. Maurice presented the cheque belonging to that about three quarters of an hour ago. The manager was not satisfied and rang me up. The cheque was made out to you and endorsed to Maurice. It was for ten thousand pounds."

Ernest Wadlow's mouth fell open. His chin dropped and his eyes stared. They were pale eyes, and with the white showing all about them in a ring they looked paler still. The open mouth was pale too, and the furrowed cheeks were grey.

Miss Silver got up from her chair and came over to him. She put a hand on his shoulder and said firmly and quietly,

"Pull yourself together, Mr. Wadlow. This has been a shock. I will get you a glass of water."

He still had that dazed look when she came back with a tumbler from Rachel's bathroom. He gulped the water down, and then bent forward, still clasping the glass.

"You did not know—did you?" said Miss Silver. She looked over his bowed head at Rachel. "I think it is Mrs. Wadlow whom you must ask for an explanation. This cheque was made out for the sum to which she considered Mr. Maurice Wadlow was entitled. I find no difficulty in believing that she forged it. No one who had ever had anything to do with the management of money could have supposed for a moment that a cheque for so large an amount could be cashed across the counter without reference to the drawer. I suspected Mrs. Wadlow immediately. It is probable that Mr. Maurice believed the cheque to be genuine. I can hardly imagine—"

Ernest Wadlow leaned to the writing-table and set down the tumbler with a force that cracked it. He said in a loud, unsteady voice,

"Stop—stop! You're driving me mad!" He blazed at Rachel. "What's this woman talking about? I don't know who she is, and I don't know what she's saying. Ten thousand pounds—across the counter—an open cheque! It's lunacy! I never heard of such a thing! And you ask me to believe that Mabel—that Maurice—"

Miss Silver had seen the door move as he began to speak. It was opened now with a jerk and Mabel Wadlow walked in. She was highly flushed, and she appeared to have forgotten

144

that the stairs brought on her palpitations. She shut the door with quite a vigorous push and said angrily,

"Maurice doesn't know anything about it!"

Ernest sprang up.

"Mabel!"

"I knew Rachel would try and put it on Maurice! She has never made the slightest effort to understand him or appreciate him. It isn't any good her saying she has, because she hasn't. If she had the slightest feeling for a mother's anxieties she would have given him the money when I told her how necessary it was that he should have it and be prevented from going to Russia, where he might catch anything, and if he brought me a Bolshevist daughter-in-law, it would break my heart. But what does Rachel care about that? She only cares about the money. And it isn't even as if it was her own money—it was my father's, and *morally* half of it is mine! Are you going to send me to prison, Rachel, for taking some of my own money in order to save my only son from getting shot in a cellar or poisoned with bad drains?"

"Mabel," said Ernest in a shaking voice—"you can't know what you're saying. Rachel, she doesn't know what she's saying. Mabel—"

"Be quiet!" said Mabel at the top of her voice. "I know perfectly well what I'm saying. I did the whole thing myself. I thought of it the minute I saw the cheque Rachel had given you. And how she had the nerve—what was the good of a miserable hundred pounds when Maurice wanted ten thousand? So I made up my mind what I was going to do, and I did it very well." Mabel actually preened herself. "I got another cheque, and I copied the hundred pounds one, only I put ten thousand instead of a hundred. And nobody could possibly have told that it wasn't Rachel's signature, so I can't imagine what all the fuss is about."

All this time Rachel Treherne had been sitting back in her chair, her face quite without expression, her eyes raised to her sister's face. She might have been watching a scene in which

145

she had no concern. She spoke now in a cool and level voice.

"Banks are not usually asked to pay so large a sum across the counter on an open cheque. The manager asked Maurice to wait, and rang me up."

Mabel's face became convulsed.

"What have they done to him?" She caught at Ernest, and he put his arm about her.

"To Maurice? Nothing at all. Hadn't you better sit down, Mabel?"

Mrs. Wadlow allowed herself to be piloted to the most comfortable armchair. She clutched her side and enquired eagerly,

"Then you told them it was all right?"

Rachel's eyebrows went up.

"Certainly not. I stopped the cheque."

"But Maurice—Rachel, have you no feelings? Can't you see that you are torturing me?"

"I told the manager there was some mistake," said Rachel coldly.

Ernest bent solicitously over his wife.

"My dear, I beg of you—you will suffer for this."

"What will he *think?*" said Mabel with a rending sob.

"That you or Ernest have forged my name." Rachel's tone was extremely dry. "I am afraid that Maurice will not get that ten thousand."

The sound of the lunch bell came up from the hall below. Neusel, who throughout these agitations had remained plunged in slumber, sprang up instantly and trotted to the door.

CHAPTER 28

Civilized life is at the mercy of its own routine. Whatever may be happening in a household, breakfast, lunch, tea and dinner follow one another inexorably. Birth, marriage, divorce, meetings, partings, estrangements, love, hate, suspicion, jealousy, battle, murder, and sudden death—through all these comes the sound of the domestic bell or gong, with its summons to eat and drink. Whether you die tomorrow or today, another meal is served.

Rachel Treherne paused at Caroline's door, heard no sound, and followed the Wadlows downstairs. She was glad to concern herself with ordering a tray to be sent up, and when she turned to the room again discovered that there would have to be two trays. Mabel had disappeared, and Ernest, with reproach in eye and voice, informed her that an attack of palpitations was imminent, and that he had taken it upon himself to insist upon a recumbent position and perfect quiet.

"She overtaxes her strength. We should not have allowed her to excite herself. She will be prostrated for the rest of the day. Yes, certainly some lunch—her strength must be maintained. Light and nutritious food at very frequent intervals, and she should never be thwarted or allowed to overtax her strength—those are the exact expressions used by Dr. Levitas. No one has understood Mabel's constitution as he did. I blame myself, but I cannot exonerate you, Rachel—no sisterly kindness, no attempt to calm her, no concern about her health." All this in low, agitated tones, with a nervous polishing of the *pince-nez* and small fidgeting movements.

Actually, the arrival of Ella Comperton was a relief. Ella's range of subjects, from leper colonies to slums, might not be ideal as table topics, but they were at least preferable to a discussion of Mabel's health and the unsisterly harshness with which she had been thwarted in her maiden attempt at forgery.

Richard and Cosmo both came in extremely late. Richard cut himself a plateful of cold beef and ate it in silence. Cosmo, on the contrary, made an excellent lunch and was in quite his best vein—social anecdotes, art gossip, the Surrealist exhibition in Paris. The flow was easy and continuous, and Rachel blessed him in her heart. She never felt fonder of Cosmo than when she had just refused him. No scowls, no sulks, no lowering of the social temperature. Not like poor Richard. What had gone wrong between him and Caroline? Some stupid little thing. Lovers did quarrel about stupid little things. It couldn't be anything more. *It—couldn't—be—anything— worse—*

She jerked her thoughts away and heard Cosmo say,

"Nightmare, not art, my dear Miss Silver."

Miss Silver crumbled her bread.

"I speak under correction of course—you will know far more of these subjects than I do—but is it not the aim of the Surrealists to get away from the presentation of externals and present those ideas which are commonly submerged in the unconscious mind?"

Cosmo laughed.

"And very unpleasant minds they must have, if the ideas are a fair sample."

Miss Silver gave a slight cough.

"Just a little like the Day of Judgment, if I may say so without irreverence—the secrets of all hearts being opened. There are, I suppose, very few of us who would not be afraid to see that happen." She continued to crumble the bread. "If our thoughts—our intimate, secret thoughts—were to take shape and stand before us now, I wonder what we should think of them."

Cosmo smiled his most genial smile. It was turned upon Rachel.

"You at least would be safe, my dear. I can imagine that your thoughts would make charming pictures."

Rachel felt an almost physical pang. "My thoughts? Oh, God!" There was a horrified moment when she wondered if she had spoken the words aloud. Her thoughts—fear, suspicion, agony, resentment, terror—how dreadfully might these take shape.

Cosmo was still leaning to her and smiling.

"Singing birds and lilies, my dear."

Ernest Wadlow straightened his *pince-nez.*

"It is an interesting theory. I remember discussing it with Dr. Levitas. He compared the balance of Mabel's mind, I remember, to a chime of silver bells. She was very much pleased with the image. We both thought it a very apt one. The least disturbing element, and the delicate tuning suffers. I remember quoting Shakespeare's 'Sweet bells jangled out of tune.'"

Ella Comperton fixed him with an offended stare.

"Good heavens, Ernest—what will you say next? That was Ophelia, and she was mad. There has never been any madness in our family."

Richard Treherne pushed back his chair, excused himself briefly, and went out. Rachel, listening, heard him go up the stair. Ernest was still talking, but she had lost the thread. Her mind seemed to have closed, and what came through was meaningless sound which made no sense.

The telephone bell rang, and she got up to answer it with relief. With the receiver at her ear, she heard Cherry's light laugh, like the echo of a laugh from a very long way off.

"That you, Rachel? I haven't a minute. I'm speaking from a perfectly foul call-box right off the map. There's a village, but I don't know what it's called."

The familiar desire to box Cherry's ears restored Rachel to her normal self. She said quite sharply,

"What are you doing there?"

"My dear, what *does* one do in a call-box? I'm telephoning. It smells of paint and shag."

"What do you want?" said Rachel.

The light laugh came along the wire.

"My dear—how practical! Well, I thought the parents would like to know that Bob and I were married this morning. The most expensive sort of special licence—to make up for no bridesmaids. I couldn't very well ask Mildred or any of the lot who were going to be hers—could I? Anyhow it's quite legal without. And tell Mummy it was in a church, because Bob's Aunt Matilda would have altered her will if it had been a register office—at least Bob said she would, so I gave in."

"Cherry, do you really mean all this?"

"Absolutely. Tell Mummy to save all fits for the divorce."

Rachel hung up and came back to her place. She addressed Ernest in a perfectly expressionless voice.

"Cherry has married Bob Hedderwick. You had better let Mabel finish her lunch before you tell her."

Ella Comperton uttered a faint shriek.

"But he was engaged to Mildred Ross! Cherry was going to be a bridesmaid!"

A spark came and went in Rachel's eyes.

"A little thing like that wouldn't worry her."

Ernest Wadlow said nothing. His *pince-nez* fell off. His mouth fell open.

Miss Silver turned her head to listen. The faint sound which she had caught became a sound which everyone could hear— the clatter of feet on the stair—running feet. The door was flung open and Richard Treherne came halfway into the room. He looked for Rachel, and spoke to her in a loud, angry voice.

"She's gone! Taken her car! She shouldn't have been left— she wasn't fit!"

They were all up and round him. Rachel put a hand on his arm, and felt it rigid.

She said "Caroline?" on a mere breath of sound. "Are you sure?"

His face frightened her. He shook off her hand.

"I tell you her car's gone! And she's not fit to drive. What's going on in this house? What have you done to her?"

"Richard," said Rachel—"*please*. You must go after her."

He said violently, "Where? Do you suppose I'd lose a moment if I knew where to go? She gave up her flat last month. Where would she go?"

Miss Silver came forward.

"Where did she garage her car when she was in London?"

Richard flung round.

"I'll try that. I'll try and catch her on the road."

He was gone.

CHAPTER 29

Rachel stood quite still and looked after him. She was aware of Miss Silver leaving the room and going upstairs. Ernest Wadlow went past her, making small nervous sounds of disapproval. It was a relief to feel that Cherry's elopement would be likely to keep him occupied for the rest of the afternoon. Mabel would certainly be prostrated, and a prostrated Mabel meant an attendant Ernest. Neither of them would have time to think about Caroline.

Caroline—she winced away from the name—Caroline in trouble should have run to her, not away. But she had run away. Why?

Miss Silver was there again, a little out of breath.

"I went to see if she had left a note. There is nothing."

Rachel looked at her with wretched eyes.

"Why did she go?"

"She knew something, Miss Treherne."

"How do you know that?"

"She did not deny it. I urged her to speak. She wept, and buried her face in her pillow. I foolishly gave her time to think it over. She has used it to run away. If she is running away she will want to hide herself. Do you know what money she has?"

Rachel shook her head. Her lips were trembling. She caught the lower one between her teeth and held it hard.

"Not much," said Cosmo Frith. There was a disturbed look on his ruddy face. He addressed Miss Silver. "I know she hadn't much money, because she asked me—let me see—yes, it was yesterday—whether I could let her have five pounds as a loan."

"Then she had five pounds."

"Oh, no—" he laughed a little—"I hadn't got it myself."

Miss Silver's eyes went from him to Rachel.

"Then where would she go—without money?"

Rachel said, "I don't know."

Cosmo Frith shook his head.

"With your permission," said Miss Silver, "I will make a more thorough examination of the room she has been occupying."

Ella Comperton finished the glass of wine which she had poured out for herself. She put out her hand to the decanter and drew it back again.

"Girls are quite unaccountable," she said. "Of course nothing that Cherry did would surprise me. I always said that girl would come to a bad end. But Caroline—she seemed quiet enough. As a matter of fact they are often the worst. No manners—running off in the middle of lunch like this and disturbing everyone, though I don't know why you should look so tragic about it, Rachel. It's quite obvious to my mind that she

152

and Richard have quarrelled, and that they are now going to make it up. Exceedingly ill bred and mannerless I call it, but no need to be tragic. Well, I shall go to my room and lie down. I don't seem to get on very fast with all the literature Mrs. Barber has lent me, but I do find it so difficult to keep awake in this strong air."

Rachel followed her into the hall with Cosmo. He put a kindly hand on her shoulder.

"My dear, for once Ella is right. You take all this too seriously. It's just a tiff, and Richard will be bringing her back to tea. But I hate to leave you looking like this."

She turned her head.

"Are you going? I didn't know."

"My dear, I must. Poor Lazenby is really very ill. You must have heard me speak of him. Poor fellow—his own enemy, if there ever was one, and I'm about the only friend he's got left. But I don't like leaving you."

Rachel tried to smile. He was probably right. It was this weight upon her spirits which burdened everything. Richard would come back and bring Caroline with him. It was a lovers' quarrel. There was nothing to be afraid of. But the fear did not move from her heart.

The clang of the front door bell took her back a pace or two into the dining-room. She could not imagine who could be ringing at this hour, but at the sound of Gale Brandon's voice she came forward with both hands outstretched, so glad to see him that all her reasons for telling him to stay away were scattered and forgotten.

Her hands were taken and held in a grasp that hurt. He said,

"Well, I'm here. Are you going to be angry about it?"

She had tried to smile, but now she did not have to try. She looked up at him with all her heart in her eyes and said,

"I'm glad."

"The reward of mutiny!" said Gale Brandon. "You told me not to come. I came. You're glad. What happens to discipline? You'll never get over with it again."

They were still holding hands, but at this point a movement from Cosmo Frith attracted their attention. Tact might have indicated a retreat, but men are very seldom gifted with tact. Mr. Frith approached. The hands fell apart. Rachel flushed high and knew a moment of confusion. If it had been anyone but Cosmo. He had been so kind. She would not for the world have hurt his feelings.

But when the moment passed there was no discernible wound. The two men were talking. Cosmo was saying something about Caroline.

"She's gone off in her car, and Rachel is upset about it—thinks she isn't fit to drive. She fainted this morning."

It was all so much in Rachel's mind that it seemed quite natural that they should be talking about it. It was only afterwards that she wondered how the subject had come up, because after all Gale knew so little of Caroline. She said,

"I'm dreadfully worried, and that's the truth. She oughtn't to be driving, and we don't know which way she's gone. She hasn't any money."

As she spoke, the distress which she had felt before came back like a wave which has retreated only to break with redoubled force. She looked at him piteously, as if for help, and heard him say,

"But we'll go after her—if you're worried. She drives a small blue Austin, doesn't she? If she went through Ledlington, someone will have noticed it. Anyhow we can try. Get your things on."

The prospect of doing something put heart into Rachel. She nodded, ran upstairs, and was putting on her hat, when she was aware of Louisa behind her looking a good deal like Lot's wife. She said as briskly as she could,

"My coat, Louisa—the very thick brown one. I'm going after Miss Caroline."

Louisa did not move. She stood with folded hands and stared at Rachel's reflection in the glass.

"Can't you let well alone?" she said. "Them that's gone from this house, they'd stay gone if you'd let them."

"Louie!"

Louisa Barnet raised her voice.

"And why did they go, Miss Rachel? Answer me that! Because what they've got on their conscience wouldn't let them stay—that's why. And no wonder. Who was out on the cliff when you was pushed over? Mr. Richard for one, and Miss Caroline for another. And she come in crying, as Gladys could tell you. And three handkerchiefs soaked through in her clothes-basket that I saw for myself. There isn't no one cries like that but what they've brought it on themselves—you can't get from it. And why did she faint? Will you tell me that, Miss Rachel? No, you won't. But Miss Ella, she talked of it free enough—said Miss Caroline just sat there like an image and might have been deaf and dumb whilst you was telling how you was pushed over, but when it came to you being asked whether you had a sight of the one that pushed you and you said 'No,' well, right there and then Miss Caroline fainted."

Rachel stood up and turned round.

"That will do, Louie. You are hardly in a position to accuse other people, you know. I should like my coat."

This time Louisa brought it. Her hands shook as she held it for Miss Treherne to slip on. And then she caught a fold of it and spoke in a strained whisper.

"Miss Rachel—you're not going—to send me away?"

Rachel released herself.

"Where could I send you, Louie?"

The dark eyes flashed.

"To my grave. And that's the truth, for I'd not live."

Rachel walked towards the door. Just before she reached it she said without looking round,

"You talk a lot of nonsense, Louie. It isn't kind, and it isn't helpful. If you want to stay you mustn't say everything that comes into your head."

She went out, and found Cosmo waiting for her.

"Rachel—there's something I've thought of. Can I speak to you?"

She looked at him doubtfully.

"I've been too long already—"

"It's about Caroline."

She opened her sitting-room door and went in.

"Very well."

CHAPTER 30

Cosmo Frith shut the door behind him and walked over to the hearth. He stood there, picking up the old-fashioned gilt clock which had belonged to Rachel's mother and fiddling with the key. He looked troubled and serious. Rachel's heart sank.

"Cosmo, what is it? Don't keep me."

He said, "No, I won't—I won't—" But he got no further than that until she made an impatient movement. Then he put down the clock and said, "Don't, my dear. It's because it's so difficult to say."

"Difficult or easy, I think you must say it, Cosmo."

He drew a heavy breath that was like a sigh.

"Yes, I know—but one puts off—you will probably be angry—"

"Does that matter?"

He nodded.

"A good deal—to me."

A bright exasperated colour was in Rachel's cheeks.

"Oh, say it and have done!" she cried.

He gave her a wounded look.

"You see—you are angry already. But I can't help it. I can't let you go with that man and not say a word."

"You said you wanted to see me about Caroline."

"Yes, but I must say this too. I must beg that you will not go off alone with this man who calls himself Brandon. He is Gale Brent, and if you'll give me time I'll prove it. What do you know of him? He was on the cliff when you were pushed over it. Suppose he pushed you. Suppose he had some crazy notion of revenge. Oh, it sounds melodramatic enough, but isn't your morning paper full of just that sort of crude melodrama? Can't you believe that a man might grow up under a grudge and nurse it until he was crazy on just that one point? He'd be sane about everything else. He'd look sane—talk, think, and act as sane men do—and all the time there would be that one danger-point."

"You're talking nonsense," said Rachel coldly. "I can't stop, Cosmo."

He stood where he was.

"Rachel, this morning you practically accused us all. You called us together, and you called in a stranger, and in front of that stranger you informed us that there had been an attempt on your life. I think we were all under observation. Will you deny that?"

Rachel gave no answer.

"You see," said Cosmo Frith again. "I say—and you don't deny it—that we were all under suspicion. Poor little Caroline broke under it. She fainted, and she has run away. I suppose that proves her guilty—"

"Cosmo, stop! I can't listen to this."

He said, "I am afraid you will have to. Don't you see, it's the fact that you've put us all in the pillory which gives me the right to tell you to look elsewhere. My dear, do you really believe that any one of *us*—It's too monstrous!"

The phrase which he had used about the morning paper flickered through Rachel's mind. She could not bring it across her lips. She said mournfully,

"What is the good of this?"

He returned her look with one as sad.

"No good at all. And you want to go, don't you? Rachel, I

157

only ask that you don't go alone with him. I don't say come with me, though you know I'd be proud and happy, but I do say this—go in your own car with your own chauffeur. Don't risk yourself alone with Gale Brandon."

Rachel's chin lifted.

"Is that all, Cosmo? Because if it is—"

"No, it isn't. There's still Caroline."

"Yes?"

He stood aside from the door and opened it.

"I have been thinking it over, and I am sure that she would go to town. You see, she has a key to my flat. I let her have one when she gave up her own flat a month ago. And she spoke of running up there—oh, one day this week, I can't remember which."

"Why didn't you say this before? Why didn't you tell Richard?"

The concerned look was back on his face.

"I know—that's what I've been saying to myself. But it had gone clean out of my mind. It wasn't until I came to go over it all—You know, I could go straight up there myself. There's no need for you—"

She shook her head.

"No—I must go. I must see her."

She went past him into the passage, and this time he made no attempt to stop her, but as she emerged, the half open door of Caroline's room was opened wide and Miss Silver appeared.

"Miss Treherne—will you spare me a moment?"

It seemed as if everyone was in a conspiracy to keep her. She said quickly,

"I ought not to. Won't later do?"

Miss Silver shook her head with a kind of mild obstinacy.

"Oh, no, I am afraid not. I really must beg—"

Rachel resigned herself.

"Cosmo, will you tell Mr. Brandon that I won't be a moment?"

She went into Caroline's room, and found evidences of a thorough search. Drawers stood open. The bed had been stripped. On the dressing-table some torn scraps were laid out to form part of a typewritten sheet. Some of the words were damaged, and some of the pieces missing. She leaned with a hand on either side of the table and read what was there to read:

"Better get away at once whilst we are all at lunch. You'll get a good start. That woman is a detective. If you don't get away, she'll make you speak. Take your car to . . . " Here there was a piece missing from the right-hand side of the paper. The next line began on the left. "I'll make an excuse and . . . " The end of the line was gone. Below again was a whole sentence. "We can talk things over and decide what had better be done."

The bottom part of the paper was torn away. On an isolated scrap was the name—"Richard."

Miss Silver said briskly, "Who has a typewriter?"

With her eyes on that last fragment, Rachel Treherne said, "Richard."

"Do you know if this was typed on his machine? Are there any peculiarities which you could recognize?"

Rachel said, "Yes." She put her finger on the first word. "The capital B—it always blurs like that." Her eyes went back to the fragment with the name on it. "Is that the signature?"

Miss Silver said, "It might be."

Rachel spoke in a dazed voice.

"Richard went after her . . . If he wrote this . . . Where did you find the pieces?"

"In the bed-clothes. She got the note. She tore it up. She was in great distress—probably her hand was shaking. The bits dropped and scattered. Some were on the floor. She managed to destroy the part that mattered most. We don't know where they were to meet. Then she hurried on her things. I found the cupboard door open. A dress had fallen from its hanger. That drawer was pulled out. The pin-cushion was on the floor, the bed left anyhow, the lunch-tray not touched. You can see what a hurry she was in."

Rachel's heart cried out in her. Caroline—in such a desperate hurry to be gone! And where was she going? Where were they all going?

She straightened up slowly, and spoke as if answering her own thoughts.

"I am going after her. Cosmo thinks she will be at his flat. He says she has a key. They are like uncle and niece, you know."

"And is Mr. Frith driving you?" said Miss Silver.

"No—I am going with Mr. Brandon."

There was a slight, definite pause. Rachel braced herself. Cosmo had warned her. Was Miss Silver going to warn her too? She knew that if they all warned her she would still go with Gale Brandon.

But Miss Silver did not appear to have any warning to give. She said thoughtfully,

"Quite so. And Mr. Frith stays here?"

"No. He is going up to town to see a friend who is ill."

"Can you give me the telephone number of his flat? If Miss Caroline is there—"

"No, no, you mustn't ring her up—it would be fatal."

Miss Silver detained her with a touch on the arm.

"Suppose she is not there—is there anywhere else she might go—to talk things over?"

Rachel hesitated.

"She actually spoke of going to town. I think she would go to the flat. Cosmo seemed sure—"

"Miss Treherne, is there anywhere else—any lonelier place than a London flat?"

"There's Cosmo's cottage. I did think of that, but he was so sure—and she wouldn't go there by herself. It's—very lonely. Oh, no, she'd never go there alone."

"She was not to be alone. You forget that. She was to meet

the person who wrote that letter, and talk things over. Where is this cottage?"

"At Brookenden—about fifteen miles from Ledlington."

"In the direction of London?"

"No, the other way. The cottage is a mile out of the village. Cosmo goes down there to paint. When he's not there it's shut up. Caroline wouldn't go there—she didn't like it."

"If she did go there, could she get in?"

"Oh, yes. He hides the key in the tool-shed. There's nothing there to steal, you know."

"Is there a telephone?"

"Yes—he had one put in. I can give you the number. Look here, get Louisa to ring through. That wouldn't frighten her— if she's there. But she wouldn't be there yet. Miss Silver, I'm sure she wouldn't go there."

"If you will give me the address and the telephone number—"

She was offered pencil and paper. She scribbled quickly— Pewitt's Corner, Brookenden.

Miss Silver bent her brows.

"A very curious name."

Rachel turned in the doorway.

"It's a corruption of the French *puits*. There was a well there, and the house was built over it. I've always thought it must make it horribly damp. And Caroline says it gives her the creeps—that's why I feel sure she wouldn't go there. I'll ring you up if she's at the flat."

Miss Silver stood looking at the piece of paper in her hand.

CHAPTER 31

The car moved away. Rachel Treherne leaned back with relief. She had taken her way, and she was past caring where it led her. The strain lessened and she could relax. Whincliff Edge was left behind and its problems with it. London lay ahead, and problems there to meet her. But between Whincliff and London for the space of an hour or two there was only herself and Gale, in a swift moving world of their own. All that mattered was that they were here together—shut off—shut in.

As they turned out of the drive on to the Ledlington road, she looked at him, and found pleasure in the strong set of his head. Everything about him was strong. She thought, "If he hadn't been so strong, I shouldn't be here now." And that gave her pleasure too. She said, without any effort at all,

"Are you Gale Brent?"

The road was empty. He took a look at her and smiled with his eyes.

"Now fancy your asking me that! Who's been talking?"

"Cosmo. It was in a letter that my mother wrote to his— *Gale Brent*. Nanny only remembers him as Sonny. *Are* you Gale Brent?"

He laughed a little. It was a very unembarrassed laugh.

"I'm Gale Brandon sure enough. That's my real name. I haven't come courting you under false pretences. At least— well, in a way I suppose I have. But I was going to tell you—I just wanted a clear start. You know, I fell for you the moment we met—again. And I was going to tell you all about it as soon as I'd got you safe." Her heart beat hard. He put out his

162

left hand and dropped it on her knee, covering both of hers. "Have I got you?"

She said rather inaudibly, "You seem to think so."

The hand closed in a harsh grip that made her gasp.

"It's for you to say—at least that seems to be the idea. I don't know that I'm dead struck on it. I'll get you one way or another, but"—his grip tightened—"you can say it if you like."

Rachel found herself laughing without much breath.

"And if I don't like?"

His voice changed, took on a boyish, coaxing note.

"Maybe I'd like to hear you say it after all. I've got an idea it would sound good. Have I got you?"

Rachel said "Yes," and the hand that was gripping hers let go and came about her shoulders. The car described a rather odd curve and narrowly missed the ditch. The hand came back to the wheel, and the voice said ruefully,

"That was a bad break. I'll have to put off making love to you till we get some place. It's liable to go to my head, and I wouldn't like to get sent to gaol for disorderly driving, or being drunk in charge of a car, or anything like that. I'd better tell you about being Gale Brent."

Rachel said, "Oh!" Her mind felt perfectly light, bright, and empty—a house stripped but not yet garnished. The light was very bright indeed. She heard Gale say, "I'd better tell you about being Gale Brent," and in that light, empty house which was her mind she thought, "Then I'd better listen."

He said, in the voice she knew best,

"Well, it's this way. My father's name was Sterling Brandon. He quarrelled with his father about marrying my mother. So then he went away—cut the old folks right out—didn't write—didn't so much as tell them when I came along—wouldn't use the name. They must have said things he couldn't get over. Anyhow he called himself Sterling Brent. My mother died when I was about four years old, and

163

that made things worse. He kind of set up the quarrel for a monument to her. Well, about a year after that he met your father. They were partners for a bit—something like a year, I think it was—and that's when I got acquainted with you. I'd never seen such a little baby before. I can remember standing there looking at you and wondering if you were real. I expect I fell for you then. Your mother was mighty good to me, but I never rightly got on with Mabel—I didn't like her, and she didn't like me. But I was mighty happy. And then it all came to an end. My father quarrelled with your father, and I'm bound to confess it's the likeliest thing in the world that it was my father's fault. The fact is he'd a genius for quarrelling—couldn't see anyone else's point of view, and always thought the other man must be disagreeing with him out of spite. Then he'd go all hot and kick up a shindy, and the next thing would be you couldn't see him for the dust. Well, we went off to some other place—I forget where. Then he picked up a paper one day and saw that his father had had a stroke, so he went back. The old man was head of a big real estate business, and as he didn't live long enough for them to get quarrelling again, my father came in for everything. So now you know."

Rachel wondered whether she did. The words seemed to float round in her mind without meaning very much. She said vaguely,

"My father was sorry about the quarrel. He found oil after they broke the partnership. He wanted your father to have his share. It doesn't matter now, does it? I'll tell you some time."

He said, "No, it doesn't matter. But there are other things that matter very much. Look here, could we pull up and talk, because there's plenty to talk about."

It came to Rachel then with an absolute shock that she had forgotten Caroline. But she remembered her now. Caroline, and her fear for Caroline—they both came back to her together. She said only just above her breath,

"No, no, we mustn't stop. I must find Caroline. I don't know what is happening, and I'm—frightened—"

He put his hand down over hers again, but this time the clasp was gentle as well as strong.

"Don't be frightened, honey—it'll be all right."

"It's like a bad dream."

"Well, you're going to wake right up. Like to tell me about it?"

"I don't know where to begin."

"Perhaps I know some already. The little woman in brown, that Miss Silver—what is she, a detective?—she told me some."

He felt her start.

"But—but when—you've never met—"

He laughed.

"That's where you're wrong. You went up to put on your hat, your cousin went after you, and she came down."

Rachel stared at him.

"But there wasn't time."

"You can say a lot in five minutes if you don't waste time handing bouquets. She got off the mark quicker than anyone I've ever known, and first I reckoned she was crazy, and then I reckoned she wasn't. She's got a way of looking at you that makes you take notice of what she says, and the first thing she said to me gave me one of the worst jolts I've ever had. She said you didn't fall over that cliff last night. She said you were pushed. What have you got to say about that?"

She drew a long sighing breath.

"It's true."

"Any guess who did it?"

The colour rushed into her cheeks. She dragged her hand away and leaned back into the corner of the car.

"That's the horrible part of it—it might be anyone. It's been like that every time, only of course some of the things were just Louisa trying to frighten me."

"Rachel—what are you saying?" He brought the car to a standstill and turned to face her. "We've got to have this out.

165

What is all this? You know, I can't drive a car and listen to this sort of thing. You've got to tell me."

Rachel told him with simplicity and relief.

The money. That was the first thing—the burden of the money—the responsibility which she was not allowed to pass on or to share.

The family—always there. "And it's nice to have a family, but they oughtn't to be always there. One ought to have a life of one's own. I didn't see that in time, but I see it now. You can't live all those other people's lives, and that's what I've been trying to do. I've drained myself, but I've never satisfied them. I don't mean just the money, but because of the money they've looked to me, depended on me. They've expected more and more. It's all been wrong, and it's kept on getting worse—like something out of focus. And then this last week it's been a nightmare. When I couldn't bear it any longer I went to see Miss Silver. She helped someone I know, so I went to her. She came down here yesterday evening, and she found out right away that Louisa had been playing tricks on me. She really is clever, you know."

"Why was Louisa playing tricks, and what sort of tricks did she play?"

He saw her colour fade and her eyes darken. Her voice went to an uneven whisper.

"She wanted to make me believe that someone was—attempting my life."

"And how did she do that?"

"A slippery step—my curtains on fire—chocolates doctored with ammoniated quinine—snakes in my bed—"

"*What?*"

"Two of Mr. Tollage's adders. Noisy killed them. But Louie didn't mean to hurt me—she only wanted to make me believe that someone else was trying to hurt me. Gale, she swears that there was another slippery step before she polished hers, and that one of the chocolates had been tampered with before she touched them. She swears someone was really trying to kill me. And, Gale, she was right. It wasn't Louie who pushed me over the cliff."

She saw his face hard with anger.

"How do you know that? She was there, wasn't she—came along with the lantern just as soon as I'd pulled you up."

She shook her head.

"She loves me. It couldn't be Louie any more than it could be you."

He nodded slowly.

"Yes—I was there too—wasn't I? Sure it couldn't have been me?"

Their eyes met. Time stayed. Then she said,

"You see. That's all I've got—the people I love. That's something secure. When that is shaken I can't bear it. Outside that it's all suspicion—no one trusting anyone else—Louie trying to make me believe it was Caroline, or Richard, or both of them—Cosmo trying to make me believe it was you—and I, God forgive me, only too ready to believe it might be Maurice or Ernest, because, you see, I don't love them."

He put the Wadlows aside with an odd sweeping gesture.

"So Cosmo thinks it was me. I'd like you to tell me why."

He caught the flicker of a smile.

"Revenge of course—because of your father and my father—the real full-dress, old-fashioned feud—"

She had the feeling of having stepped over the edge of an unseen drop. She got a quite unmistakable jolt. It stopped her. She saw his face harden. There was as sudden an effect of change as if she had looked from him to his presentment cut in stone. The light was bad. It might have been an illusion, for before she could draw a breath it was gone and he was saying,

"So I pushed you over. But why did I pull you up again?"

She said rather breathlessly, "Because you saw Louisa's lantern of course. Or you might have had a brain-storm and then felt sorry about it."

"I see—"

He looked up and down the road. A *Home and Colonial* van

went past. Three young men on bicycles came from the Ledlington direction and flitted noiselessly by, bodies stooped, heads down, hands gripping. Gloom swallowed them.

Gale Brandon said roughly,

"That's enough about that. I haven't kissed you yet."

CHAPTER 32

Rachel drew away at last. She had not known that she could feel like this—to be two people and yet one, to have a double strength and a double joy, to be the giver of joy and the giver of love to someone whose only thought was to give and give again. A line of Browning's came to her and stayed: "Men have died, trying to find this place which we have found." She felt the triumph of that, and its disregard of death.

She wrenched herself as from a dream, putting him away with her two hands.

"Gale, we must go on—we must."

He said reflectively, "I don't know what you want to go on for, honey."

She shook his arm.

"I've got to find Caroline."

"And you don't know where she is, so how are you going to find her? See here, if she left while you were at lunch, that would be somewhere before two o'clock."

"We went down to lunch at a quarter past one. Her tray went up about five minutes after that. She wasn't undressed— she could have got away easily by half past one. She had had a note telling her to go. It said, 'Better get away while we're all at lunch—you'll get a good start,' and something about Miss Silver being a detective. And then, 'They'll make you speak if you don't get away. We can talk things over and decide what had better be done.' And a bit half torn off, with, 'I'll make an excuse and—' I thought it meant I'll make an excuse and come after you."

"How do you know all this?"

"Miss Silver found the bits all torn up. Some of the pieces were missing. Richard's name was on one piece—just the name by itself. That doesn't mean he wrote it. It was typed—on his machine. But that *doesn't* mean he wrote it. We don't know who wrote it, and we don't know who she's gone to meet, because just those bits were destroyed. I suppose she took care about that."

"But Treherne followed her. He did just what the note said—he made an excuse and followed her." He was starting the car as he spoke. "Would you worry about her if you thought she was with Treherne?"

Rachel looked at him.

"I'm frightened," she said. "I've been frightened all the time. But what frightens me most is that I can see Miss Silver is frightened too. And I oughtn't to be frightened if Caroline is with Richard, because he loves her."

Gale Brandon looked straight ahead of him. Visibility was not too good. He thought, "There's a fog coming up. It's a bad business." He said out loud,

"I liked Treherne a good deal, but I don't know him. Miss Silver said two things to me, and I'm going to tell you one of them. She said not to let you out of my sight, so I'd like you to bear that in mind."

"What was the other thing?"

"I'm not telling you that yet. Let's get back to Caroline. If she got off by half past one, she wouldn't be far off getting to London now. It's after three, and I suppose she'd make it in two hours at the outside."

"Not if she had to wait for the person who wrote that letter. And if it was Richard, he—it must have been quite two o'clock before he got away."

"And you don't know where he would take her?"

"No—Cosmo thought. . . . She has the key of Cosmo's flat. We thought—"

"But wasn't that when you were thinking she had gone alone? Would Treherne take her there? That's the point."

Rachel hesitated.

"He might—if they wanted to talk—if he wanted to get her away. She knows something—my poor Caroline—and she's frightened of being made to speak. Oh, if I could only find her! She needn't be frightened—she needn't be frightened about anything. She's got such a tender heart, and she's easily hurt. I'm blaming myself terribly, because I've seen for some time that she was upset. But I thought that it was Richard, and I didn't like to interfere."

"And he's in love with her you say?"

"But she has refused him. That is what I can't make out. I've been so sure that they cared for each other." Gale Brandon was thinking of the second thing which Miss Silver had said to him—the thing which he had refused to tell Rachel. "Miss Caroline is in great danger." That was what she had said, and that was what had made him wonder if she was crazy. If she was, then they could have the laugh on her. But if she wasn't—well, in that case things didn't look too good. And one of the people they didn't look too good for was Richard Treherne. He said abruptly,

"Are you sure she's not crazy, that Miss Silver?"

"Quite, quite sure."

He accelerated sharply. The hedgerows became a mere streak on either side, with the fog smudging them.

They came to the ugly outskirts of Ledlington, and had to drop again to thirty. Rows and rows of little new houses, with names like *Happicot* and *Mon Abri*. Then the older streets, with the older, dingier houses. And ultimately the narrow High Street with a big new multiple store or a cinema crammed in here and there among the relics of an Elizabethan, a Georgian, or a Victorian day.

Right through the town and out on the other side to the London road. Ledlington talks about a by-pass, but has not yet achieved one. Away from the lights of the shop windows dusk and the fog darkened the landscape. Flat fields, cropped hedges, a row of bare elm trees marching on either side of a lane, a signpost with the words "To Slepham Halt."

They were five miles out of Ledlington, and in that five miles neither of them had spoken. Rachel said suddenly,

"Stop, Gale!"

He glanced round at her, his foot on the brake.

"What is it?"

She said, "I don't know. I feel as if we were going the wrong way. Do you believe in that sort of feeling?"

"I should call it a hunch." The car slowed down and stopped. "Well, I don't know. They're very unreliable things hunches. I've had them and I've acted on them and they've come off, and I've had them and I've acted on them and they've let me down flat. The only sure thing about them is that you never can tell. What's your hunch?"

Rachel looked at him rather helplessly. The impulse which had made her say "Stop!" had spent itself. She felt lost and rudderless. She said uncertainly,

"I don't know. I felt we were going the wrong way. I can't explain it, but you know—when you wake up in the dark and you don't know where you are, and you move, and run into something, and it comes over you that you're all wrong— well, that's the nearest I can get to it."

"We haven't run into anything yet," said Gale, with a laugh in his voice.

"It was a very strong feeling," said Rachel.

"Haven't you got it still?"

Her voice sounded forlorn as she said, "I haven't got any-thing—I'm all lost."

He put a consoling arm about her.

"What do you want to do about it, honey?"

Through the lost feeling something pricked.

"I think I want to go back."

"To Whincliff Edge?"

"No—no, I don't think so."

When he had turned the car he said, "All right, where do we go?"

"Back past the turning for Slepham Halt, and then take the left-hand fork instead of the one that goes to Ledlington."

"And where does that take us to?"

"It takes us to Pewitt's Corner," said Rachel.

CHAPTER 33

When Miss Silver had gone out of the room and shut the door Caroline Ponsonby sank back upon the pillow and hid her face. She could shut out the light and her own power to see, but she could not shut out Miss Silver's words. She kept on hearing them just as if they were being actually spoken: "What is it that you know? It would be better for everyone if you would say. . . . It will be better for everyone if you will make up your mind as quickly as possible." The same words over and over, and over and over again. And the door shutting softly. Her mind was tormented, and through the torment the senseless repetition went on, and on, and on.

When the door was opened again she pressed her face deeper into the pillow and brought her hands up over her ears so that she might not hear. She was past coherent thought and at the mercy of one of the oldest instincts in the world. Hide your eyes, and stop your ears—make yourself very small and very still, and perhaps they will think you are dead, perhaps the hunt will go by. Every muscle tensed as she pressed herself down against the bed, eyes darkened and ears hearing only the beat of her own blood. She held her breath and waited. No voice came through the silence. No one touched her.

With an infinite strained caution she slackened the pressure upon her ears and listened. There was no sound of breathing but her own. She waited a long time, or what seemed to her a long time, before she lifted her head and looked about her. There was no one there. She was alone in the room and the door was shut, but on the table beside her head there was a folded note with her name typed across it—just Caroline. She stared at it, and then sat up and pushed back her hair. Everything in the room stood out very hard, and sharp, and clear. Her name on the note was black and distinct.

She took up the paper and opened it. There were some lines of typing, but no beginning. She read:

"Better get away at once whilst they are all at lunch. You'll get a good start. That woman is a detective."

A shaft of terror pierced her to the very quick. The hard, clear outlines were blurred. The typed lines wavered in a mist. She said, "I won't faint—I won't—I *won't!*" She fought the mist until it went away and left the paper clear again. She forced her eyes to the sheet and read:

"That woman is a detective. If you don't get away, she'll make you speak. Take your car to Slepham Old House. I'll make an excuse and meet you there. We can talk things over and decide what had better be done. You'll have some time to wait, but you must get out of this or they'll make you talk. Drive right into the stable yard and wait."

There was a line or two more which terrified her. She sat staring at these lines and at Richard's name. *Richard—*

173

*Richard—Richard—*No, she mustn't think about Richard, she must only think about getting away.

She ran to the door and locked it, and as she stood there with her hand on the key she heard the lunch bell ring. Suppose someone came to ask her how she was. Suppose it was Rachel. *It would surely be Rachel.* And at the thought Caroline's heart stood still. This was misery—to feel an anguish of dread at the thought that it might be Rachel who would come. "But I've locked the door. Nobody can come if I've locked the door." She leaned her forehead against it and closed her lids over eyes which were hot and dry. They burned behind the lids. She heard Ernest's voice, and Mabel's, and Miss Silver's. She heard Rachel's step, she heard it pause. Then the footsteps went past and the voices died away.

She unlocked the door and went back to the bed. Ivy would come up with a tray, and she mustn't find her up.

She began to tear up the typewritten note, but her hands were shaking so much that she bungled it, and before she had finished Ivy came.

As soon as the girl was gone she jumped up. The torn pieces of the letter spilled. She found some of them and crammed them into her pocket.

A coat—something to cover her head—that old brown hat—some things in a bag—brush—comb. . . . No, what did it matter? Her hands shook too much. Just her handbag then. Money—it doesn't matter. Nothing matters except to get away. A scarf? Yes. Only hurry, hurry, hurry!

Then along to the end of the house, past Richard's rooms, and down the stair that gave on the garage door. No one there. Rachel's car—Cosmo's—Richard's—her own little Austin. And the tank was full.

She got in, and found her hands were steady on the wheel. The garage slipped away. The drive slipped away. The empty Ledlington road began to slip away. The worst of the terror that had been gripping her relaxed. She was no longer trapped

174

there in that room for anyone to find, to question, to torture. She was out of the trap and away. If she was to be hunted she had a good start, and no one would look for her at Slepham. That was clever. They would make sure that she had gone to London. She had talked of going there—was it yesterday or the day before? She couldn't remember. Everything was such a long way off. . . . She stopped thinking and watched the road.

It was just after half past two when she turned into the lane with its bordering elm trees which led to Slepham Halt and the Old House. There is a deserted lodge on the right-hand side about half way between the line and the London road. Caroline drove in through moss-grown pillars and along a moss-grown drive to the stable yard.

Slepham Old House had stood empty for twenty years. It was a big ramshackle place of no particular period, and entirely lacking in modern conveniences. Since there is nowadays no market for an ugly house which has thirty bedrooms, one bathroom, no electric light, and a range which takes a ton of coal at a gulp and asks for more, it was likely that it would continue to stand empty until it fell down.

The stable yard was much enclosed. It had that peculiarly chill, deserted feeling which settles about places which have been used by men and left for a long time derelict. There was nothing to bring anyone there, and so from year's end to year's end no one came. The house was stripped, the out-houses empty and locked, the stables falling down.

Caroline leaned back in the car and closed her eyes. It was very cold, and it was dreadfully still. She had wanted to be alone, and now she had her wish. The loneliness of the place began to rise about her like a tide.

CHAPTER 34

It's pretty thick ahead," said Gale Brandon. "How much farther is it?"

"I think that last village was Milstead. We ought to have asked. Everything looks different in a fog," said Rachel doubtfully.

"And if it was Milstead?"

"Then it's about three miles on."

"I'd like to make it before the last of the light goes."

"It's pretty well gone as it is. It's nearly four o'clock."

He looked round at her for a moment.

"What's the hurry, honey?"

Everything in Rachel protested. Words rushed to her tongue.

"There isn't any hurry—there can't be. It was you who said there was, because of the light."

His eyes went back to the road again.

"I know—I said it all right. But do you think I haven't felt you sitting here beside me trying to push the car? Even when we were doing fifty I could feel you pushing. A hundred wouldn't have been fast enough for you. What's in your mind, Rachel?"

She struck her hands together.

"Nothing—nothing—I just want to get there."

Gale Brandon frowned.

"There's no need to tell me if you don't want to, but we've got too close for me not to know when you're frightened—and that's what you are right now."

Physically, they were so near that he felt her shudder. She said quickly.

"Do you believe that? Do you think that what is in someone else's mind can reach one? Because that—that's what is frightening me."

"Then you'd better tell me about it," said Gale Brandon. "You'll do better if you don't have secrets from me, because I shall always know when you've got them, and I shall always find out what they are, so it'll save a heap of trouble if you tell me right away. Now—what is it?"

She slipped a hand inside his arm.

"When we were going to London and I said 'Stop!' I told you I didn't know why I said it, and that was true. Something made me, and I didn't know what it was. But I know now. Just before I came away from Whincliff Edge Miss Silver asked me if there wasn't anywhere else that Caroline might be. We'd been talking about her going to London to Cosmo's flat, and she asked if there wasn't anywhere else. I told her about Pewitt's Corner, and when she said what everyone always does say, 'What an odd name!' I told her about the house being built over an old well, and about Pewitt's being a corruption of *puits*. And I told her Caroline couldn't bear the place and I didn't think she'd go there. She always did so hate the thought of that well under the scullery floor. There's a lid of course, but she hated it all the same, and I made sure she wouldn't go there. But—oh, Gale, it was the well that made me say 'Stop!'" Her hand closed desperately on his arm.

"Yes, honey? Go on. You thought about the well—"

She pressed against him.

"I didn't know it was the well. Something frightened me and made me say 'Stop!' Afterwards, when you had turned the car, I knew that it was the well. I remembered she was afraid of it, and sometimes—when you're afraid of something—Gale, do you think it was because Caroline was thinking about the well that I thought of it?"

It was out. She sat empty and shaking, with the horror put into words.

His left arm came round her.

"You're just frightening yourself. Why should she think about the well?"

Her voice came to him, hesitating and stumbling.

"I—don't know—it—came to me. I didn't frighten myself— it frightened me. Why should I have thought about the well— suddenly—like that—unless someone—someone else—was thinking about it? And—and Caroline—the well—it always frightened her."

She was held in a strong clasp.

"That doesn't sound like sense to me."

"It's not sense," said Rachel desperately. "The things that have been happening aren't sense at all. They're like the things in a bad dream—they're nonsense. But oh, Gale, they're horrible nonsense—wicked, horrible nonsense."

"Steady, Rachel! You've got to keep to sense, and so have I. Do we go straight on here, or is there a turn?"

"We keep straight on. If that was the turn to Linford, we're nearly there—another two miles at most."

"That's better. Does your cousin come down here much?"

"Cosmo? He lives here most of the summer. He hasn't been down since the end of September. He doesn't care about it in the winter."

"And Caroline?"

"She doesn't care about it at all."

"Then I don't see—"

She steadied her voice carefully.

"She—she's in bad trouble. I don't know what it is. That's my fault—I ought to have made it my business to know. I didn't like to interfere between her and Richard, but I oughtn't to have let it go on—so long. Only—" she stopped and looked round at him in a bewildered way—"it—it isn't really so long, you know. It isn't really long at all—it's just that this week has seemed like a year."

"Well, it's nearly over now, honey," said Gale Brandon.

CHAPTER 35

The car came to a standstill with the fog thick about it and the last of the light no more than a memory.

"Did you say this was a corner?" said Gale. "Because it's asking for trouble to leave the car on a corner in this fog. The first thing anyone would know about the lights is where they'd hit them."

"Yes, it's a corner. If you turn up the lane, there's a gate into a field. You can run the car in there."

It was easier said than done. Astonishingly difficult to find the gate and, when found, to back the car in. A narrow lane; deep ruts; a bramble that scratched her cheek; a smell of straw and cows; the glare of an electric torch reflected back from an impenetrable wall of fog but shining suddenly right into Gale's eyes as he blundered into her—these things made up Rachel's picture of the next few minutes. Gale's eyes—startling and strange to see them like that—looking out of the dark, looking for her.

When the car was in the field, they linked arms and began a search for the wicket gate which led to the house. The ruts were really deep. There was a ditch on one side of the lane, and a holly hedge on the other. They groped their way by the hedge, and found it a safe but uncomfortable guide. At last the gate clicked and let them in upon a paved stone path with rose bushes, wild and unpruned, all their summer growth upon them to fling a spray of damp against the cheek or catch at the groping hand. Rachel discovered that you may know a place quite well and yet feel lost in a fog like this. She knew that they must skirt the house, but they blundered into soft earth on the one hand and a very hard wall on the other before they succeeded in doing it. The torch was extraordinarily little help. It showed the path and nothing much besides, but when they had felt for and found the tool-shed it did pick out the key for them, hanging from a nail in the wall, all rusty—a big, old-fashioned key on a loop of tarry string.

The back door next, and a good deal of fumbling to get the key into the lock. And all the time Rachel keeping back her own fear with the insistent thought, "There's nobody here. No car. No light. No sound. No anything." The key went home, and turned easily enough for all its rusty look. The door swung in. Rachel put out her hand for the torch, missed it in the dark, and heard it drop between them on the flagged step. She said "Oh!" on a quick breath, and Gale exclaimed. Their hands met, and she left the picking up to him. But the torch might just as well have been left lying on the step, since prod, poke or push as he would, Gale Brandon could get no spark out of it.

"If I was a smoker, I'd have matches," he said ruefully. "I've never fancied it somehow, but here's where it would have come in useful."

"There'll be matches on the dresser," said Rachel—"and a candle. Stay where you are and I'll find them. I know just where they are." She took a step from the door and stopped, hands stretched out before her, eyes straining against the dark, ears straining too. But there was no need to strain for the sound which had stopped her. It filled the empty room—the homeliest, most comfortable sound in the world, the ticking of a clock.

Rachel stood where she was without moving and listened to it. She knew the clock quite well—a cheap shiny anachronism which lived on the scullery dresser and gained a steady five minutes a day. She turned her head and said in a strained voice,

"Gale—the clock—it's ticking."

He laughed behind her in the dark.

"That's just a way they have."

She drew in her breath sharply.

"Not when they haven't been wound for a month. It's an

eight-day clock. Cosmo hasn't been down here since the end of September. He said so yesterday—he said he hadn't been down. But the clock's ticking."

"Well, honey, anyone could get in with that key. Let's get those matches."

He moved to pass her, but she caught his arm.

"Wait! Gale, please wait. I don't like it. I won't go on without a light. Have you got matches in the car?"

"Not a match. But there's another torch—a small one I keep for a spare. Do you want me to get it? It's a long way back to that field."

Rachel hesitated. To go stumbling and groping back to the car, with matches a couple of yards away on the dresser? Not reasonable. She said "No—" in a hesitating tone and took a half step forward. And then, in a rush of terror, reason was suspended.

With that suspense what asserted itself was the oldest fear in the world—the trap, the snare, the gin, the pit, the terror that lurks unknown in the dark. She went back, and as Gale Brandon moved to pass her, she caught at him and held him.

"I won't go on without a light. There's something—"

She heard him laugh.

"What's wrong with this place is the damp. It smells like the inside of a well."

And with that Rachel knew. She said,

"Will you stop here—quite still? Will you promise me not to move—at all?"

"What's this?"

"Will you promise, Gale—will you *promise?*"

"If you want me to."

She let go of his arm and began to feel her way round the edge of the room. First to the corner by the sink, and then to the larder door. Then to the dresser, feeling, always feeling, with her left hand on the wall and her right hand at arm's length to grope in the empty dark.

She came to the dresser, felt her way along it until her fingers touched the matches, and struck one. The tiny spirt of light dazzled and sputtered out, but it had shown her an old brass candlestick, the candle half burned down. With her back to the door she struck another match, and this time reached the candle wick. There was a moment whilst the flame took hold, and another when it flagged and failed. Then the wax melted and fed it, and the flame rose bright and clear. She turned with the candle in her hand and held it up. A yard from her feet on the one side, a yard from Gale's feet on the other, was the open mouth of the well, three feet across. If she had taken the second step where she had taken the first, it would have taken her over the edge. The well was two hundred feet deep. There was twenty feet of water in it all the three years when half the wells in the country failed and dried out. There it was, as black as death, between her and Gale—the old well of the Well Corner, dug four, five, six hundred years ago for the refreshment of man and beast. Her thought stood still, and could not move from the well.

Her hand held up the candle, stiff and steady, as if the wax, the brass and her arm were all of one piece. She stared at Gale, and for a moment he stood rigid, staring back at her. Then he came round the well, walking slowly and carefully, and took the candle from her hand and set it down on the dresser and put his arms about her.

They stood like that, locked together, without speaking a word, hardly drawing breath, because death had been so close and life was immeasurably sweet.

Presently, when he lifted her face and kissed her, she could feel that his was wet, and that moved her very much. Her own eyes were dry. The danger had been hers, not his. Her heart contracted as she thought of what he might have heard in the dark if she had taken that other step. She would have cried out, but the sound would have been swallowed up by the well. . . . And then there would have been the splash—a long way down—a horribly long way down.

She found words then to comfort him, as one finds words

to comfort a child who has waked afraid—stumbling words, broken words, that brought tears to her eyes and a great gush of love to her heart. As he held her and kissed the tears away, they came so near that it was as if they took each other then with a true marriage vow—to love and to cherish—till death us do part—and thereto I give thee my troth.

They drew apart slowly and reluctantly. The candlelight showed the room with the door open upon the back door step, a tin can standing in the sink, a deal table pushed against the left-hand wall, and, tilted against it, damp from the breath of the water, the wooden cover which had been taken away from the well.

Gale let go of her and walked over to it. He touched it and looked back over his shoulder.

"Do they keep the well open like this?"

Rachel said, "Never."

In her mind words formed themselves—part of a verse which she knew quite well, but now she could only remember how it began: "They have digged a pit . . . " The words said themselves over and over. "They have digged a pit—they have digged a pit—they have digged a pit—" But she couldn't remember how the verse should end.

Gale came back to her.

"Rachel—what does this mean?"

She said, "I don't know." But it wasn't true, because the answer was in those words which repeated themselves without ceasing in her mind: "They have digged a pit . . . "

CHAPTER 36

They stood there, very close but not touching one another. The candle behind them on the dresser threw their shadows forward across the well, and the uneven brick, and the damp stone of the doorstep beyond it. The two long shadows lay there and were still.

At last Gale said, "What's in your mind? You'd better tell me."

She turned towards him then and spoke in an odd clear voice,

"Someone wound the clock, and someone uncovered the well—" She turned a little more and pointed. "The clock says half past four. It gains five minutes a day. What is the right time?"

They looked together at the watch on his wrist. The hands stood at five-and-twenty past.

"Then it was wound yesterday," he said.

Rachel said, "Yes."

"And the person who wound it uncovered the well. Why?"

She had no answer to that.

"But the clock," said Gale Brandon—"that's what I can't understand. If that cover was taken off the well for the only reason that I can think of, why in thunder should the person who did it wind the clock?"

Rachel was cold to her feet. There was just one person who could never keep his hands from a clock. If Cosmo had come here yesterday he could no more have helped picking up that clock and winding it than he could have helped breathing. Because the clock would have stopped—it would have been stopped for nearly six weeks. Cosmo could never pass a clock that had stopped without winding it. But Cosmo had not been here since the end of September. He had said so yesterday.

Someone had been here.

Someone had wound the clock.

The person who had wound the clock had uncovered the well.

They had digged a pit—

She turned slowly and looked at Gale. His eyes were horrified and stern. A most dreadful thought came to her. Her lips were suddenly dry as she said,

"Caroline!" She could not get past the name. Her eyes said the rest, and said it with anguish. "Did she come here before us? Are we too late?"

He said "No—no—the door was locked. The key was in the shed."

Rachel's hand went to her throat.

"He could have put it there."

"Who? My God, Rachel!"

She shook her head, tried to speak, spoke in a whisper.

"I—don't—know. Someone—uncovered—the well. Some-one—tried—to—kill me. Perhaps Caroline—knew—who it was—"

"Rachel, don't look like that! She hasn't been here—" He paused, and added, "yet."

"How do you—know?"

"It's easy. Look here—if this trap was set for Caroline and she had fallen into it, would the man who had set it lock up and go away and leave the well uncovered? You can see he wouldn't. Why, the first thing he'd do would be to cover up the well."

Rachel tried twice before she said, "Unless he meant it to look—as if—she had done it herself—"

Gale took her by the shoulders and shook her lightly.

"Wake up, honey—you're dreaming. If anyone was plan-ning to make this look like suicide, he'd have to leave the door open the way it is now, with the key sticking in it. Quit frightening yourself. Caroline isn't here."

"Then where is she?" said Rachel with trembling lips.

"Well, there are a few good places besides this, honey."

She put a hand on his arm and stared at the well.

"That wasn't done—for nothing. Someone was meant to come in like we did, and to fall—Oh, Gale!—as I should have fallen if I had taken just one more step!"

Her clasp tightened suddenly. He turned his head. They both held their breath.

"There's someone coming now," he said.

For a moment Rachel heard nothing. Then it seemed to her as if she heard too much. A vague sound without direction which might have been the sound of a car, but whether coming or going she could not tell. The drip of a fog from the eaves, from the holly hedge. The faint scuttering which some small creature would make if it were disturbed—mouse, or mole, or rabbit—any one of them might be abroad in the dark. And, first faintly and then clear and distinct, footsteps coming nearer.

She held on to Gale, and they watched the door.

It was Miss Maud Silver who came out of the fog and stood looking in on them from the worn step. She was dressed with her usual dowdy neatness—a three-quarter length jacket of black cloth with some rather worn brown fur at the neck and wrists, and a curious head-dress, half cap half toque, made of the same stuff as the coat and trimmed with what was quite obviously a piece of the fur which had been left over. A black handbag with a shiny clasp depended from her left wrist. She put a hand in a black kid glove on the jamb of the door and looked in upon the candle-lit room.

Two doors, one to the left by the sink, one to the right beyond the dresser. The open well, not flush with the rough brick floor but sunk. The cover that would bring it to the floor level leaning against that table on the right. But the well was open now, and the two people who stared at her across it might have been looking at a ghost instead of at Maud Silver.

Miss Silver could not remember when she had been frightened last, but she was frightened now. Under her breath she said "Oh dear!" She then called up her courage and addressed Gale.

"Mr. Brandon, where is Miss Caroline?"

Gale Brandon said, "Not here."

Miss Silver came across the threshold and closed the door behind her.

"Are you sure?"

"Quite," said Gale coolly.

"Why?"

186

He told her, using the same arguments with which he had comforted Rachel.

"We found the door locked, and the key on its nail in the shed. This damnable thing as you see it. Rachel nearly walked into it. Someone was meant to walk into it."

"Miss Caroline," said Maud Silver.

"Well then, we got here first. If it had been meant to look like suicide and the trap had been sprung, the door wouldn't have been locked or the key in the shed. If it was murder and meant to be hushed up, the cover would have been put back."

"But she may come at any time," said Miss Silver—"unless the plan has gone wrong. Plans do go wrong, you know. It is not in mortals to command success."

All this time Rachel had neither spoken nor moved, but now her hand dropped from Gale's arm and she gave Miss Silver back her own question. Her voice was agonized.

"Where is Caroline?"

Miss Silver said, "I don't know. I think she will either come here or be brought here—I feel sure of it. I have been in great anxiety lest I should get here too late, but the fog delayed us."

"Us?"

"I took the liberty of employing your chauffeur and car, Miss Treherne. A most reliable man and a very careful driver. He is putting the car in a place of security, and will then report here. We may be glad of him. In the meanwhile it is of the first importance that we should show no light, and that this door should be locked and the key replaced in the shed. If you will do that, Mr. Brandon, and then come to the front door, I will admit you."

When he was gone Miss Silver skirted the well, picked up the candle, and led the way through the kitchen to the living-room. The old beams hung low and made a trap for innumerable shadows. The front door opened directly upon the room, and a very steep, narrow stair ran up in the far corner. Here too the floor was of brick, with a rug or two to soften it. The cold of the fog and the November night was everywhere. The chill hearth was clean and bare. A draught came leaking down the stairs. A faint smell of tobacco hung stale upon the air. The three small windows, one on either side of the door and one in the left-hand wall, were curtained with a brightly patterned chintz. Behind the curtains wooden shutters fitted close and were secured by an old-fashioned iron bar.

Miss Silver applied herself to withdrawing the bolts of the door and unlocking it. This done, she turned to Rachel.

"Miss Treherne, we can only do our best. I think he will bring her here."

Rachel said in a harsh voice that was strange to her, "Why didn't you go to the police?"

Miss Silver looked at her steadily.

"What could I have said to them? I know, but I have no proof. You cannot accuse a man without proof. I was sure that he pushed you over the cliff last night. I was sure that he would try again in some other way. If I had come to you and accused him, would you have believed me? I think that you would not. Because I had no proof—no proof at all. It would have required more than a stranger's word to break down the affectionate trust of years. I thought it best to remain silent, and to keep as close a watch upon you as possible. But until just before the lunch-bell rang today I did not know that Miss Caroline might be in danger too. I blame myself. I should have acted more quickly, but I was, I must confess, outwitted. He is very cunning, and he has a great deal at stake. He contrived to get her out of the house whilst we were at lunch—"

Rachel interrupted her.

"She has been gone for more than three hours. Miss Silver, where is she? It would have taken her no more than an hour and a half to get here—before the fog came down."

Miss Silver shook her head.

"She was certainly not to come straight here. Oh, no, that wouldn't have suited his book at all. If she was to stumble into the well in the dark, then it must be dark before she got here. The torn-off piece of the letter would have told her where she was to wait for him, and when he thought it was safe he would pick her up and bring her here—in her own car if it was meant to look like suicide. Everyone in the house would have had to say how uncertain and depressed she had been. There would be no mark of violence, no sign that anyone had laid a hand upon her—no one *would* have laid a hand upon her. He would have had the whole night to make his way to some station from which he could take a train to town. Yes, I think that it was meant to look like suicide."

The cold of the house must have got under Rachel's skin. There was no warmth in her. The cold seeped into her bones and settled about her heart. And coldest of all—fear. She said in a dead voice, but quite calmly,

"Suppose she wouldn't come. She was afraid of this place—she hated the well. Suppose he killed her first. Have you thought of that?"

Miss Silver said, "Yes." Then she added in her briskest voice, "It is useless to speculate. We will not anticipate evil. We need coolness and courage. And here is Mr. Brandon who has plenty of both."

CHAPTER 37

When Rachel looked back afterwards at the next half hour it seemed to her the longest she had ever known. She would have said the most dreadful too, if the culmination of that time of waiting had not been more dreadful still.

At first she was too cold and numb to feel. Prim and efficient as a governess in her own schoolroom, Miss Silver took command. She talked apart with Gale. They admitted the chauffeur, Barlow, and talked with him. Finally they took up their positions. Barlow in the kitchen, with a candle well shaded and the window made light-proof by hanging a table-cloth over the drawn curtains. Rachel and Gale together where the back door opened and, opening, would hide them from view. Miss Silver on the other side of the door, halfway between the well and the larder, with the larder door left open as a line of retreat. A log of wood on the floor beside her.

Rachel's glance had passed over the log without really seeing it in the candle-light, but as she stood in the dark and waited, a picture of it formed on the surface of her mind, as a broken reflection forms again on water that has grown still. An odd picture. Miss Silver and that log of wood. Miss Silver pushing the log until it lay right on the edge of the well. A heavy log. An odd picture. She thought about it with the kind of apathy which dwells on some trifle because the thing is there and it is too much trouble to stop thinking about it.

The silence and the cold of the scullery settled about them. The darkness was unbroken—a darkness that could be felt. The damp of the well came up with a breath of decay. Rachel's thought came slowly and most unwillingly back to the well. It was so very old. More than twice as old as the house which had been standing over it for three hundred and three score years. An old well. Very deep, very dangerous. Was this the first time that a man had made use of its secret danger? No wonder Caroline was afraid of it.

The numbness of the apathy left her. Her heart turned over. *Caroline. . . .* She shuddered from head to foot.

Gale's hands came down on her shoulders and turned her to him. He held her, and kissed her again and again. Agony and joy were together in her mind. She thought, "I can't go on feeling like this—I shall die." And then she thought, "This isn't death, it's life." And then she stopped thinking at all, and time stopped too.

It began again with the sound of the telephone bell. The bell rang in the living-room, and with both doors closed the sound had something ghostly about it, like a sound caught between sleep and waking.

Miss Silver said at once, "You go, Miss Treherne—and pray do not forget the well."

Rachel wondered whether she would ever be able to forget the well. She left Gale's arms—left warmth, protection, comfort—and skirting the right-hand wall, came past the table to the kitchen door, actually brushing the well cover as she passed. Her hip touched it, and her hand. The wood was soft and smooth, almost slimy. The feel of it set her shuddering again.

Barlow was in the kitchen, sitting up stiff and straight on one of the kitchen chairs with his candle on the table beside him shaded by an elaborate contrivance of books and saucepan lids. She signed to him not to get up, and went through into the living-room, leaving the door ajar.

The telephone was on the wall half way to the window. The bell was ringing again, and now it sounded horrifyingly loud. Her heart beat, and the hand that lifted the receiver shook, and then stiffened into rigidity, because it was Richard's voice which struck insistently upon her ear: "Hullo—hullo—*hullo!* Who is there? Is there anyone there?"

Richard—but Richard . . . What was the good of saying but? What was the good—

She put her left hand up to her throat and managed his name.

"Richard—"

His voice leapt at her.

"Who is that? Is that Rachel? Oh, for God's sake!"

Rachel Treherne took a hard pull at herself.

"Yes, it's Rachel."

"Where is Caroline?"

"Richard—I—don't—know—"

"Where is she? She wasn't at Cosmo's flat. Her car wasn't in the garage. I thought about the cottage, and started to come down, but this damned fog is so thick. I thought I'd ring up and tell her I was coming—if she was there."

Rachel said steadily, "She isn't here, Richard. Miss Silver thinks—she may be on her way."

There was a harsh anger in his voice as he said, "After four hours! It's nearly four hours since she left Whincliff Edge!"

"Miss Silver says—"

He broke in more harshly still.

"What are you doing at the cottage? And Miss Silver—what is she doing there?"

Her control was slipping. Her voice flinched.

"She came—to look—for Caroline. I came—with Gale. She isn't here. Miss Silver thinks—We're waiting to see if she'll come."

There was a sound that might have been a laugh or a groan.

"Then I might as well wait with you. I'll push on."

"Where are you?"

"Linford."

She heard the receiver jerk back and the line go dead.

But she ought to have warned him not to drive up to the Corner. She ought to have thought of that. It was too late now.

She hung up, went back across the kitchen, and opened the farther door. But as she opened it, there came to her ears the sound of the back door key grating in the cumbrous lock. Instantly she was alive. She felt a vital apprehension, a tingling excitement that was partly fear and partly an astounding relief, because now, at last, the waiting was over. She stood on the threshold with the door drawn to behind her—listening—intent.

The lock went back, the back door handle turned, and the door swung in, covering Gale. Only now he was to move, come forward to the edge of the door, and be ready. She could see the doorway breaking the solid dark of the room, and something—someone—like a shadow standing there. The wet step caught a glimmer from the fog. The shadow stood there and did not move. Then from the fog a voice called cheerfully,

"Get a light—there's a good child. Right across to the dresser. There are matches there, and a candle."

The shadow on the threshold stirred. Caroline's voice said faintly, "It's so dark." And at the sound of that faint voice three people in their hearts said, "Thank God!"

The man's voice came out of the fog again with a bantering sound.

"Afraid of the dark? You poor tired child! Well, the best way is to make haste and light that candle. I've got my hands too full to do anything about it myself. Hurry up, child! Don't you want a cup of tea? I do."

Caroline said, "*Oh, yes!*" She took a step forward. And then, as Gale's arm came round her, she screamed, and Miss Maud Silver pushed the heavy log out over the edge of the well. . . . It seemed a long time before the splash came.

There was no second scream. Even if Gale Brandon's hand had not closed down over her mouth, Caroline would not have screamed again. For twenty-four hours she had walked the edge of an abyss. Now she slipped over the edge. She let go. She went down.

There is a point at which you no longer care. Caroline reached it and let go. She did not quite lose consciousness, but she no longer cared what happened.

Miss Silver moved noiselessly back till she touched the jamb of the larder door. She stood there with the door in her hand, ready to move forward or back.

Rachel did not move at all. She had no consciousness of her body. She was set there in judgment. She was a burning flame of justice.

She waited, looking to the doorway. A second shadow had come up, and stood there as Caroline had stood a moment before. So little time had passed—so much had passed—

Cosmo Frith stood between the fog and the well. He was breathing hard. He stared in upon the dark. The sound of a scream and the sound of a splash were still in his ears. The dark was before his eyes. But he was safe. He had only to skirt the well, light the candle which stood ready upon the dresser, replace the wooden cover, and be gone. There would be no one to say he had ever come. If the night had been clear, if there had been the remotest chance that the car—Caroline's car—might have been seen and traced, he would have left the well as it was. And the door open and the car outside. But now he had a better plan than that. Cover the well and lock the door, and take the car as far from Pewitt's Corner as it would go, and then set about an alibi. Town for him. Telephone calls to friends. Dinner and a theatre. Lights. Music. People ...

It came to him that he had only to walk into that life and be safe. Caroline had been the danger, and Caroline was gone—the little fool. He threw up his head and laughed. It had been so easy.

"You little fool!" he said aloud, and laughed again. "You damned little fool!"

The words went into the dark. The damp of the well came up against his face. Get on with it! Get on with the job and get away!

He stepped over the threshold, felt his way by the left-hand wall, and came to the dresser. The ticking of the clock struck on his ear and startled him. He must have wound it last night. What a damnable fool's trick! What ailed him that he couldn't keep his hands from a clock? He must stop that ticking before he left.

Candle and matches were to his hand. Miss Silver had seen to the replacing of them. He struck a match, bent over the candle, and watched it light. And looked up to see Rachel standing against the kitchen door. She was bare-headed. The dark coat which she wore hung open over a dark dress, and both were indistinguishable against the background of old time-blackened wood. Her hair showed faintly. Her face was white and wet. Her eyes took up the candle-light and turned it into flame. She said in a whispering voice,

"What have you done with Caroline?"

Cosmo looked back at her, the match with which he had lit the candle still in his hand. A little smoulder of fire crept up the wood and burned him. He dropped the match.

194

CHAPTER 38

Caroline stirred in the dark shadow behind the door. Gale Brandon had set her down there, and she had fallen in a crouching heap and neither known nor cared what would happen next. But now she stirred, opened her eyes upon candle-light, and saw past Gale, who stood between her and the room, to Rachel whose voice had called her back.

If Rachel was here, she was safe. That was the first thought that came to her. An old association of safety with the familiar voice. Her eyelids began to droop, until a second and dreadful thought startled them wide again. If Rachel was here, nothing was safe any more. The man in front of her moved forward away from the door. Caroline got to her knees, and from her knees to her feet. She had run away from Rachel, and Rachel was here. She must run away again. If she stayed, they would make her speak. She mustn't speak. All that was left alive in her said that—"You mustn't speak."

She held the edge of the door, slid round it, and reached the step. She had to go farther than that. She had somehow to reach the car and drive it away into the fog. Blind and beaten she must do it—for Richard—*Richard*. The name was like a stab, and the pain of it roused her. Behind her in the room she heard Rachel say in a strained, whispering voice,

"What have you done, Cosmo? You knew the well was open. You sent her in—Caroline. You heard her scream. You laughed—I heard you laugh."

"Better for you if you hadn't," said Cosmo Frith.

Rachel said, "Better for both of us." And with that Caroline turned and looked back into the room.

She saw then what she had not seen before—the open well. And beyond it Cosmo at the dresser, and Rachel leaning back against the kitchen door.

Gale Brandon stood where the well cover tilted against the table. He was watching Cosmo and Rachel, but she thought they did not see him. They only saw each other.

Caroline watched too. Rachel's words said themselves over in her mind—"You knew the well was open. You sent her in. You heard her scream. You laughed." She saw Cosmo as if she was seeing him for the first time. All the easy geniality was gone. There was about him something which even to her dim and exhausted sense spelled danger. If a dog looked at you like that, you went warily. But for Cosmo to have that twisted look of hate for Rachel—for Rachel—

Caroline opened her lips to cry out, but no sound came. She was a yard from the step. She tried to move, but she had no power. They spoke in the room—Rachel—Cosmo. Rachel's words went by her, but she thought she heard Cosmo say, "I've always hated you."

Gale Brandon took a long stride forward. The thing had gone far enough—too far in his opinion. He stood between Rachel and Cosmo Frith and spoke his mind.

"That's enough of that! You sent that girl to her death, and you'll have to account for it!"

His voice rang loud where the other voices had been low. He had come out of nowhere with the extreme of suddenness.

Cosmo took the shock with a visible stiffening of every muscle. He straightened up, measured Gale with the eyes which had reminded Caroline of a dangerous dog, and stepped back. The odds were out of all reason, and he was not beyond reason yet. There was still the car. If he could get a start—get away—get over to France. After all, there was no proof—no possible proof. They could never prove that he had uncovered the well. Rachel would keep the police out of it if she could. . . . No, they'd be bound to come in, with Caroline dead—with Caroline dead. But it would be an accident. No one could ever prove that it wasn't an accident.

All this in the flash between danger and decision. He said aloud,

"I've nothing to say to you, and nothing to account for—to you. There's been an accident, and there's an end to it."

With the last word he had turned his back and was skirting the well as he had skirted it before, going right-handed past the larder and the sink, with his head up and his shoulders squared. Miss Silver saw him go. And then he came to the open door and stood there face to face with Caroline. She was a yard away on the flagged path which led up to the step. A glimmer of candle-light showed him her face drowned in the fog. Her eyes were open and empty. They looked at him as drowned eyes look from a dead face. She stood quite still. Everything stood still for a heart-breaking second. It was when she put out her hand with a wavering motion that reason went out of Cosmo Frith. He broke suddenly, dreadfully, screamed some incoherence of horror, and went back from that weak, groping hand—and back—and back.

Gale Brandon tried to reach him, but was too late. It was no more than three steps from the doorway to the well—three steps taken at a rush. And then, hands clutching and balance gone, over the edge and down.

The verse which Rachel had not been able to finish finished itself:

"They have digged a pit and fallen into it themselves."

CHAPTER 39

The inquest was over, and a verdict returned of death by misadventure, with a recommendation by the jury that the well should be permanently boarded over or furnished with a parapet. There had been terrible moments of strain, but, with so much else that was over, they were over now.

"Will you describe what happened, Miss Treherne?"

The grey-haired coroner was a friend of nearly twenty years' standing. Thank God for that.

Rachel could hear her own voice now.

"Mr. Brandon and I found the well uncovered. I very nearly fell into it. We warned Miss Silver. Mr. Brandon and Miss Silver stayed in the scullery. I went to answer the telephone. When I came back the door was opening. Miss Ponsonby came in, and Mr. Brandon pulled her out of the way of the well. Mr. Frith followed her. He came round the well and lit a candle."

"The room was in darkness?"

"Yes."

"May I ask why?"

"There was a candle in the kitchen. I spoke to Mr. Frith about the danger of leaving the well uncovered."

"Was there a quarrel?"

"No—I should not have called it a quarrel. I had had a terrible fright."

"Was there any quarrel with Mr. Brandon?"

"No. Mr. Brandon told Mr. Frith he was accountable for leaving the well uncovered. Mr. Frith turned away and went round the well to the door. Miss Ponsonby was just outside. I think he did not expect to see her there. He was startled, and he must have forgotten about the well. He stepped back, and before Mr. Brandon could reach him he overbalanced and fell."

"Mr. Brandon did not touch him?"

"Oh, no."

"Did anyone touch him?"

"No."

Gale Brandon's evidence, on the same lines. Then:

"What did you do after Mr. Frith fell?"

"Miss Silver rang up the police. The chauffeur and I went to try and get a rope. He must have sunk at once. We did what we could."

"I am sure of it, Mr. Brandon. Oh, there is one thing—can you account for the log of wood which was found floating in the well?"

"I think I can. It was lying near the edge of the well. It got pushed over."

"You noticed it?"

"Yes, I noticed it."

Miss Silver's evidence, very precise and composed:

"Where were you when Mr. Frith fell?"

"I was just inside the larder, sir."

"And why were you in the larder?"

"I stepped back just inside the door when Mr. Frith came in. I wished to leave him room to pass safely round the well."

"And from first to last no one touched Mr. Frith?"

"No, sir—no one touched him."

"He was startled at seeing Miss Ponsonby and stepped back?"

"Yes, sir."

They had all given their evidence, and it had all been true, only no one had spoken the key-word which would have resolved death by misadventure into something darker and more dreadful. If the coroner had his thoughts, he did not speak them—at least not in that place or at that time. The jury returned their verdict and dispersed.

The talk at the Magpie went that there was something queer about the business:

"What did he want with the girl anyway, taking her off to his place in all that fog? No good, I'll be bound."

"Scared to death she was, for fear what they'd ask her."

"The crowner let her down easy."

"Funny thing, all of them rolling up like that, one after the other."

"Well, I'd nothing against Mr. Frith myself, but they do say . . ."

They said a lot.

The inquest was over. The verdict stood. The nine days' wonder would pass. Life would go on.

But there was another reckoning, here in the family. A private inquest where something more than the bare truth would have to be spoken if the life that went on was to be worth living.

Richard Treherne had come to Pewitt's Corner to find Rachel sitting on the step with Caroline unconscious in her arms. Upon that a coming and going—men with a rope, and the rope too short—the police—the whole dreadful business of plumbing the well. He had taken Rachel and Caroline back to Whincliff Edge, and had not seen Caroline again until he saw her, a sight to wring the heart, across the crowded coroner's court.

He saw her now on the couch in Rachel's sitting-room, where this second, intimate inquest was to take place. He stood inside the door and, seeing Caroline, saw no one else. A rage against Cosmo took him. She looked so drained of everything. But her eyes met his, and they were clear. He thought of the sky after rain, clear above the sea—only Caroline's eyes were brown. He came forward, took her hand, kissed it, and sat down.

Rachel was there; Gale Brandon; Miss Silver in a very odd grey dress which looked as if it had been trimmed with black tape; and Louisa Barnet—Louisa stiffly apart, wearing her Sunday black and the expression which she reserved for funerals. Rachel wore black too, but bright at her breast was the oak sprig she had chosen with Gale. And he had said he wanted it for the woman whom he had loved all her life. The diamond leaves and the acorn cups gave out a frosty sparkle. The pearls had their own soft, changing sheen.

There was a silence, and then Rachel said,

"We've got to talk this out, and then we needn't ever speak

of it again. I have asked Louisa to be present—she and Miss Silver know why. Miss Silver has something to tell us, and so has Caroline."

Noisy, stretched out in front of the fire, opened one eye, rolled over, and began very delicately to wash his face in exactly the same way as a cat, except that cats, to whom the toilet is a sacred rite, sit up and give it their entire attention. Noisy licked lazily, stroked a somnolent face, and presently sank again into a dream of badgers.

The room was very quiet as Miss Silver said,

"Where would you like me to begin, Miss Treherne?"

"I leave it to you."

Miss Silver moved her chair a little. She could now see everyone quite comfortably. Dear me, how pale they all were! All except Mr. Brandon. It was impossible to imagine Mr. Brandon looking pale. A very forcible type. He would be a great support to poor Miss Treherne. Wealth was certainly a terrible responsibility, and the cause of a great deal of crime, but if you had it you just had to make the best of it.

She cleared her throat, coughed slightly, and began to speak.

"I came down here at Miss Treherne's request. She had furnished me with a list of her relatives and some information regarding them. But members of the same family are not always the best judges of one another's characters. They are apt to be biased by such things as early association, custom, and personal predilection. I became aware immediately of the presence of these three factors. Of Mr. Richard Treherne and Miss Caroline Ponsonby Miss Treherne could believe no wrong. Of Mr. Maurice and Miss Cherry Wadlow she was, on the contrary, quite prepared to believe anything. Between these two extremes there were Mr. Wadlow and Miss Comperton who irritated her but whom she found herself unable to suspect, Mrs. Wadlow whom she took for granted, and Mr. Frith for whom she had a strong cousinly affection."

Richard said, frowning, "Is all this really necessary?"

It was Rachel who answered.

"I think so. Please go on, Miss Silver."

Miss Silver continued.

"I arrived to find that Miss Treherne had met with a very serious accident. I was at once placed in a considerable dilemma. The circumstances were such that the police should have been called in. Miss Treherne positively refused to allow this. She even went so far as to declare that she would deny the whole thing if the police were sent for. I had therefore to do the best I could, and I may say that I have never had a more serious responsibility laid upon me. I was convinced that Miss Treherne's life was being attempted by one of her relatives, and that this person was a very cool and daring criminal with a great deal at stake. I discovered that I was not the only person to be convinced of this. Louisa Barnet was so much convinced of it that she had for some time been risking her situation and her character in a series of foolish attempts to alarm Miss Treherne."

Louisa sniffed. Her eyelids were red, her mouth made a straight, hard line. At the mention of her name she stared fiercely at Rachel for a moment and then looked down again at the hands which were clenched in her lap.

Miss Silver coughed slightly.

"The attempts were foolish and rather alarming, but I am convinced that her motive was concern for her mistress. Miss Treherne did become alarmed, and her alarm brought her to me. I quickly discovered Louisa's activities. But Miss Treherne's accident on the cliff was quite another matter. In this case I exonerated Louisa immediately. Real devotion is unmistakable, and it was plain to me that she would have died for Miss Treherne."

This time Louisa did not look up. The rigid line of her mouth set itself more rigidly. Her clenched hands were more tightly clenched.

Miss Silver looked away.

"I turned my attention to the family circle. In all but Mr. Frith I found uneasiness, nervousness, worry. I took particular notice of Mr. Frith from the beginning. Miss Treherne remaining upstairs after her fall, I was a complete stranger to everyone present. To everyone but Mr. Frith I was a retired governess of no importance, a *protégée* of Miss Treherne's, quite a negligible person. I therefore saw them all behaving in a perfectly natural way. They were polite, but they did not trouble to put on a social manner—they were just themselves. Mrs. Wadlow talked because she likes talking. Mr. Wadlow indulged an inclination to fidget. Miss Comperton endeavoured to enlist my interest pecuniarily in a scheme for slum clearance. Mr. Richard and Miss Caroline were silent because they were much occupied with their own thoughts. But Mr. Frith went out of his way to make himself agreeable, and I asked myself why he should do so. He was not the type of man who devotes an evening to the entertainment of an elderly governess. His conversation convinced me that he desired to impress me with his talent, his social position, and his devotion to Miss Treherne. I asked myself why he should be at so much pains, and it occurred to me that Mr. Frith knew who I was, and for what purpose I had been brought down to Whincliff Edge.

"As a first step in my investigation into Miss Treherne's fall over the cliff, I had to find out where all the other members of the household had been between five o'clock and six-fifteen. The servants were out of it, with the exception of Gladys, whose story interested me very much. First of all, Mr. Frith rang for her at half past five and asked to have a letter posted should anyone be going out. Secondly, she had taken advantage of this to run down to the post herself. Now why should Mr. Frith have rung for her? Letters for the post are placed on the chest in the hall. The chauffeur had just driven into Ledlington to fetch me. If the letter was not sufficiently important for Mr. Frith to have completed it in time for Barlow to take, why did it suddenly become so important that he rang for Gladys to ensure its being posted? Or, the pillar-box being just at the bottom of the drive, why did he not walk down with the letter himself? It seemed to me that Mr. Frith had been anxious to establish the fact that not only was he in the house at half past five, but that he had no intention of going out. He would, however, have had plenty of time after ringing for Gladys to slip out through his own room and reach Mrs. Capper's cottage before Miss Treherne emerged. Nobody else had any sort of alibi, and what looked like an attempt on Mr. Frith's part to establish one actually aroused my suspicion."

Gale Brandon was standing on one side of the hearth. He had been watching Miss Silver as she spoke. He laughed now in a sudden boyish manner and enquired,

"Do you always suspect the person who has an alibi?"

Miss Silver shook her head.

"Not always. But when a person has taken pains to have an alibi, it is of course a suspicious circumstance."

"I was thinking that I hadn't one of any kind," said Gale— "I was right there. But I didn't mean to interrupt you."

Miss Silver acknowledged the excuse with a slight inclination.

"To continue. At breakfast next morning Mr. Frith's behaviour confirmed my suspicions. It was obvious that Miss Treherne's electric torch had been tampered with. Mr. Richard had put in a fresh battery in view of her coming home by the cliff path in the dark, yet when she emerged from Mrs. Capper's cottage the torch gave so feeble a light that she turned it off and used it only when she came to the worst bit of the road. It was, in point of fact, too feeble to disclose the identity of any person who might be following her. Now what did Mr. Frith do? He became very much concerned to prove that there was some mistake, and that the torch was all right. The mistake, if I may say so, was his, since he once more attracted my attention. He had no sooner demonstrated that the battery was in perfect working order than I was convinced that he had first changed the new battery for an old one and then replaced the new one. And that is where he made a bad mistake. It is a fatal weakness of the criminal mind not to be able to leave well alone. If he had been content to leave the run-down battery in the torch, it would have been much more possible to attribute its failure to an accident. The battery might have been defective, or Mr. Richard might have put in an old one by mistake."

Richard Treherne lifted his frowning gaze and said abruptly,

"Or on purpose. Didn't you consider that?"

A little prim smile met the frown.

"Certainly I did, Mr. Richard. But you would not in that case have replaced the battery."

"Wouldn't I?"

Miss Silver shook her head.

"I think not, Mr. Richard. In fact, the whole business of the battery would be out of keeping with your character. If you will forgive me for saying so, you have strong feelings and you show them easily. If you were to commit a crime, it would not be premeditated, nor would it occur to you to cover up your tracks afterwards. The affair of the battery is entirely out of keeping with your character as I read it."

The dark colour came into Richard's face.

"And you are never wrong?"

Miss Silver gave a modest cough.

"Not very often, Mr. Richard. So, you see, I was convinced that Mr. Frith was attempting his cousin's life. He was in embarrassed circumstances, and her death would have brought him a large sum of money. Miss Treherne admits that she kept the draft of her will in a drawer, and that she is careless about her keys. I am persuaded that Mr. Frith did not neglect such an opportunity. And now, you see, I was quite sure in my own mind about Mr. Frith, but I had not one iota of evidence to support my conviction. Miss Treherne was resolved not to call in the police, and Mr. Frith felt so secure that he actually urged her to do so. Meanwhile Miss Caroline was behaving in such a suspicious manner that had the police been called in, she would certainly have been the first object of their attention."

CHAPTER 40

And now, Caroline," said Rachel, "will you tell us why you behaved in this suspicious manner?"

Caroline raised herself, flushed, looked across at Louisa, and then turned imploring eyes on Rachel.

"Louisa is one of those who has suspected you," said Rachel. "If she does not hear your explanation she will always suspect you. This would hurt me so much that I ask you for my sake to speak."

Caroline hung her head. Then she said, speaking very low to Richard,

"Please go away—a little farther off. Please don't look at me. I can't bear it if you do."

He took her hand and put it to his lips, then got to his feet with a jerk and went over to the window, where he stood with his back to the room, eyes staring blindly and ears straining for the sound of Caroline's faint words.

They were very faint indeed. She sat up, put her feet to the ground, and leaned against the shoulder of the couch, one elbow propped and her forehead resting on her hand. She said,

"I didn't know what to do. I wasn't fond of Cosmo, but he's always been there—like an uncle. I don't think I thought whether I was fond of him or not—I don't know. When you've known someone always like that you don't think whether they're telling you the truth."

Miss Silver spoke in a very kind voice.

"What did he tell you, Miss Caroline?"

"It was about Richard—" She stopped, drew a long sighing breath, and forced the flagging words. "He said when Richard was at college he had got into difficulties. He said it wasn't really Richard's fault—he took the blame for a friend. He knew I wouldn't believe anything against Richard, but he made it seem as if Richard would get into most dreadful trouble if it came out. He said there was a forged cheque, and if it came out Richard would go to prison."

Richard swung round, came back, and stood over her.

"My darling little lunatic! What are you saying?"

Caroline lifted swimming eyes and said in a choked voice,

"Go away—I told you to go away."

"Well, I'm not going!" said Richard.

He was so angry, and so relieved, that he would have liked to pick her up, shake her till her teeth chattered, and then kiss her until she cried for mercy. He restrained these barbaric desires, sat down beside her on the couch, and put a firm arm about her waist.

"So I'm a forger? And a damned fool into the bargain? Go on, darling!"

"*Please* go away."

He did actually shake her a very little.

"I'm not going. Have you got that? Now get on with this blithering story. Cosmo told you I had forged a cheque in a spasm of nobility to save a friend, and you lapped it all up. Is that it?"

Quite a bright colour came into Caroline's cheeks. She blinked away the brimming tears and said in a soft, indignant voice,

"I didn't! Of course you can make it sound stupid, but if you'd heard him—"

"I should have believed I'd forged that cheque. All right, we've got that—he convinced you I was a philanthropic forger. What then?"

Her colour faded again. She looked across to Miss Silver and spoke to her.

"I can't put it the way he put it—I'm not nearly clever enough. And I trusted him. He said someone had got hold of the story and unless he could be persuaded to hold his tongue it would ruin Richard. So I gave him fifty pounds—he said he hoped that would be enough. But afterwards he said it wasn't, and I managed another ten. And that wasn't enough either."

Gale Brandon said something into the fire, and Rachel said, "Oh, Caroline *darling!*" Richard's arm tightened, and he said angrily.

"Why on earth didn't you come to me?"

The brown eyes looked at him with reproach.

"I couldn't, because, you see, what he said was quite true. It would always have been between us if you had known that I knew. That's true, Richard—you wouldn't have liked me to know."

"That I was a forger! I suppose I wouldn't! Go on!"

Her eyes went back to Miss Silver.

"I'm not clever. He made it sound quite reasonable. He said this man had got the cheque, and if I wouldn't buy it he would go to Richard. I thought that would hurt him so frightfully— oh, can't you see what I thought? It was all years and years ago. I felt I would do anything to prevent him from dragging it up—I *didn't* want Richard to know. I couldn't touch most of my money because of its being in trust. I sold out two hundred pounds that Aunt Mary left me, and I gave up my flat. And when that wasn't enough, I sold my mother's ring."

Richard said "*Caroline!*" in a shaken voice.

She turned to him at once.

"I didn't mind, darling—I didn't really. Only Cherry found out and was horrid. And then—then there was that dreadful Thursday evening."

"Yes, Miss Caroline? Will you tell us exactly what happened on the Thursday evening?"

Caroline looked very pale.

"I went out with Richard after tea. We went up on to the

cliff. He asked me to marry him. And I said I couldn't. I didn't feel I could with this dreadful secret going on. I didn't feel as if I could keep a secret from him if we were going to be married. So I said no. And Richard went on up the cliff, but I came back. And when I was quite near the house I met Cosmo. I was crying, and he was very kind. He said the only thing to do was to offer the blackmailer a really large sum and that would finish the whole thing. And he said I could get the money from Rachel if I told her I was in trouble and that I must have it. And that made me cry more than ever, because the one thing I couldn't, couldn't bear was for Rachel to think it was money I wanted from her. So I ran in through the garden gate. But there was someone there, and I came back and ran down the path to the road and came in that way. I didn't see Cosmo, so I knew that he must have gone along the cliff. And afterwards he came to me and said I mustn't ever say I'd seen him, because if I did, he would be obliged to say that he had seen Richard near the place where Rachel fell. That's why I fainted when Rachel told us she had been pushed. I knew that Richard and Cosmo had both been there on the cliff."

"As a matter of fact I went across the downs to the road, and came in the same way that you did," said Richard.

"Cosmo said he went a little way along the cliff path and turned back. He said Richard passed him and went along towards Nanny Capper's—walking very fast. He said if I spoke of having seen him, he would have to say this, and then Rachel would believe that it was Richard who had pushed her. And when Richard didn't say he had been on the cliff path, I thought—I thought—I didn't know what to think."

At this point Louisa gave a rending sniff. It might have been the sniff of affliction, or it might, on the other hand, have signified acute disbelief. Her face, like her hands, remained clenched upon whatever it was that she was feeling.

Richard's arm dropped from Caroline's waist.

"You thought—you thought that I had pushed Rachel over the cliff!"

She broke into a childish sob.

"Richard—I didn't—I wouldn't! He said he'd seen you. He said you were angry with Rachel, and he was afraid you had lost your head. I didn't *believe* it—but I'd got so that I couldn't think."

"And why was I angry with Rachel? Did he tell you that?"

"He said—he said he was afraid the blackmailer had got tired of waiting for me to find the money. He said he thought the man had been to you, and that you had tried to get the money from Rachel and—and failed."

"So I went and pushed her over the cliff! Caroline, did you really believe all this stuff?"

They had both forgotten that there was anyone else in the room. She said in the voice of a scolded child,

"He kept on saying things. I couldn't think about them any more. They just hurt."

"You see," said Miss Silver with a small preliminary cough—"you see what a strong motive there was for silencing Miss Caroline. Mr. Frith must have been in desperate straits for money. In fact we now know that this was the case. He was very much afraid of losing his footing with Miss Treherne, yet if Miss Caroline were to confide in her or in Mr. Richard, he would lose that footing once and for all. He was running a frightful risk and he dared not go on. Hence the attempt on Miss Treherne's life. It was cleverly planned and boldly executed. If it had succeeded, it would have been quite impossible to bring it home to him, but thanks to Mr. Brandon it did not succeed. He was still desperate for money, alarmed by my presence, and afraid of what Miss Caroline would say when she was questioned. He might well be afraid, because now not only was she likely to give away the falsehoods he had made her believe about Mr. Richard, but she was also in a position to say that his story of having been in the house between five and six-fifteen was untrue, since she had actually met him on his way to the cliff path. His guilty conscience pushed him on. Some time on the Thursday night he took out his car and ran over to Pewitt's Corner to uncover the well. Barlow, whose room is over the garage, is known to be an extremely heavy sleeper. Mr. Maurice was away. Mr. Richard might have heard the car—"

Richard shook his head.

"I'm like Barlow—nothing wakes me."

"Mr. Frith would naturally be aware of that. He chose to take the slight risk of being heard rather than the risk of being seen by daylight at Pewitt's Corner. There really was very little risk at all. It was, I feel, an interposition of Providence that Miss Treherne mentioned the cottage and the well to me before she left with Mr. Brandon. I had to wait until Mr. Frith took his departure. He was so very explicit as to his movements that my suspicions were redoubled. Why, in the midst of all this anxiety about Miss Caroline, should he go out of his way to inform me that he was leaving his car at a garage in Ledlington whilst he continued his journey to London by train? When I found that he had actually done this I realized that Miss Caroline was in very great danger. But I did not believe that the danger lay in London. No, if Mr. Frith wished to direct everyone's attention to London, then the danger lay elsewhere, and when I asked myself where, I remembered the lonely cottage at Pewitt's Corner with its very convenient well. As we now know, Mr. Frith alighted at Slepham and joined Miss Caroline who was waiting for him with her car at the old house near the halt. Mercifully, I had a five mile start of him. The fog was an equal handicap to both cars, and thanks to Barlow's skilful driving we reached the cottage in time to prevent a terrible tragedy. I was naturally much surprised to find that Miss Treherne and Mr. Brandon were already there. You have never told me how that happened, Miss Treherne."

Rachel coloured.

"I couldn't stop thinking about the well," she said in a low voice.

Miss Silver nodded.

"We were all thinking about the well—Mr. Frith—and myself—and you. A very dangerous contrivance, and lamentably out of date. Modern plumbing is not only a great deal more convenient, but it does not so readily lend itself to a criminal intent. Survivals from the dark ages may be romantic, but I must confess I prefer modern conveniences."

Gale Brandon slid his hand over his mouth. Rachel turned rather hastily to Louisa.

"Now, Louie—you have heard everything. I should like to hear you beg Miss Caroline's pardon."

Louisa lifted her eyes. They looked first fiercely and then imploringly, but Rachel met them with something implacable in her own level gaze. Louisa received an ultimatum, opposed it, hung irresolute, and suddenly gave way. Her hands still gripping one another, she got up, stared over the top of Caroline's head, and said in a hard, mechanical voice,

"I'm sure I beg your pardon, Miss Caroline, but none of it wouldn't have happened if so be you'd spoken up."

After which she retired in good order upon Rachel's bedroom, where she could be heard relieving her feelings by a vigorous opening and shutting of drawers and cupboard doors.

Caroline cast a wavering look at Richard's angry face, burst into tears, and ran out of the room. Richard, to all appearances angrier than before, jumped up and went after her, slamming the door behind him with so much violence as to wake Noisy, who, opening both eyes this time, uttered a protesting grunt, rolled over to face the fire, and once more sank deep into a dream.

Miss Silver said, "Dear me!" patted her neat front as if she feared that the draught of the slammed door might have disarranged it, murmured a polite unheeded excuse, and withdrew.

Gale Brandon went over to the bedroom door and shut it

firmly. The sound of Louisa working off her temper receded. He turned and held out his arms to Rachel, and she came into them with a sob.

"I've been a terrible failure, Gale. I wonder you're not afraid to try me for a wife."

Mr. Brandon's lips being muffled by her hair, his answer was not very plainly audible, but she inferred that he was quite willing to try. After an interval he elaborated the theme.

"You know, honey, I think you're the finest woman on the earth, so if you couldn't make a go of it, there isn't anyone in the world who could. And that's just where it got you. There isn't anyone who could make a go of all that money, and this will business, and those relations of yours. I don't know what they were like to start with, but this show was just naturally bound to bring out every single bad quality they'd got. That's hard talking, but there's got to be some hard talking between us. I don't blame you, because you were nothing but a girl— you hadn't any experience to go on, and your father landed you in for it. And I don't blame him, because first he was a very sick man, and then he was so sick that he died, and it stands to reason that he wasn't in a state to think clearly. It always beats me why people attach so much importance to a dying wish. If there's one kind of wish that oughtn't to be taken any notice of, it's that, because it stands to reason that a man who's so sick he's going to die isn't in a fit state to go binding wishes on other people. Anyhow, honey, it's all got to stop now. You give your sister what you think she ought to have—tied up in trust if you like—and do the same by the others. Let them have their money and stand on their own feet, and if they ditch themselves, you just leave them there till they get enough horse sense to climb out again. Don't you go feeding them pap any more. It don't do them any good and it don't do you any good, and anyhow I'm not going to have it."

Rachel felt rather as if she were out in a high wind. The

wind seemed to be blowing quite a lot of things away. And she didn't care. She let them go down the wind. The rough tweed of Gale's coat was pleasant and harsh under her cheek. Half her life was gone, but there was another half to come.

Gale tipped up her chin with a strong, gentle hand.

"What you really want is a family of your own," he said.